Fade to Red
and
Other Stories

Peggy Gardner

ISBN: 979-8-89079-315-7 (hardcover)
ISBN: 979-8-89079-283-9 (paperback)
ISBN: 979-8-89079-284-6 (ebook)

DEDICATION

For my children, Morgan and Wade,
and all my nieces and nephews.

FADE TO RED

"All lovely things will have an ending
All lovely things will fade and die."

—Conrad Aiken

THE GOAL

CHAPTER 1

ETHEL:

In our galaxy of the Milky Way, astronomers predict that about three times in a century a supernova explodes, spewing elemental particles like oxygen and gold to form new worlds. The crushed remnants, called neutron stars or black holes, are left behind. Right here in Kansas, I have made my home in one of those black holes while my supernova of a sister, Thalia, inhabits a world that should have been mine.

Einstein would have perfectly understood the physics of my relationship with my sister—all her energy and matter warp the geometry of space while I provide gravity, the way a heavy body sags a mattress. But, in 1940, while Einstein was making his appeal for a rational approach to universal questions, I was an only child on a farm in Kansas where my-not-blood-kin grandmother considers philosophical questions to be ill-mannered.

Wartime radio did its dead-level best to distract us from the truth that Hitler was busily bombing England's Dover coast. "Truth or Consequences" with Ralph Edwards had a two-second limit for truth, before zany consequences tickled the audience. Farm families like mine weren't much in the mood for anything more serious than crops and weather.

The muffled words coming out of our old Zenith frizzled like static as the radio warmed up to report a disrupted world. Our family listened in a curious state of malaise to what Hitler might be doing in Belgium and France—before Thalia arrived to play havoc with our lives.

After the Dustbowl and the Great Depression, Kansans feared a drought more than a Nazi invasion. The annexation of Latvia and Estonia by Russia was of less interest than what Wallis Simpson and the disgraced heir to the British throne might be getting themselves up to in the Bahamas.

Every evening after supper, the four of us, Papa, Mama, Grandma Ethel and I, crouched around the burnished wood veneer of the radio as though it might emit the chemicals that helped the Delphic Oracle speak the truth.

Grandma Ethel never hesitated to voice her own version of truth. "Voodoo and love potions. That's how a divorced woman got that poor Edward to give up his kingdom and manages to keep him under her thumb. We talked about it at the Temperance meeting today. Strong drink, too. Those royals imbibe. That's how she got him to leave his country. Otherwise, he'd never have left his mother."

Squinting her sharp, dark eyes under that epicanthic fold that made her look like a disgruntled walrus, Grandma Ethel would stare into space, careful not to cast her eyes at Mama, who knew exactly where they were directed.

Grandma Ethel came with the house; it had been her husband's and his father's before him. I will have to say this for the house. It has stubbornly held onto every odor that ever wafted through its dreary, chopped up, cordoned-off spaces. No amount of soda or vinegar nor charcoal briquettes covered with Epsom salts removes the odors of chimney smoke, tobacco, camphor, wallpaper paste and the mold of stale lives.

I was born without much ado in this pseudo-Victorian house perched on the far edge of a middling town in north-central Kansas. It was the same farmhouse where my father had been born, in the same bed, and probably on the same soiled mattress. I popped into the world to the sound of Grandma Ethel chastising

Mama for "carrying on and bothering the menfolk" just before Grandma slipped on the stairs and broke her ankle.

My father was so grateful that the only mother he had ever known managed to limp down the stairs to bring him the good news that his wife had survived the rigors of childbirth that he didn't ask if the scrawny girl with hair the texture and color of a dead mouse was alive. That's what Grandma Ethel told me. That's why he named me Ethel after a woman who is not my blood grandmother, in gratitude for the news about his wife—not about the birth of his daughter.

When Grandma Ethel told that story to anyone with a willing ear, she would clutch her belly with the same pained expression of the Spartan boy holding a gnawing fox under his coat, unwilling to reveal the fact that his intestines were being consumed along with his secret. "It could have been worse news. My namesake Ethel had all her limbs while I was nursing a broken one from that fall. Not sure about her wits."

Grandma Ethel's cruel witticisms could hook into the skin of the unwary as fast as her crochet hook could produce yet another antimacassar for our chairs. I began to size her up long before she realized that I had her number.

When there was only Mama, Papa, and Grandma Ethel, the saving grace for me was the nice chunk of the beautiful prairie and hills beyond it that Papa owned. Wheat fields as far as the eye could see coursed east and west like an undulating green ocean in the spring and golden as a mythical Sahara in the summer.

Our house, with those Nineteenth Century, factory-produced bibelots fashioned to resemble turrets and flowery vines, crouched uncomfortably along this prairie like a misguided guest who has entered the wrong door but is too embarrassed to leave.

My Grandpa Hector Ellis had inherited the house, 640 acres of good wheat land and grass pastures, and a free-flowing, spring-fed creek from his father, my Great- Grandpa Nestor Ellis, who built a house with five bedrooms, two bathrooms, and three chimneys, so a large family would thrive as well as wheat in Kansas, where the winter sweeps down from the North Pole.

Instead of a troop of children, Great-Grandpa Nestor had to settle for a dead wife and a healthy twelve-pound son; he finally christened his son Hector after six months of grieving. He tried to settle his grief with a five-hundred pound pink granite tombstone hauled all the way from Topeka with these words carved on it:

Serena Ellis, beloved wife of Nestor
"Those who in living fill the smallest space
In death have often left the greatest void."

—W.S. Landor

According to Papa, his father Hector filled the void left by Great-Grandpa Nestor and then some by taking over responsibility for the farm by the time he was twelve.

After Serena's death, Great-Grandpa Nestor planted his feet into a pair of lace-up, ankle-high black boots, kept a chaw of tobacco in his cheek except on Sundays, and listlessly directed farming operations from a chair under the diseased elm near the north forty.

Hector lived up to his Trojan namesake, according to Grandma Ethel. "By the time he was eighteen, they say there wasn't a hired hand on the place he couldn't lick. When I set eyes on him at his wife's funeral, a timid girl like me couldn't say no."

Grandma Ethel had ways of saying no even when she didn't say no. She soldiered on, fully in command, until the day of her eighty-ninth birthday when she disappeared, along with Mama and Papa, into the funnel of a tornado.

Not to speak ill of the dead, I do have to say that four years earlier Grandma Ethel at eighty-five proved her mettle after her unfortunate run-in—or should I say fall-in—with near death in the old well.

Of her 206 bones, six major ones—her femur, tibia, fibula, humerus, ulna and radius—on the right side of her body cracked and popped like green firewood before Grandma Ethel hit the cooling water of that old well. She managed to float like a fisherman's cork until Gus Talbert, Papa's hired man, heard something he couldn't believe.

From below the great mass of white roses that I had planted months earlier near the abandoned well to deal with my own grief over my sister's betrayal, Gus could hear a faint melody and muffled words of an old Baptist hymn. ". . . heard my distressing cry . . . from the waters lifted me . . ."

It took four volunteers with two ladders from the Ellsworth Fire Department to hoist Grandma Ethel out of the well. Papa said she didn't stop singing "Love Lifted Me" until they gave her an overload of morphine in the hospital.

Of course, Grandma Ethel blamed me for "hiding a dangerous well with that screen of sweet smelling roses to lure the unsuspecting." I got to hear about it for four long years as Grandma Ethel pushed her walker around the house like a mean-tempered mule fighting its harness.

She would perk up and step lively whenever Thalia came prancing up the sidewalk for a visit with little Lance. So like Thalia to name her son after an adulterous knight. Considering what my sister did to me, "Shaft" would have been more fitting.

As a way of getting even with all of our family who were left in the house after Thalia moved to town, Grandma Ethel prettified every room with her idea of an English garden. Long stripes of delphiniums wound their deadly cobalt blues along every bedroom wall. Great puffs of pink petunias, quickly foxed with brown spots, exploded on the dining room walls.

When Grandma Ethel conscripted our hired man to wallpaper, she did it the cheapest way, showing him how to make paste from high gluten flour mixed with warm water. Mold spewed its colonies behind the flowers. I'm sure of that. It accounts for the allergies that were rampant in our household until the house vanished in the blink of a tornado's eye.

CHAPTER 2

I need to digress so that I don't tell things out of order. Life takes its own twists and turns without me helping it along. At the center of the story is a terrible question: What could I have done differently?

Misapprehension settles around me like coal smoke—sooty and clinging. The subtext of possible answers bubbles into my mind like one of those artesian wells in the canyon on our farm, bitter with the taste of gyp. Mostly, I try to repress the questions. It's better not to know.

I will say this up front. Between the two of us, I'm the rational sister. Thalia's reasoning is spurious at best. Helping anyone understand my family requires me to go back at least three generations. When my Grandpa Hector was only eighteen, he found his pa, Nester, facedown under a tree that was just beginning to show signs of the devastating Dutch elm disease. Grandpa Hector said only six words when the undertaker came to get his father's corpse: "He can't blame me no more."

That's what Grandma Ethel reported though she hadn't arrived on the scene back then. She claimed to have heard it later from the undertakers who have long memories because their business is sporadic, not routine like farming.

I don't see how she'd know what anybody said back then, although shouldering blame appears to be a genetic trait for some of us. Grandma Ethel didn't come under the Ellis roof until Papa was two years old, but she tucked into our family history like a farmhand with a steaming plate at the dinner table, claiming it as her own before it could cool.

My grandpa, Hector Ellis, married the neighbor's oldest daughter, Rebecca Bergson, before his own father's grave had settled flat enough so it could be nicely mowed.

"He wed Rebecca with unseemly haste," Grandma Ethel would always add, careful that her husband Hector couldn't hear. "They say she was not a modest girl like her Biblical namesake, but she was doomed to suffer the same birthing trials." Grandma Ethel always got a little pinched look about her mouth when she talked about Grandpa Hector's first wife, as though bile was charging up her throat to be released in nasty little spurts.

"Old Dr. Lontrey said them twins waged a battle in Rebecca's womb the like of which he never saw before. He said that their birthing must have rivaled the Biblical Rebecca's with Esau and Jacob."

The wrinkles around Grandma Ethel's tight, little mouth would purse like someone was pulling the string. I guessed it might have been the ghost of Rebecca who couldn't tell her own story, since Grandma Ethel had taken it over.

"Praise be that Rebecca's first-born didn't resemble that hairy Esau. When the glint of early morning sunlight lit the thatch of hair atop a wailing newborn, Rebecca was struck silly and said: 'Jason of the golden fleece.'"

Grandma Ethel said that she heard tell that four more hours of labor were so agonizing that Rebecca made no sound when she popped out the second twin, my own dark-haired father. Dr. Lontrey called him Jacob. Grandma said the name was "fitting," considering that female trouble after the birth had taken Rebecca to a better place. She said Jacob means "supplanter."

Sometimes I sit and stare at the photograph of Papa's brother, that other twin, Jason, who was not quite two years old when he climbed onto the back of a cultivator pulled by two skittish mules, and I wonder why the color of hair has come to matter so much in our Ellis family's lives.

"That peculiar shade of gold, like the yolk of a duck egg, crops up on the head of an Ellis baby in just about every generation," said Grandma Ethel, squinting sagely, as though eyeing the Ellis chromosomes through a microscope as she dusted the only photograph of my dark-haired father and his fair-haired twin and replaced it on the mantel.

"Bitter reminder. Don't know why Jacob leaves this portrait out in the open where his pa always kept it." Grandma Ethel would always replace the ornate brass frame precariously close to the edge of the mantel.

Two children stared back at us, rooted before a studio photographer. They wore Lord Fauntleroy shirts and ankle high boots—plump, smiling Jason of the Golden Fleece and Jacob, his eyes dark with apprehension.

"I've said it a hundred times, and I'd lay anything on it." Grandma Ethel's faint mustache crinkled above her small mouth. "My husband's first wife, Rebecca, speak no ill of the dead, had some high-flown notions if you look at all the do-dads in this house. She didn't have the wherewithal to be the wife of a man's man like Hector."

She eyed the photograph critically again. "Lived long enough to name one twin after a Greek philanderer; the doctor got the other name from the Bible; thank God that Jacob has a decent name."

Before Grandma Ethel—who I will say again is not my blood grandmother—could continue her monologue about how Grandpa Hector was so needy for a competent woman to sort out his household and be a mother to little Jacob, I would seal my ears for the hundredth time.

Small towns like Ellsworth, Kansas, have ears and eyes that outlive every citizen and make for very long memories. I knew that my would-be grandmother, Ethel Harkness, when she was a thirty-year-old spinster daughter of the newly arrived Baptist preacher from Liberal, had clamped onto Hector Ellis tighter than a suckerfish—as he stood grieving over an oak casket that held the multiple pieces of his son Jason.

It seemed to me that Grandpa Hector might have been conditioned to accept the death of his wife Rebecca after the hard birth of his twins. His own mother, Serena Ellis, fell to the fever and chills of what Grandma Ethel called a "bad birthing" in less than a week after Hector was born; the baby boy was sent to suckle a "field hand's missus with a newborn."

What Grandpa Hector could not accept was his own negligence in letting his golden-haired son Jason perch behind him on the cultivator. Big, red, sweating mules, their muscles straining to pull the razor-sharp disks left Hector distracted as he plowed up shining curls of deep silt loam.

And the parts and pieces of Jason as he silently joined the soil of Kansas. The screams of the dark-haired twin Jacob, left pouting on the porch, because he feared the mules, sounded only after the cultivator had made a wide sweep at the turn and Hector saw the wisp of a white cotton shirt sprouting where nothing had been planted nor would ever be planted again.

From the minute she first set her squinty eyes on my grandpa, Hector Ellis—whose own eyes were probably rheumy with pain—Ethel Harkness was quick to build her own mythology around the day they met. "My father, who had never formally been acquainted with Hector or his boy Jason, beings as we were new to the church, preached a fine burial service on the foolish and wise virgins."

Grandma Ethel would glare at me when she recounted that day, because I always rolled my eyes, trying to sort out why that parable made any sense for the funeral of the hapless golden child in that old photograph.

"Be prepared for judgment and a new beginning. That's what he was preaching about. That's what my father often preached about," she'd add, reflectively. "I began to take that as a divine sign that judgment was at hand for a wise virgin with a big heart, and I'd best be figuring out a way to get on with my future."

Grandma Ethel delighted in remolding a destitute widower with one dead child into a pugnacious landowner who just happened to have a needy son. "I heard tell that by the time he was half grown, there wasn't a hired hand on the place Hector couldn't lick. When I saw him grieving over Jason at the funeral, I was struck dumb by such suffering in a big man."

I remember her glancing slyly over to the corner of the room where Grandpa Hector had layered himself like a marooned seal in the Stickley rocker. "A big man with a ruddy complexion and such a forceful nature that I couldn't say no when he come calling."

Or she came calling with her beef tongue casseroles and soggy layer cakes to claim little Jacob Ellis as more dear to her than a natural-born son could be. Grandma Ethel could wind the truth faster than a spindle could turn.

Just this side of comatose before he was eighty, Grandpa Hector managed to keep the rocker moving in absolute time to some metronome ticking away in his head. All of us in the room knew that the beat was Ja-son, Ja-son, Ja-son, the son that he had been distracted from watching for just that instant it took for his child to fall into eternity.

My own papa, Jacob, had a maimed air about him, like one of those soldiers coming home from war with a peg leg or an empty sleeve. He never spoke of his missing twin but occasionally straightened the photograph on the mantel so that Jason could see out the window to the field this side of the north forty where he had died.

"That photograph is a sore reminder of the past, Jacob. Dwelling on what's beyond fixing can impair a person's wits," Grandma Ethel would say every time she saw Papa fiddling with that old photo. "It's a good thing that the Lord saw fit to put someone with common sense here to look after this family." Then she'd cackle like a nesting hen.

Using my wits to avoid Grandma Ethel's serpent tongue should have prepared me for anything in this life. I watched her peel Mama's hide like an onion, layer at a time, to maximize the tears.

"It's not your fault, Eula, that your folks never had the where-withal to get land of their own. It's tiring to be beholden. I feel for your mother, her man working like a field hand all his life. Teeth gone. Old before his time." Grandma Ethel's new dentures would clatter away in an orthodontic frenzy at the recollection of my Grandpa Tull's vacant mouth.

Just as Mama's pellucid blue eyes would fill to the point of overflowing, Grandma Ethel would turn her rhetoric on a dime. "We old people need to know when it's our time. When we get to be a bother. In the way, so to speak. Hear things we shouldn't. We have a way of knowing when we outlive our welcome. That's why I always choose the back piece of the fried chicken and close my bedroom door to troublesome sounds at night."

That little speech, offered up with open palms like a communicant waiting for the wafer, always got the response it expected. "Never, Mother Ethel. We never tire of having you with us," Mama would protest halfheartedly.

Speak for yourself, Mama, I always wanted to add. But never did, because Grandma Ethel's witchy, blue-veined fingers could pinch clear down to the bone.

"I know a man must cleave to his wife, and they should be one flesh, as it says in the Bible. But not behind walls as thin as these. Not seemly," Grandma Ethel would add cryptically.

When Grandma Ethel wasn't dredging up the failings of her daughter-in-law, she watched me out of one of her sly little eyes— the one not coated over with cataract hoarfrost like a late-season buckeye. She watched and pinched and waited and cautioned Mama not to trust what comes out of a child's mouth. Grandma Ethel made sure that I would grow up under a pall of suspicion.

For as long as I can remember, the odor of mistrust emanated from Grandma Ethel, try as she might to overpower it with the Arpège perfume that Papa mail-ordered for her every birthday. I might have become as misanthropic as Grandma Ethel if I hadn't escaped from Lanvin's odor of one thousand flowers to run through fields where sunflowers smelled only of green and yellow.

Escaping outdoors became my safety net until I was six. When the sun tipped like molten lava just where our land drops off the edge of the world, the fevered crimson sky could restore me until Grandma Ethel's caterwauling brought me inside for supper and things that went bump in the night. Or, as I was to learn, a bump that would change life as I knew it.

CHAPTER 3

I try to suppress the memory of my parents in their late forties threshing about on a lumpy cotton mattress, but those old-fashioned bed springs screeched like a banshee through open windows on those hot Kansas nights. I read somewhere that banshees are female spirits that wail to announce an impending death. A little death, I suppose. I read about that too, somewhere. I wouldn't know where.

My younger sister Thalia would know. Sex, for her, is a recreational sport. If someone on the opposite team is about to score a touchdown, there is Thalia, waving her pom poms down by the goalpost, flashing her tight little apple butt, distracting the players with pure-dee purpose.

Every single thing that Thalia does is purposeful. Not reasonable, but purposeful. When she hatched in the middle of an aisle in Fletcher's Hardware on that bleak January day with seven-year-old Ethan Fletcher peeking between the hoe handles, it was an intentional act so that Ethan could see her buck naked. Thalia is all about timing.

Her entrance was timed before she could possibly know the impact of timing. As a miniscule fertilized egg embedding itself in a forty-six-old uterus, Thalia scheduled her gestation in what I'd say was the nick of time.

Mama claimed that Thalia was a surprise. That's what women always said back then when their roots were going gray and their bellies blossomed. Old elves like Santa Claus left surprises; Surprise lilies (known in coarser circles as Naked Ladies) popped out of dry August soil in our front yard; a surprise meant that only nice mythologies and Mother Nature were complicit in the unexpected.

I spend an inordinate amount of time thinking about how Thalia came to be so I can understand what she's come to be. A fiancé thief. A sister's burden. A virtuoso of vengeance. Hardly the namesake muse of comedy and idyllic poetry.

Our path in this life begins with naming. Sets the stage for what might happen. Mama wanted to name me Joanna, because God had been gracious in sending them a child after ten years of marriage. Papa insisted on Ethel after his stepmother, a noble woman to assume the care of a son not her own, he said. Papa claimed that Ethel Ellis had a nice ring to it.

Most of what Grandma Ethel said had a ring to it, like the front doorbell she made Grandpa Hector rig up. But, instead of a pleasing ding-dong sound, it made a nasty splat-splat noise, like water popping in hot grease. As the charge traveled from terminal to terminal, it erupted in a warning that pleased Grandma Ethel no end. "Tinkers and Mormons will know they're not welcome here. Kinfolk and people used to doing business with us won't be put off by the sound."

Neighboring farmers who stopped by to report a bull out or a fence down knew to use the back door. The last time I could remember anyone but Mama's folks paying one of their monthly, edgy visits was a scraggly group of Baptists come to view Grandpa Hector belly side up in his oversized wooden coffin.

I remember how a yellow, sulfurous haze contracted around the house that damp and foggy February day in 1945 as Baptists filed through the front door in silence, waiting for Grandma Ethel to break the spell. She obliged: "Lying face down in the dirt for so long caused no end of trouble for the funeral home to fix him like normal. Now, he looks like he might rise up and speak his mind."

Once the normalcy of the well-powdered corpse in our parlor was established, the Baptists bubbled over like ecstatic arsonists with the news of the firebombing of Dresden. Thalia screamed in the throes of colic. My papa, Jacob, sat like a brown study beside the casket.

Grandma Ethel positioned herself with open palms and a desolate expression by the front door, as though someone had stolen her widow's mite. "My husband passed without so much as a warning. Toppled over in that old chair under the elm without making a sound. Said he had an ache. Wouldn't say where. Said not to bother him. So, we didn't. When Jacob found him face down in the dirt, his hands were still warm and his arms flexible. Like he just had a little fainting spell and might wake up." Grandma Ethel stood expectantly, like a diva before the final applause.

"His heart just gave out. Hearts have to work double time in a big man like Hector. I told him time and time again to take an afternoon rest upstairs. He wouldn't listen. He was a man with a set mind."

A set mind that couldn't let go of its grief over a lost, golden-haired son. I remember watching nods of what was supposed to pass for sympathy going from Baptist to Baptist, like dominoes falling one by one. Even as a seven-year-old, I knew that Grandpa Hector couldn't move his three hundred pounds up the stairs and had slept in the closed-in sun porch since I could remember.

If memory serves me right, I'm the one who found Grandpa Hector under the diseased elm, his mouth fused to the red soil as though he had planted a last, lingering kiss against the land that had swallowed his son Jason.

"My namesake Ethel never thought once to check on her grandpa, knowing how busy we was with little Thalia and her colic. I fault that girl for lack of diligence," Grandma Ethel whispered just within my hearing to any Baptist who would listen as they paraded by Grandpa Hector's open casket.

Finding fault with me did nothing to ameliorate the sly, self-satisfied expression on Grandpa Hector's face that looked like one of those wax or plaster casts made from the death heads of famous people.

Surrounded by folds of white satin, his cheeks puffed into half spheres just below his sunken eyes. In spite of Grandma Ethel's complaints to the undertaker that "his mouth don't look quite normal," Grandpa Hector's pale, stone lips were frozen in a grin, the only smile I had ever seen on his face.

My sad Grandpa Hector always sat under that blighted elm on summer days and sometimes in the winter twiddling his thumbs and saying "Jason, Jason, Jason" so softly that I had to strain my ears to make out the words.

Grandma Ethel made excuses for a husband who didn't fit her notion of "normal." She said that Grandpa Hector got kicked in the head by a mule just after they got married and had an epileptic fit—just once—right at the dinner table she'd set with her own wedding china.

"His tongue lolled about like a cow licking a salt block, slobbering into the mashed potatoes. Then his legs jerked like he had St. Vitus Dance. I managed to get on top of him and clamp a serving spoon in his mouth. Broke two good china plates. Kept him from swallowing his tongue. I knew exactly what to do to save him." She'd beam over at Papa as she recalled her act of mercy.

Once she had a captive audience, Grandma Ethel couldn't omit the prologue. "We was talking about you, Jacob, about your unholy fear of the farm machinery when you were just a little boy. Well, actually, I was talking, because your father kept you penned up in the yard whenever the fields were being worked. I suggested that he take you on the tractor for a little spin to help you get over it."

In a dark whisper, she'd add within my hearing: "I hope little Ethel didn't get that epilepsy gene. It's a frightful thing to watch. Hector was never the same after that night."

When I was old enough to realize that something besides the specter of a seizure ailed my Grandpa Hector, Mama said: "Rue. My father-in-law suffers from rue." That's all she would say, but I noticed that for every sharp word Grandma Ethel said to Grandpa Hector, Mama offered a kindness to him.

"I could warm your coffee, Father Hector. I could get you a pillow for your back. I could take little Ethel outside so her noise won't bother you." The voice Mama used with Grandpa Hector was velvety as molasses.

With Grandma Ethel, Mama might have been Charlie McCarthy's dummy, her responses just on the tipping point of being disrespectful to his ventriloquist, but never going too far. In looking back, I see Mama as a controlled puppet, loving Papa too much to get her back up over Grandma Ethel's spite.

CHAPTER 4

Years later, I think about the three of them—Papa, Mama, and Grandma Ethel—that day when the sky turned purple with rage while I sat in the courthouse basement reading Nabokov's *Lolita* (a risqué book that would never be shelved). While the crepe myrtles outside the dirty window frothed into the wind, I prayed that the entire collection of the Cootenah Public Library didn't blow away, along with me and Lolita's molester, Humbert Humbert.

Unable to draw a decent breath in the vacuum of a tornado roping high above the town square, I had to force away a notion that crossed my mind. Thalia, with that by-blow of hers who looked like a miniature version of her high school boyfriend, Buff Pennington, could be on the road to our farm at this very minute. Just like Dorothy and Toto in that Oz movie, Thalia and her whiny child might be flying off among farm implements, never to return.

And that would have suited me just fine. What happened next didn't. Except for a few shingles atop the Methodist church, the town was spared. The Ellis homestead with Mama, Papa and Grandma Ethel whipped up and out of the county with not so much as a splinter of wood to show that four generations had spun out their lives on that patch of loam.

Driving with Thalia, Ethan and little Lance on a road covered with the debris of the tornado—sticks of furniture, a set of unbroken china, pages from a photograph album stacked neatly under a brick—I felt as though I were peering into closets, looking into forbidden cupboards.

Then, there was a perfectly still and empty atmosphere that seeped in through the car windows, as though we were in the eye of the tornado. But it had long since gone, leaving only the humped grave of the dirt cellar where once three stories of Victoriana had graced the wheat fields.

"Fluttering and dancing in the breeze." Only Wordsworth might be inspired by that single line of daffodils left where Mama's flowerbed once flourished. I never thought of Wordsworth as mawkish until I knew how his lonely, puffy clouds could pull themselves into a killing vortex to blast someone's life away.

I can remember to this very day how I stood, fearful of moving, hopeful that Papa and Mama were safe in the cellar.

Thalia, pushy as ever, denying me that one last moment of optimism, rushed over to yank up the cellar door, revealing row after row after row of canned peaches gleaming in the pale shaft of light. Nothing more.

As though the same shaft of light had moved into her imprudent pale blue eyes, Thalia looked right through me to Ethan Fletcher, who should have been my husband, not hers, to affirm my future. "Ethel will be moving in with us tonight, Ethan. There's not a scrap of hers left here."

Not an arm or a shoe from Mama or Papa. Not odd things that tornados sometimes leave behind like photographs in mint condition, even Grandma Ethel's dimity handkerchiefs still in a box, nothing to remind us that they had ever breathed this air in this place for almost three quarters of a century.

I might have resisted Thalia's offer to move in with her, but the temptation to prowl around the edges of her life with Ethan overcame my good judgment.

The edges of *my* life had curled in and withered like pages of those old foxed books in the Cootenah Library. And, it was all Thalia's doing. She might have had some help from Buff Pennington.

Like teenage Nordic skiers poised at the top of an impossible jump, Thalia and Buff knew that no one would blink when they flew over. They were the town's darlings, Romeo at seventeen making the winning touchdowns and fifteen-year-old Juliet waving pompoms where no pompom should be. Risky behavior like climbing up the water tower on a starry night while tanked up on choc beer simply confirmed their immunity from mishaps.

"Golden lads and girls all must, as chimney sweepers, come to dust." Shakespeare never encountered the likes of Thalia. Neither had Buff's mother, a sixth generation member of the DAR who could intimidate a small Kansas town with her ancestry and blue hair. A farmer's daughter had no hope of dangling off that family's tree.

When she was only sixteen, Thalia's predicament was as old as Eve's when she said to Adam: "I have got a manchild with the help of the Lord."

With the help of his mother and banker father, Buff Pennington skedaddled off to a private school back East, and my almost-fiancé Ethan Fletcher stepped in to fill the breech so to speak. And break my heart.

THALIA:

The remembrance of a certain evening has lodged itself in my memory with an imminent aching, like a bad tooth just on the edge of being painful. Ethie was fourteen that summer and worked like a field hand with Papa. After dinner, we'd sit in the front room with all the windows open, trying to catch a breeze. Mama's thin, beautiful fingers, the nails worn to the quick, stroked her Kimball spinet. She sometimes played old Methodist hymns and often Stephen Foster.

That particular night, Mama said: "Ethie, sing."

In a marvelous contralto, smoky and dark with just a bit of a catch, like Marlene Dietrich, Ethie sang: "I'll be seeing you in all the old familiar places."

Papa sat in his black socks, worn by washing, clinging in limpet patches to his thin ankles, his eyes somber and watchful, smiling at Ethie, as though her voice might be pulling every one of those lost Ellis souls out of the shadows to harmonize: "And when the night is new, I'll be looking at the moon but I'll be seeing you."

"Your voice sounds downright gravelly, like you're pretending to be one of those juke joint girls and don't know how. You're not cut out to be a vamp. I'd give considerable thought to putting myself out there with no talent," Grandma Ethel said with such gratuitous spite that I gasped out loud. Then she backhanded Ethie with a follow-up summary: "Some girls are born to fade into the wallpaper. Don't mean they aren't useful. You're as good on that tractor as a hired hand."

Although Mama encouraged Ethie to sing with her, after that night she always made an excuse. She buttoned herself into ugly, plaid homemade dresses, pulled her hair into an unflattering ponytail low on her neck, and retreated into a book after dinner.

That evening's little family melodrama ended like all the others with no one saying anything but Grandma Ethel who knew which buttons to push. I was decorative; Ethie was useful; and, Mama could always be persuaded to end our evenings with "Beulah Land," Grandma Ethel's favorite, "because you can see Heaven from there." Then she'd always add: "Don't tinkle the keys, Eula. Just play it simple. You weren't born to be a concert pianist."

I shuddered for Mama, wondering what could lie under Grandma Ethel's impulse to such savagery. My papa had married a girl from a poor farm. Grandma Ethel had set her sights on someone with airs; her stepson should have stepped up a notch on the town of Ellsworth's social scale. She might be dreaming that a banker's wife with DAR credentials would roll out the welcome mat for me. Buff's mother never would.

CHAPTER 5

ETHEL:

Like Holden Caulfield, I am fond of digressions. They let us draw our breath before we get on with the story that has an ending we might not want to tell. As the county librarian, I have felt obligated to do considerable reading of the books my clientele request.

Secretly, hidden back in the stacks, I squat and speed read. I have no interest in ladies' book clubs or monitoring what is age appropriate for those grimy little hellions that bring back cracked spines and stained buckram.

My interests lie between the borrower and the book. Why has Luann Scales, the Baptist minister's wife, checked out *Tobacco Road* a dozen times? Is she fond of turnips or titillated by the rape of Jeeter Lester's daughter? Why did Harvey Schmidt, the high school history teacher, take the octavo edition of *Birds of America* into the bathroom and put it back on the reference shelf with five of the plates neatly cut away?

Grandma Ethel was right in one sense. The county librarian has an interesting job if she can get past the ordering, mending, stacking, and organizing to get at the heart of the job—who is reading what and why.

I developed distrust for novels when my own life parted company with logic and reason—about the same time that my should-have-been fiancé Ethan went haywire. The storylines of most novels wander about, double back on themselves, try to engage the reader in fictional lives, and then sputter out in some kind of resolution.

That isn't how real lives work. Most people plod along with some sense of hopefulness that their lives will get better. Then, along comes a femme fatale or a younger sister who puts the kibosh on that notion. Next, comes a tornado that wipes the slate clean but leaves anger etched in a heart.

Anyone who has branded a squalling calf understands etching. After the first wave of nausea passed when I saw the eyeballs roll and the tongue thrust forward and smelled the singed hair and hide, I could slam that white-hot iron with a big E onto the rump of our cattle without flinching. "My best helper," Papa called me whenever Thalia was out of earshot.

In spite of the identical ruffled big sister/little sister dresses that Mama stitched on the old treadle sewing machine, Thalia and I would never be as companionable as the Dashwood or March sisters. Grandma Ethel saw to that.

In a nobler moment, I could see myself like Elinor Dashwood, sorrowful by the bedside of my dying, impetuous sister or maybe Josephine March weeping as shy Beth faded away. But then, I could hear Grandma Ethel reminding everyone that the wrong sister had been stricken; I would remember that one of the Graces from Mount Olympus like Thalia is above human suffering. Or, had the Fates not had a misstep, she might have been.

When she was newborn, what looked to me like the yellow fuzz of a flattened baby chicken on Thalia's head appeared to Grandma Ethel as the hair of a resurrected Jason. "She'll be the family beauty, just like him, your other boy," she shouted into Grandpa Hector's deaf ear.

Papa was right put off by that comment and went to be alone out by the livestock corral with me trailing behind him. What he said was meant for only the cattle to hear, but I heard him just the same. "She can't let it be. She can't let the dead stay dead. She's the sulfur in our house."

Spotting me hunkered down by the water trough, Papa had smiled ruefully. "Your Grandma says hurtful things sometimes, Ethie, but she loves you and me more than she'll let on. Thalia has just caught her attention because she never had a baby of her own. Just me. I was over two years old when she married your Grandpa Hector. She's just excited over the novelty of a new baby in the house. She misspeaks sometimes."

As a child who had been born under the same roof with Grandma Ethel, I wasn't swayed by Papa's defense of his step-mother. I remember keeping my lips zipped and holding back all the angry things I wanted to say. For years, I had watched her pecking away at Mama, the way a healthy chicken will go after the eyeball of a droopy hen.

I had watched her huddling over Grandpa Hector as he slumped dormant in his old rocker facing the patch of ground that gulped down Jason's life. When she thought no one was listening, she'd hiss: "Looking for a ghost, Hector? He's up on the mantel wondering why his father was so careless." Then she'd pat Grandpa Hector on the shoulder and say loud enough for the bats in the barn rafters and the hired hands to hear: "I worry about you out here in this sharp air. You'll catch a death of cold."

By the time Thalia was a year old, she walked with the careful balance of a tightrope artist, pushing Grandma Ethel's interfering hands away. At the age of two, Thalia could backtalk faster than Grandma Ethel could listen. "She talk mean to Ethie. She talk mean to Mama. Bad Grandma."

A bar of carbolic-tasting Lifebuoy soap wielded by Grandma Ethel cured both Thalia and me of talking back, but we never fought the truth in our heads and devised small ways to get even, although we never discussed our small acts of revenge. Salt in her preserves. Sweater sleeves turned inside out. Skeins of wool knotted.

No one seriously dared to contradict Grandma Ethel. The ritual of ignoring her vicious little jibes comforted both Thalia and me that we were living in a world of bright normality. We were bound by some invisible code to never say aloud what we were thinking so we could sustain the fantasy that Grandma Ethel's cruelties were simply eccentricities.

Even Mama cultivated the elaborate fairy tale of herself as a devoted daughter-in- law of a wise and benevolent older woman. The reality of Grandma Ethel, a mean-spirited, waspish stepmother who tried to control every moment of our family's existence, would be too terrifying.

Grandma Ethel's ecclesiastical canons ranged from the practical to the personal: "Them sheets need to be gathered in right now before they blow down to Oklahoma. It's a sorrowful fact that you never left the Methodist fold to be saved as a Baptist. Your husband oughten to be familiar with you in front of the children." That, after one of Papa's chaste, cheek kisses.

After Thalia was born, a kind of telepathy developed between Papa and Mama that helped avoid any kind of confrontation that might be seen as critical of Grandma Ethel's partiality for Thalia. "Why don't you let Ethel help you today, Jacob? She loves being with her papa."

I did. I really did. Clinging to Papa on the John Deere tractor as great plumes of dust from the dry fields sent us into asthmatic fits of coughing was as sweet to me as breathing incense. That green slotted tractor seat was just big enough for me to kneel behind him and bury my face into the damp cotton of his work shirt. Together, we were defying the past of him as a boy fearful of mules.

Leaving the house in the mornings were special moments for me as I looked behind at Thalia. She would race from one old veined glass window to the next like a goldfish trapped behind curved space.

Then, on a special day that should have belonged to me, Thalia, at just two and a half years old, hogged the limelight again. Papa had often let me sit on his lap to steer and help him shift the gears on the tractor, but this fine August morning, he announced: "Time for you to work the gears all by yourself, Ethie." He always called me Ethie out of the hearing of Grandma Ethel.

The big green model H tractor with its two-cylinder engine and three-speed transmission plus a reverse gear put Grandpa Hector's old Allis Chalmers to shame. I moved confidently up into the seat by myself that morning.

"You just ease it forward slowly and line it up right alongside the shed. This little honey will go over seven miles an hour with the foot throttle cranked all the way open, but you keep it at a safe crawl. I don't want anything happening to my good right hand." Papa had ruffled my absolutely straight hair as though he expected it to bounce into curls. "Jeanie with the light brown hair. I should have named you Jeanie. I like the sound of that," Papa had been in a jovial mood that morning. "Floating like a vapor, on the soft summer air," I echoed back, well-schooled in Stephen Foster that Mama played every evening on the Kimball Papa had bought her.

"Nothing vaporish about you, Ethie. You're my sturdy side-kick. I'll have you driving this tractor like a top hand before your grandma spots us." I was concentrating on the gears so that the tractor didn't lurch forward or turn into Papa as he walked beside the big back tire.

Then, I saw the flash of Thalia's dress behind the silo. Or maybe I just saw the vapor of something that might have been a child's dress. The silo was off limits to children. That glimpse of bright color couldn't have been Thalia. Papa had warned us time and again. "Unstable pockets of grain in a silo can engulf a grown man."

Popping the first gear smoothly, I edged forward, so if Grandma Ethel or Mama did come looking for Thalia, they would see me first, all by myself on the tractor seat. Papa followed not a foot away, beaming as his Jeanie with the light brown hair turned the front wheel left and then right, slow and easy.

I hoped Mama would come outside before Grandma Ethel so I could show her how I could move the first gear with both hands. She'd be that proud of me. Mama was making wild sand plum jelly that morning, Papa's favorite, and had to keep adding pectin, because that kind of jelly is so tart that it won't set up.

Thalia should have stayed in the porch swing where Grandma Ethel left her while she went inside for a glass of ice tea with not enough sugar, because Mama had used it all in the jelly.

I might have heard her first scream, but finding the exact notch for that gear lever took all my concentration as I grated it back and forth, forcing the noise to drown out everything, especially my sister who might be drowning in a vat of grain.

A strip of cloth flapping on the door at the top level of the silo caught Papa's attention just as I wrestled that lever into gear and chugged proudly forward, shouting: "Look at me, Papa! I've got the hang of it."

I'm likely never to forget his shriek. At that moment, he flung himself away from a moving tractor without so much as a backward glance at me, grabbed an old two by four off a pile of scrap wood, and drug it behind him as he scaled the footholds on the curved side of the silo.

As I banged the tractor into the corral just to show him, I watched Papa tearing up that rickety little ladder on the silo and thought about that fine day a year ago when Papa had taken me all the way to McPherson to see Johnnie J. Woosh, billed as the Human Fly.

Just as this day should have done, that day in McPherson almost a year before belonged exclusively to Papa and me. Thalia was croopy; Grandma Ethel claimed she'd caught her sore throat from Thalia and was in a blaming mood, so Mama stayed at home with both of them. It was just Papa and me off for a little adventure of our own.

As we pulled into the town square, the local high school band, sweating under their pre-WWII thick wool uniforms, blasted out something that might have been a Sousa march. Or not. Papa bought us hot dogs and lemonade at the Lions Club tent and found us a place to sit on the curb with a good view of the courthouse. The brass ball at the top of the cupola shown like gold when Papa said: "You and me, Ethie, need more time together."

I was just about to add "without Thalia" when the crowd pushed forward, blocking our view. Papa boosted me onto a slatted wooden courthouse bench, pulled me tightly against him, and pointed to two men following the band down the street.

Holding up a big sign that said: "J.W. Groton Automotive Supplies," the Human Fly pranced along main street like a show pony in his flesh-colored tights that showed some amazing bulges. Hot on his heels was a man with a thick coil of rope and an inner tube; he smiled and waved at Papa.

"That's Mr. Groton. I bought Firestone tires from him. He hired the Human Fly to show how strong Butaprene is. It's synthetic rubber, Ethie. Mr. Groton claims we might not have won the war without synthetic rubber. I doubt that." Papa winked at me as though we shared the same doubt, the way he did when Grandma Ethel wasn't looking.

I was looking as the Human Fly who, within minutes, had scaled five stories, lassoed the spire, and was poised at the base of the pyramidal roof.

Like a belly dancer with amazing stomach muscles, he stepped into the circle of that inner tube and wiggled it, hands-free, right up to his protruding belly button. The band stopped playing as Mr. Groton stepped up on the platform by the Lions Club tent, fiddled with the microphone that splatted with static, and grinned apologetically at the small crowd. "Blasted thing ain't working. What I sell works."

Mr. Groton flung an arm up to where the Human Fly peered down on the crowd from about seventy feet over our heads; at his signal, the Human Fly unfurled an American flag down the side of the courthouse. The stars and stripes drooped into a listless August sky as he moved to the edge of the building and flexed his toes like a prima ballerina about to go on point.

With arms stretched wide, he flung himself out, over, and plummeted down the façade of the county courthouse in front of an awe-struck crowd. About two feet from the ground, the inner tube around his waist flexed like Grandma Ethel's girdle and popped him to his feet.

That special day with Papa had been a year ago. Now, as I cranked my neck back, I could see Papa just like the Human Fly climbing and climbing toward the small doorway at the top of the silo. He was almost there with the long board clattering behind him. There was no inner tube around his middle to save Papa.

After shutting off the fuel to let the tractor die just the way Papa showed me, I jumped down and sprinted over to the silo. Wherever Papa was headed, he might need his good right hand. The ladder was easier to climb than I expected. I imagined myself in tights with a flag in one hand and more courage than the Human Fly as I stepped up and up and up toward that small, dark space at the top where Papa had disappeared.

When I poked my head inside the hinged door, I could see him lying facedown on an unstable board atop a sea of shifting grain, probing and probing. One fist full of yellow hair surfaced through a wave of wheat and kept going heavenward as Papa screamed: "Got her!"

All I could think about at that moment was that old fairy tale illustration of Rapunzel tossing her golden mane out the window of the tower so the prince could climb up.

Thalia looked more like a rag doll with snot-covered grain oozing out of her nose than the heroine of a fairy tale. "Out of the way, for God's sake, Ethel! Get down. Go get help! Get help!" As he balanced on that tipsy board with one arm around Thalia and the other clamped to the side of the opening, the stentorian breathing of Papa frightened me more than the odd wheezing of my sister.

Mama and Papa rode in the ambulance clear to Manhattan and stayed at the hospital with Thalia, leaving me behind with Grandma Ethel, who spent every waking hour asking me how I could have missed seeing Thalia climb up the silo when I was right there on a tractor next to it. My best mournful face couldn't stop the Inquisitor General from prying out sins, much less Grandma Ethel. For the rest of the summer, she blamed Papa, Mama, and me for our carelessness, never directly, but with sly innuendos.

"If God had seen fit to bless me with such a beautiful child, I wouldn't let her out of my sight for a second." Grandma Ethel would try to pull a struggling Thalia onto her lap. "Making preserves shouldn't cause a lapse in concentration." This one aimed directly at Mama. "Your oldest daughter doesn't deserve unbridled attention, Jacob, no matter how hard she tries to get it." This was a double against Papa and me.

So, Thalia recovered after two days in the hospital and took up everyone's time and sympathy for the rest of the summer while I worked harder and harder to be that good right hand that Papa had called me more times than I can count.

An Inuit in Alaska must have an easier life than a farmer in Kansas. Hanging about on an ice floe waiting for a seal to surface must be a walk in the park compared to watching an ice storm freeze your cattle in their tracks.

Trying to forget Thalia's limp body tucked under Papa's arm as he scrambled down the silo shrieking at the top of his lungs for help, I make myself recall the prideful way that Papa had shouted to me just as I made a careful turn with the tractor and headed back in his direction: "We're feeding the world, Ethie. That's what farmers in this country are doing. We had a bumper harvest this year. Our silo is full up with wheat."

Those big tractors, now insulated against the wind, and huge combines that whip through wheat fields in a day might look like giant toys. Overhead, depreciation, interest, insurance, repairs, and hired labor can slash profits to losses in the space of a single hot summer. Without price controls, a bumper harvest didn't mean much back then.

A bumper harvest meant even less when something planted itself in Papa's eye as he looked at me across the limp and wheezing body of my sister that morning. It wasn't a judgment so much as an appraisal. Just the inkling of a doubt. I could see it flickering there. Then I couldn't. Both of his eyes were fixed on the golden-haired child in his arms.

CHAPTER 6

THALIA:

My earliest memory is of drowning. Not in water, but in tiny pellets of gold that moved like waves above a current, sucking me further and further down into an ocean of blackness. I don't remember how I got in the silo or how I got out. Mama and Papa and Grandma Ethel have told me the story about my near miss with death so often that the story has become mythology, like one of those tales that a troubadour spins over and over so it will be repeated long after the narrator is gone.

My sister Ethie, who never embellishes anything—not her clothes or her very determined straight path through life—only said one thing when I asked her, years later, about the time I fell into the silo and ended up in a hospital in Manhattan: "It was a defining moment."

"For you? For me? For Mama and Papa? For the universe?"

Ethie just pursed her lips, narrowed her eyes and stared past me at our acres of tawny wheat as though the word "defining" was traveling out there marking boundaries that only she could see.

Ethie is the most selfless, older sister imaginable. Restrictions, limits, and confinements are her protective armor. She hides out in the bowels of the county courthouse stacking library books by the hour. She's known to have a sharp tongue when someone loses a book or cracks a buckram spine. "Just doing my civic duty protecting county property," she says.

"Protective" is the word that comes to mind most easily when I think about my sister. When I was growing up, she did her dead-level best to keep me from harm's way, tying me into the porch swing so I couldn't get caught up in the cultivator like our poor dead Uncle Jason.

She didn't exactly hover over me or pamper me like Mama and Grandma Ethel did as I screamed the house down, demanding what I wanted whenever the spirit moved me. It was the little things I remember most: sliding her piece of cake onto my plate until I ate so much sugar I would puke; twisting the head off the ugly rag doll that Grandma Ethel made so Papa would buy me a new china one; prodding me to sass Grandma when she was hateful to Mama and claiming all the picture space for herself.

Grandma Ethel subscribed to the *Saturday Evening Post* just so she could clip Norman Rockwell's covers to line the dining room wall. Her favorite was of the graying grandmother hoisting a twenty-five pound turkey onto the table with her wrist slightly bent and not a single clenched muscle in either arm. Everyone around Rockwell's table is gap-jawed with pleasure.

When I look back to my childhood, our Kansas farm appeared to be a kind of perverse Eden. When a member of the family thinks that one child is a princess, and the other a handmaiden, both of those children's worlds are skewed. Our Eden housed a snake. Grandma Ethel. She could have found a worm in the apple that Adam ate. Fault-finding was Grandma Ethel's way of keeping the world balanced, I suppose.

She lost her balance only once. The oddest thing. The old spring-fed, hand-dug well next to a cistern in the corner of the back yard hadn't been in use for years. Papa had nailed a grid of wooden slats across the top of it and warned us: "The water table here was higher when my great-grandpa dug this well. It's clayey soil on top, but friable underneath. The sides keep caving in. I don't want to ever catch you girls playing out there."

Grandma Ethel had complained for years that the old concrete cistern was an eyesore. So, my sister Ethie fixed the eyesore and got nothing but blame for her trouble. She had planted rose bushes in front of the well as a kind of tribute I suppose when Ethan announced our engagement at Thanksgiving. Three months later, when the well caved in, Grandma Ethel held Ethie accountable for her mishap even though my sister was at Kansas State University, learning how to shush people in a library.

If Grandma Ethel's tumble into the well had been her intention, Ethie would have said. She's a forthright kind of person, acts decisively, and doesn't explain after the fact. Mostly, she doesn't explain at all, but reveals her loving heart in symbolic acts, as Mama often reminds me.

The morning after Ethie learned about Ethan and me, she drove the pickup into town and loaded it with every White Rose of York that Ethan had in stock. Then, all by herself, she chopped through half-frozen soil to plant what she called Rose alba in an odd geometric pattern in front of the old cistern and well. To keep the Kansas frost at bay, she piled straw clear up to the stubby tops of the rose canes. I guess Grandma Ethel forgot the well was there with all the excitement of a new baby that next spring.

After Grandma Ethel beat me to the punch the minute that Ethie walked in the door at Thanksgiving break, blurting out news meant to be mine, my sister just stared at me with those dark eyes like Papa's, as though she might be confounded by something but couldn't give it a name.

I had already named what was growing in me months before it had any size to it. Lance. As a noun, it's a weapon; as a verb it means to pierce. At no time did I consider that moonstruck knight of King Arthur who diddled the queen behind his back. Unlike the chivalrous Arthur, I fully intended to settle an old score with Buff Pennington and his football cronies in a way that even Ethie would approve. Carefully, logically, and rationally.

That thought would come later, after my wound had time to fester, after I learned that ravishment by a linebacker and a tight end did not lance the boil in my belly. During the months in the fall of that year, a sense of desperation blotted out any reasonable or prudent thoughts.

In rural Kansas in 1960, expediency trumped any sisterly concern I might have had about Ethie's claim on Ethan Fletcher. Wagging tongues in Ellsworth were probably in a paroxysm that I had no power to halt. Ethan did. Ethan, who drove my sister back and forth on weekends from K State, faded into the woodwork until he pieced together a life that was falling apart.

From the first day in November when he paid a visit to our farmhouse holding a scraggly bunch of yellow blossoms that he called *Ranunculus asiaticus*, Ethan made it clear that he and Ethie shared an interest in plants, nothing more.

Shuffling his feet on the door mat as though he might scoot into a buck and wing dance at any moment, he said: "Your sister showed considerable interest that I was working on this Persian buttercup variety to get the exact color of your hair."

His comment made me think back about how Ethie had pored over the *Burpee Seed Catalogue* during the summer. I suspected that there might have been something more on her mind than just friendship with Ethan. She would never say. Ethie might as well have worn a medieval curb-plate on her tongue. As for me, I never had a stiff upper lip, and at that moment, I could feel six front teeth, including the canines, exposing themselves in a wolfish grin.

On Thanksgiving Day, Ethie worked in that bitter Kansas wind, planting those rose bushes, refusing to sit down with us to Thanksgiving dinner. She did appear to be in a good mood in spite of the surprise news of my engagement to her friend Ethan, quoting Shakespeare as she loves to do with tidbits about the weather thrown in for good measure.

Stomping a light dusting of snow off her boots onto Grandma Ethel's favorite throw rug when she finished the new rose plant-ings, Ethie announced to no one in particular: "Now is the winter of our discontent" and went upstairs to lock herself in her bedroom for the entire next day to avoid Grandma Ethel's annoying refrain about how to make an intimate wedding more public.

Ethie seemed to get over any little huff she might be feeling by the time Papa pulled the pickup around to the front drive to take her back to K State on Saturday.

I don't think I'd ever seen Ethie smile so genially at Grandma Ethel when she wrapped her arm about her shoulders and told her: "Remember to fertilize the roses when the first leaves show, Grandma. They're York roses, climbers. Richard the Third's namesakes. They'll hide the hump of that old cistern if you stake them right. The other hump around here won't stay hidden long."

Well, that remark was uncalled for, but Ethie doesn't always consider the hurtfulness of her dry sense of humor.

Mama and Papa bent over backward to make things equal for their daughters, but I know my sister lived in a hurtful environment, so I never faulted her for sharp words. I never even noticed her deep bruises until I was old enough to repair anything for her. I'm trying now, but some days I question that it's working out.

Grandma Ethel simply lucked into a prosperous, respectable life when she married Grandpa Hector and left her preacher father looking for someone else to hand wash his "smalls." To hear her tell it, she had left a life of small tasks for one of hard work. She claimed that our big farmhouse had attracted half the dust bowl until she caulked the windows to keep the dirt outside.

"They say that the dustbowl air was so thick that prairie dogs had to dig their tunnels above ground," Grandma Ethel told me at least once a week. "Your mama would never notice a thing like that," she'd add, as she fished a dust bunny from under my bed. "And the crows all flew backward to keep the sand out of their eyes," she'd cackle as though saying the same thing ten times a week made it funny.

Grandma Ethel favored me over Ethie with a preference that whacked us up alongside our collective heads. I need to get that fact on the table. Why did she have to constantly remind us that "gentlemen prefer blonds"? She got her hands on those Lorelei stories by Anita Loos in an old *Harper's Bazaar* and wouldn't let them go.

It would be a stretch of anyone's imagination to think of Buff Pennington as a gentleman. In Ellsworth High School, he made quarterback in his sophomore year and me in his junior year. That's a story that needs to be sorted out.

Grandma Ethel busily sorted out my life after my first date with Buff. "Thalia is making her mark with the upper crust in this town and her not yet sixteen. That banker's boy would have been my choice. As close to gentry as anyone in this neck of the woods could be."

As my sister never hesitates to remind me, Grandma Ethel should consult the OED before making some of her pronouncements. Buff would walk away with the prize for profligate of the year. After hearing the bad news of his impending fatherhood, a member of the gentry would never stake down the love of his life in a field of wheat stubble for the fullback and halfback to sample.

CHAPTER 7

ETHEL:

At the end of summer when Ethan Fletcher went off to K State, the year before I graduated from Ellsworth High School, I made it a point to go by Fletcher's Hardware at least once a week just to let his mother know I was interested in how he was getting along.

Lona Fletcher was Church of Christ. So when Ethan invited me, a lowly junior, to his senior prom, I let his mother know I respected her admonishment that we were not to dance. Spies were everywhere, so we didn't. We sat. Ethan was never much of a talker. Our hands touched only by accident. My accident.

Nothing was accidental about Papa encouraging me to follow Ethan to K State. Papa and I had been sitting together on the front porch swing the night after my graduation from Ellsworth High, creaking rhythmically back and forth, careful not to stress the number 9 flat-headed wood screws in the bead and board porch ceiling. "I know English is your favorite subject, but you don't want to end up as a teacher," Papa said.

I nodded in agreement, reconciled to the fact that I might have to postpone college for a year or two until Papa paid off the bank loan for a sorry quarter section of grazing land to the south of us that he'd bought as a kindness to Mr. McGill, the neighbor across our south boundary.

The day Papa borrowed money for the first time ever in 1953, he drove with me across an over-grazed pasture up to a bungalow-type house with the paint peeling off its porch columns and all its windows boarded.

His voice was so soft that I had to strain to hear him. "I remember when Ditch McGill asked all the neighbors who had a truck or a spare team of mules to help him haul this Sears' house from the railroad tracks to his place. I'll never forget the day it arrived. Pretty Boy Floyd killed four FBI agents in Kansas City that very day—June 17, 1933."

Papa eased out of the pickup and moved over to a front porch that was parting company with the rest of the house. "Your Grandma Ethel said Ditch was a spendthrift to put $1,783 into a house when his fields were drying up. His wife's folks, the Adams, farmed that place since before statehood. The Adams kept to themselves, didn't socialize with the community, had only the one girl. When she married Ditch McGill, he moved out here to her folks' farm, but he kept working on the rigs in the west part of the state."

Shaking his head, Papa said: "The best farmer working full-time couldn't make a living on 160 acres like this farm during the Dirty Thirties. The water wells are marginal. This land doesn't have fresh-water springs in ponds or canyons like ours. Ditch had no choice but to stay on the rigs and farm in his off time. What happened to his wife's folks wasn't his fault no matter what your Grandma Ethel says. Nature just runs wild sometimes."

I shot a quizzical look at Papa. I didn't remember Mr. and Mrs. Adams at all; I vaguely recall the McGills, although they lived not a mile down the road from our house. "What happened to the Adams?"

Papa sat down on a corner of the sagging porch and brushed dirt off a patch next to him for me. "It was a terrible time for farmers, even us—dust blocking the sun, fields drying up from 30-mile winds every day. Your Great-Great Grandpa Nestor was a forward-thinking man. Years before anyone could imagine a dustbowl, he planted Osage Orange, cottonwood, and cedars all along the north side of our fence line—and, he planted that wide band of red cedars just north of the barn to protect the house and outbuildings. The Adams' farm had no protection. Their lean-to was on the wrong side of that grove of trees."

Closing his eyes as though to block an image he couldn't bear to see, Papa continued. "It must have been 1930 or '31. I was out of high school by then. Dust was everywhere. Your Grandma Ethel hung wet sheets over the windows and doors of our house so it couldn't come in the cracks. A wall of red dust higher than our silo came boiling across the fields early one morning. It didn't let up until almost sundown. Your Grandpa Hector and I went to check on our neighbors."

He paused for a moment, as though the telling was exhausting. "Ditch's wife was heavy with their first child and standing in the doorway when we drove up. She was frantic with worry. Her folks had gone out in the worst of the storm mid-afternoon to get their milk cows into the shed and hadn't come back."

Papa stood up, dusted the seat of his pants, and pointed toward a grove of Osage Orange. "The shed was over there. We thought bales of hay had been propped against the side to protect the shed. Big humps of red dirt, like those African termite mounds you see in *National Geographic*, were propped against the shed. One difference. A bare foot was sticking out of the side of a dirt pile."

Turning sharply on one boot heel, Papa headed toward the pickup. "Doesn't bear remembering, Ethie. Ditch's wife fell on the floor like a dead woman, lost their only child the next day. Someone got word to Ditch, and he got there in time for the burial. He didn't go back to the rigs. He worked seven days a week trying to make a decent farm out of this place."

"So he bought this house a couple of years later?" I had stayed on the sagging porch, looking up at the triangle shape of the roof over the porch. Something about the angle of the roof jutting forward, asserting itself, appealed to me, as though house intended to put its best foot forward in spite of its modest size.

"Oh, yes. Ditch wasn't too proud to ask for the neighbors' help. I never understood why your Grandma Ethel took such an adverse stand against Ditch and his wife. They were Pentecostal Holiness, but nice people as far as we knew. She said that your Grandpa Hector and I were not to help with the transport or assembly of Ditch's house." Papa smiled in that wry way of his, as though he harbored a secret for so long that he had to be careful in revealing it.

"She shouted the house down that morning when my father and I took off in his new Ford BB Stake truck to help Ditch. By then, she had stopped talking about people who speak in tongues and got on a different hobby horse, warning us that Pretty Boy Floyd could be hiding anywhere, most likely by train tracks for a quick getaway."

Papa turned around and walked warily back toward the sagging porch to inspect the peeling columns. "This model Sears' house was called The Crescent. Ditch told me he was attracted by what the advertisement called 'graceful columns' and 'a convenient bathroom' for his missus. I can't recall her first name. Don't know that she ever said."

He pressed his thumb against a bubble of peeling paint and shook his head. "The great-grandpa of Ditch's wife was one of those Free State men that traveled with John Brown. Came to Ellsworth after that trouble and settled on this piece of land. Ditch's wife grew up here, but we were never neighborly with the Adams."

He pointed toward a distant stand of Osage Orange trees. "Ditch grew up in Ellsworth. Town boy. Farm life was strange to him. That little lean-to of the Adams never had indoor plumbing. The water well was OK if you don't mind the gyp taste." Papa frowned as he flaked peeling paint off a column. "She got the TB after her folks died. Ditch said she dreamed of living in a house with white columns. He wanted to make that dream come true."

I inched closer to a boarded-up window, trying to see inside the house. "The oak floors and trim seem to be in good condition, Papa. Wallpaper's peeling off. I can see through to what must have been the dining room. It looks cozy inside."

"Well, it's your house now, Ethie. Don't know what you'd ever do with a falling-down house like this. Ditch sold everything inside that wasn't nailed down when they moved to Arizona. I'll never forget the look on the face of Ditch's wife the day we hauled the first load of the new house from the depot. Her smile lit up the county. Ditch said there were thirty thousand parts weighing almost twenty thousand tons. Some of his roustabout friends helped load and unload."

Papa wiggled a crosshatched collection of boards on one of the front windows. "Tomorrow, I'll have one of the field hands put some more plywood over the windows and patch the roof so it doesn't fall in. Maybe nail some boards over that big crack by the front door."

When Papa mentioned that crack, the file where I kept Edgar Poe in my brain popped open. For some reason, I couldn't stop hanging my head out the pickup window to look back at the McGill house. In Poe's *The Fall of the House of Usher*, a giant crack goes from the roof down the face of the house to a nearby lake. Earlier, Papa had described Ditch's wife falling on the floor "like a dead woman" when she heard her parents had been killed by the dust storm.

I could imagine Mrs. McGill in a cataleptic, deathlike trance just like Roderick Usher's sister Madeline. That little bungalow didn't resemble the huge country house of the Ushers, but it had an air of mystery and enough ghosts to make it interesting.

"So, why did you buy the McGill's land, Papa?" I asked, as we climbed into his pickup. "Grandma Ethel complains every time she remembers that you didn't take her advice and let it go to a sheriff's sale. She says Mr. McGill took advantage of your generous nature."

I was feeling a bit testy, because Grandma Ethel had just told me behind Papa's back that he might have spent my college money on that sorry land.

Papa flipped the gear shift into second and whipped back onto the main road before he answered. "By the time Ditch and his wife left for the sanatorium in Tempe, about four years ago, the TB was in her spine, twisting her body something terrible. Ditch called me from Tempe to see if I would buy the farm. He had leased the land—not the house—but I didn't have the heart to tell him that his renter had over-grazed it. Ditch said his wife couldn't bear to think of strangers living in her house."

I watched Papa clutching the wheel, holding it at the bottom and inching it back and forth, just like he used to drive our old tractor. When he came to the turn at the mailbox, he pushed in the clutch and let the pickup idle. "Do you remember when you were a little girl, before Thalia was born, and I read you *Aesop's Fables* every night? Your favorite was 'The Lion and the Mouse.' Do you remember why?"

I remembered. "It was the ending. 'No act of kindness, no matter how small, is ever wasted.'" *I also remembered that Grandma Ethel said it was a "heathen Greek book" and threw it in the trash when Thalia tried to teethe on the cardboard edges.*

"I think our acts of kindness go right up to heaven, Ethie, more selfless, less intentional than prayers. Praying takes a backseat to generosity and compassion in my book." Papa took a fractured breath, eased out the clutch and drove toward the barn behind our house.

Papa never criticized Grandma Ethel. He considered her as his mother and as close as blood kin to Thalia and me. She could nitpick until the cows come home, but Papa would praise her for "focusing on the fine points." Occasionally, an oblique criticism of Grandma Ethel would ease out of his mouth, almost as though the bile in his gallbladder couldn't hold another ounce of Grandma Ethel's carping.

"Papa, let's not tell Grandma Ethel or anyone about the McGill house being mine. I really like that old house. I might walk to it sometimes and think about how Ditch McGill brought in a house with white columns for his sick wife. No prayers. Just thoughts. I might trim those old rose bushes by the front porch."

Papa grinned, the way he did sometimes when he was pleased with me, a smile that went all the way to the frontal cortex of my brain into the place where good memories are stored.

CHAPTER 8

The seesaw weather that next year—from bone dry pastures to torrential rain on the spring wheat—had played havoc with our crops. Papa never talked about money, but Grandma Ethel loved to chant "new clothes while we're in dire straits" as I zipped up my homemade graduation dress on Mama's old pedal Singer. Grandma Ethel never said a word about Thalia's store-bought sundress.

I wouldn't say a word even though I rankled over the injustice of Thalia exposing herself while I should have been the center of attention giving my Salutatorian speech peppered with fond reflections on high school and humorous bits about beloved teachers, even though I couldn't stand most of them.

I lifted the entire speech except for the ending. I couldn't bear to look out at that sea of unfriendly faces and tell them how we need each other to succeed. So I ended with: "Getting the right answer is everything." The applause was sporadic at best, though Mama and Papa assured me that the community had never heard anything like my speech.

As we sat in the swing that evening listening to the cicadas and drumming our feet in unison, Papa reassured me: "Your Mama and me put your college money aside. I already paid the first installment on your dorm room. I do think it's wise to choose a course of study that gives you an assured future, Ethie."

Actually, I'd envisioned myself as a graduate of K State working up through the editorial ranks at Random House or Putnam's in New York, sleek in a Chanel suit, chain smoking if the spirit moved me, and unrecognizable to anyone in Ellsworth High.

"You can ride to Manhattan on weekends with Ethan. I already talked to his mother about it. He comes back and forth every weekend to help with the store, so you can be home on weekends to help with chores and maybe spend a bit of time with Thalia. Sisters should be close. You and Thalia ought to be sitting out here in the swing."

I'd rather snuggle up to Yersinia pestis, the bacteria that brought the Black Plague, than Thalia. Time to change the subject. "Papa, tell me why you think I should major in library science. You never mentioned it before tonight."

"I see an opportunity for you, Ethie. Marge Buckly won't be able to keep her job at the library for many more years. Arthritis. Can't lift but one book at a time without her knees buckling." He chuckled. "Didn't mean that the way it sounded. What's important to me is that you could be close to home. My right-hand helper."

Papa shuffled his feet back and forth to slow the swing. "I might have sounded a bit sharp about Marge. I don't wish ill for either her or her sister."

I did. I knew I should be ashamed by my dislike of both Marge Buckly and her sister Cora who ran the telephone exchange. Marge's drawn face when she groaned to lift a stack of books should have elicited pity, but the Buckly sisters were like abbots in those ancient monasteries, controlling the written and spoken words of their flocks. Marge decided on what books were suitable to be checked out or should be stabled as "reference."

Cora Buckly eavesdropped on phone conversations and littered little tidbits from private lives as she made her Main Street rounds. The Buckly sisters patronized and exploited, spreading gossip about what people were reading and saying. Like abbots, in their long, dark polyester dresses, hands clasped over paunchy midriffs, they monitored words—written and spoken—to keep the abbey of Ellsworth under control.

I would have protested that I didn't want to end up in the moldy basement of our courthouse library, whitened as an old grub like Marge Buckly, but the notion of control over what people in Ellsworth read gave me a warm glow. The glow blazed into satisfaction when Papa put his arm around me and pulled me into the comfort zone of compliance.

"Marge gets benefits and two weeks of paid vacation. It would be a fine career for a girl like you," Grandma Ethel delivered my death knell from a crack in the screen door. Even behind the hoar frost of cataracts, Grandma Ethel's beady eyes were busy peering into any future I might have imagined for myself.

The hierarchy of the Dewey Decimal System with its classes, divisions, and sections seemed to me to reflect the structure of the way things should be—but rarely were. I could be swept away by the Romantic poets when I sat on the front seat of Ethan's Chevy pickup every Friday and Sunday afternoon for the trip to Ellsworth and back to Manhattan.

The faint scent of Old Spice intensified the sense of possibility in that pickup cab. My own reticence reminded me that I was only experiencing a kind of vacuum where spontaneous and overflowing romantic feelings would be alien life forms to someone as reserved as Ethan Fletcher.

When the movie *It Came from Outer Space* finally arrived in Ellsworth, I could identify with all the locals in the film who were taken over by aliens. After the birth of Thalia, I had lived with an invasion. I knew exactly how those people in the movie felt, wandering around, wondering what had happened. It's called seizure, occupation, annexation of what no longer belongs to them—their very most internal and important selves.

When I went to K State, I began to feel more like the person I wanted to be—making the Dean's Honor Roll every semester, never missing a class, even one as boring as "A New Approach to Cutter's Seven Levels of Classification." I shared a dorm room my freshman year with Luann Sawyer, a portly home economics major balancing on scrunched-up feet that might have passed muster as bound in China. She wore size 2 shoes and owned thirty-three pairs of discounted model samples.

My three pair of shoes—black heels, black flats and brown loafers—graciously moved aside for my roommate, a pledge of Zeta Tau Alpha, who spent most of her waking hours at "the house" and talked of little else but her "sisters." I never said a word about my sister. How Luann could be euphoric about acquiring fourteen new sisters boggled my mind.

Ethan slept in a rooming house just off campus. As far as I could determine, he had no social life. I certainly didn't. Farm girls in those days had obligations at home when classes weren't in session. So, during my first three years at the university, Ethan showed up regular as clockwork to drive me home and back to Manhattan on Sundays; he sometimes pointed out patches of plants alongside the highway without me prompting him to speak.

Casting an occasional glance at Ethan's rather ordinary profile as he drove looking straight ahead, never at me, I thought about introducing a metaphysical poet into the conversation that we were not having. My favorite, John Donne. I mouthed the words silently: "I wonder by my troth, what thou and I did till we lov'd/ were we not wean'ed till then?"

I was tempted to whisper the next line; Ethan might have grasped the notion of being "suck'd on, countrey pleasures." Especially if those pleasures were plants like green foxtail or common spiderwort.

"*Setaria viridus*. Green foxtail. See those big clumps, Ethie. Some people around here call it bristle grass. It was cultivated in China over four thousand years ago. Look at those low-lying purple flowers. That's common spiderwort. *Tradescantia ohiensis*"

Ethan's face was as animated as I could ever remember. "They were used in the Seventeenth Century as ornamental plants. They close up in bright sunlight. They like cloudy days. I have a particular interest in spiderwort."

As nimbus clouds blackened the sky ahead of us, Ethan held his tongue for the rest of the trip.

"If a person is close-mouthed, it's best to fill in the gaps." That's what Grandma Ethel advised me when she found out I'd be driving with Ethan weekly. "Mrs. Fletcher told me he's enrolled in business school to keep them in a solid position if those Ace stores decide to cross the county line."

Following Grandma Ethel's advice for once, the first gap of silence that I tried to leap netted me a dour look from Ethan. "Business school? Who says? Botany. That's my major. My mother wouldn't know a Ranunculus from a dahlia. She's fixated on spreadsheets. Not me."

An idea popped into my mind at that moment. Plant classification was much like the Dewey Decimal System in libraries. So, that weekend at home, I boned up on the only plant I knew anything about and talked all the way to Manhattan on our return trip.

I knew a great deal about wheat: the *genus Triticum*; millions of tons produced annually; the leading source of vegetable protein in human diets; and, its straw could be used for thatched roofs if the wind were kinder in Kansas.

"Green foxtail doesn't have a leg up on wheat if it's only been cultivated for four thousand years," I pronounced glibly as we passed fields of grain. "Wheat cultivation dates back to 7,500 BC," I added smugly.

After that little exchange, Ethan seemed to open up—pointing out different wildflowers and grasses along the newly opened I-70. Then, one Sunday afternoon, he changed the subject abruptly to Ranunculus bulbs.

"I'm going to develop a new color of yellow—more gold than yellow. The color of your sister's hair. Thalia's hair is almost red-gold in certain lights. Like when she's doing her flips at the games—under those big stadium lamps."

That comment should have given me some inkling that Ethan had his eye on more than the goalpost. We always made it back Friday in time for home football games. Our entire community focused on football the way that serious investors watch the stock market. A promising halfback or sturdy linebacker might make it to big time at K State or KU. The town was pinning its hopes on Buff Pennington, the quarterback, who sprouted wings on his heels like Mercury as he charged down the field or out to our house too often.

Try as I might to see a cheerleader and a quarterback as legendary lovers, I couldn't seem to get Buff and Thalia out of Kansas. Undying love needn't be set in Russia or France, but as I watched Thalia sashaying in front of the football stands, she seemed to lack the potential for the emotions that overwhelmed Anna Karenina or Madame Bovary.

Thalia would never be brave enough to throw herself under a train or drown her sorrows with arsenic—even for someone with the perfect Greek profile that Buff sported.

Buff and Thalia were simply beautiful, over-indulged children playing at what they did best—courting the shallow affections of the Ellsworth sports-loving crowd. My family never missed a home game. Even Grandma Ethel swathed herself in a hideous black and red hand-knitted afghan to brave the crisp fall Friday nights so she could complain the rest of the week about freezing on bleachers.

I could count on the same words coming out of Grandma Ethel's prune of a mouth over the breakfast table every Saturday morning during football season. "I got a bone to pick with the Fletchers, though Ethan's a right nice boy. He can't help that his mother is Church of Christ. It don't seem right that the Fletchers always sit close to the corn dog stand while we're right where the wind hits."

"Tradition, Mama. The Ellis family has been sitting on the second row of the center section of those bleachers since Grandpa Nestor helped the school build them. He earned choice viewing seats. Everyone in our town knows where to sit." Papa would always give the same, pat answer to his stepmother.

"Ethel seems to have forgotten. She huddles closer than a lineman to Mrs. Fletcher. I'd think she'd have seen enough of that

Fletcher boy with all them trips back and forth to Manhattan. She could be keeping that north wind off me if she stayed put where she belongs instead of gossiping about who knows what with Lona Fletcher." Grandma Ethel's mouth seemed to be priming itself for a good gossip, but no one at our breakfast table would oblige.

I was busy speculating over my scrambled eggs that most of the population of Ellsworth were notched at birth right in the Hippocampus, that small curved formation inside the brain that harbors memories. With a recurring, uncontrollable tic, families would walk toward the bleachers at football games and settle where they always had, always would. Except for me.

Lately, I trotted right up those bleachers to sit companionably by Ethan's mother and tried to pretend that I couldn't see Thalia making a display of herself on the sidelines. I was busy dropping broad hints that I might be ripe for religious conversion to "the one true church," Mrs. Fletcher's own Church of Christ.

Subtlety was my strong suit, so I knew exactly how to approach Ethan's mother as a novitiate. Ethan had let it slip on one of our drives back from Manhattan that his mother flew into a "shit storm," his very words, when his *World Religions* humanities book fell out of his backpack.

"My dad told her she'd have to take it up with the Board of Regents, so she cooled off. Mom never went to college. She has a very black and white view of the world when it comes to religion," Ethan said.

I had a decidedly gray one. Mama had been a Methodist when she married Papa.

If you scratched Grandma Ethel, you'd find every Great Awakening since the Baptists stumbled upon the power of revivals. Mama had me sprinkled by a Methodist preacher as an infant. Grandma Ethel insisted that I be dunked as a teenager in the waist-high concrete pool in the basement of the Baptist Church so I could be saved before the mold in the pool took out my lungs.

Mrs. Fletcher let me know in no uncertain terms that all human beings on the planet were doomed heathens until they were baptized into the "restored" Church of Christ. Having been sprinkled and dunked without any sense of a conversion occurring, I shifted our theological conversations at the ballgames to something I could get my teeth into: a pitch pipe.

"I know your church doesn't allow any musical instruments, Mrs. Fletcher—just human voices like it says in the Bible for singing, but I heard that the choir director uses a pitch pipe." I might have been needling Ethan's mother just a bit, but I still harbored a modicum of resentment over her ban on dancing when Ethan had taken me to his senior prom.

My pitch pipe question wound up Ethan's mother for the rest of the football season, so between Buff's charges toward the goal post and Thalia's pompoms sprouting in provocative places, I learned that a piano has 88 keys and 220-240 strings and that a pitch pipe doesn't make music. Well, it can. It could be a kind of harmonica in a pinch, but I let Mrs. Fletcher carry the ball. I had my own goal in mind.

CHAPTER 9

In 1959, before I graduated, when I plopped myself down beside Ethan's parents in the K State stadium just before he was to walk across the stage for a diploma that said: Bachelor of Science, Botany, I felt an immense sadness for the year ahead of me. I would be traveling to Manhattan without Ethan beside me naming the wildflowers. While I was finishing my degree at K State, Ethan would be setting up a greenhouse next to his parents' hardware store in Ellsworth. They settled for a compromise: Ethan would cultivate his plants in a new nursery as part of the family store.

As Ethan's father scooted over to make room for me on the bleachers at the graduation ceremony, Mrs. Fletcher looked a bit disconcerted. "I never expected you to go out of your way to stay on at the end of the semester for Ethan's graduation, Ethel. We'd give you a lift home, but the Plymouth's full. Pastor Benbow and his daughter, Jerusha, came with us to see Ethan graduate."

Mrs. Fletcher's waved a white-gloved hand in front of the face of a bug-eyed girl who seemed to be trying too hard to focus. "Ethel Ellis, Jerusha. Ethel catches a ride home with Ethan now and then."

Beneath a mop of ginger hair, one bulbous, dark eye moved toward me. The other seemed to stay focused on Mrs. Fletcher's glove. Jerusha rose slowly and stretched a perfect, rosebud mouth over teeth too white to be real. Had it not been for the off-putting eyes, Jerusha Benbow might have been beautiful. The nasal drawl wasn't. "I think Ethan might have mentioned you in an off-hand way, Ethel. We've been in such a social swirl since moving from Salina, thanks to Mrs. Fletcher, that I do well to remember important members of our church."

With the eye that seemed to have the complex lenses of a fly, Jerusha sized me up and blinked me away. "Oh, yes. I recall that Ethan gave regular rides to a farm girl. I expect you'll miss the transportation. There's our boy, Mrs. Fletcher! They just called his name," Jerusha screeched.

Before Jerusha intruded that afternoon, I was feeling a bit of comfort, by envisioning myself as a rather washed-out version of Cleopatra, watching Antony heading off to do battle in some other land as Ethan flipped his tassel from the right side to the left of his mortarboard. Little did I know at that moment how spot-on Caesar was when he said that Antony had given up his kingdom for a whore—she would not be one with a Biblical name like Jerusha.

So as not to lose whatever ground I might have gained with Ethan on those companionable drives to school, I made it a habit that summer before my senior year to find excuses to go rattling into town in Papa's old pickup on what Grandma Ethel called "a fool's errand."

That scaly-eyed Saul had nothing on Grandma Ethel. Now, legally blinded by her cataracts, she could still see right through me. "I seen the daughter of that new Church of Christ preacher. She's walleyed as a fish, but Lona Fletcher's makin' over her with a big tea party so she feels right at home."

I felt the barb before Grandma Ethel snagged me. "Waste of time making up to a Campbellite like Lona Fletcher. Do you think she will ever let her son hook up with a Baptist?"

"I'm not a Baptist. I gave up church my freshman year at K State, Grandma Ethel. I believe that Ethan has a mind of his own, as well," I added blithely, although I'd never known him to miss a Sunday morning service with his mother.

As to having a mind of his own, I wasn't all that certain, but Ethan did have a will of his own. He got a loan from the bank to add on to the hardware store and stocked so many gardening tools that he might have been envisioning the Royal Botanic Gardens at Kew materializing right here in northwestern Kansas.

My expertise in classifying spreaders, seeders, pruners, sprayers, rakes, and hoes was just about to overwhelm all thoughts of the Dewey Decimal System that hot July morning as I swung by Fletcher's Hardware to pick up something I'd conveniently forgotten the last visit.

Making every effort to avoid the Fletcher's new clerk, Jerusha Benbow, I skirted through the back of the store, weaving in and out of the great rolls of carpet that stood alongside high shelving. Giving a wide berth to carpet bolts hanging at odd angles from storage space near the roof of the room, I headed toward the closest exit leading out to the new gardening addition.

"Track-Back!" I stopped in my tracks, trying to figure out why someone was shouting at me.

"You shouldn't be walking in this part of the store. We're under construction. Oh, Ethel. It's you. We're installing a new system for our carpet section. What are you doing back here? Don't you pay any attention to signs? You have to go around."

Like a member of the Praetorian Guard, Jerusha thrust her bare arm in the opposite direction and scowled at me disdainfully, as though I might be Caligula, just about to make my last stand.

"I'm a customer heading toward the plant area that is now blocked by rolls of carpet, Jerusha," I replied, trying to keep the annoyance out of my voice.

Jerusha propped herself between two upright rolls of carpet, blinking like blind Samson, searching for the light. "We're installing Track-Back in this part of the store so that every roll of carpet can be hoisted up and down effortlessly."

Jerusha moved her hand along the roll of carpet as though she were stroking a pet dog. "Don't you just love shag? Everybody will want wall-to-wall carpet. It's the American dream. Your old farmhouse probably has wood floors. They are so out of date. The Fletchers have given me a free hand in our new carpet section." She glanced in the direction of the greenhouse.

"Ethan's expertise is in the plant and garden part of the store. I have considerable experience in wall-to-wall carpet. They was right sorry to see me go from the Salina store when the plurality of elders moved Daddy to Ellsworth." Jerusha's mouth worked faster than her eyes, one of which seemed fixed on me while the other wandered.

She stepped closer to me as I eyed a wobbling cylinder of carpet on the make- shift shelving above us. "Without being tethered, these rolls can be dangerous. I saw one break a grown man's leg when it fell off a truck. Those old bolts up in the storage area are a real hazard. I need to get up there to inventory them today, so the men who've delivered Track-Back can move them. It's automated and so modern. The safest lifter ever invented. By a single switch. I don't want Ethan taking any risks."

Jerusha shot a meaningful glance at me with a single, glaring eye. "He took the truck to Emporia today. He's really too busy to be bothered. Can I help you with something, Ethel?"

She could help me by moving just to the left a couple feet while I sprinted up that rickety wooden staircase to the upper level. One good shove, and a roll of carpet could flatten Jerusha into a human piecrust. I smiled ingratiatingly at the preacher's daughter and hissed, *"Rudbeckia hirta."*

"Rud what? Speak up, Ethel," she snapped at me.

"It's Latin for a plant that you might know as Black-eyed Susan. Two flats. I'm sure that Ethan could drop them by the house when he gets back from Emporia. Give him the message from me. *Rudbeckia* or *Black-eyed* Susan if you can't remember the Latin."

I wasn't the kind of person to jibe at someone's infirmity, but I took particular delight in the flush of anger that set Jerusha's eyes wobbling off course like errant pinballs.

As she moved uncomfortably close to me, a hand with perfect vermillion nails shot out faster than the bar on our cattle squeeze chute and locked my arm in a grip.

"Let me give you a piece of friendly advice, just between us girls." One of Jerusha's meandering eyes fixated me like a cobra with a mouse, as the other eye scanned me from my scuffed boots and worn jeans to the top of my scraggly hair.

Still keeping the arm lock on me, Jerusha extended a very shapely foot, shod with a wicked stiletto high heel, and barred my exit.

"Ethan's mother said you came into the store four times last week and stood around talking Greek with Ethan about those plants of his. Men don't like girls who act like they know too much. They certainly don't like girls who hang on like cockleburs."

Jerusha gave me the tiniest shove away from her and began stroking imaginary chaff off a teal-colored dress that clung to her perfect figure.

"Night-blooming *Xanthium*, Jerusha," I retorted as I checked her perfectly oval face for flaws beyond those diverging eyes.

"*Xanthium*! Why don't you speak like a normal person, Ethel? It's very irritating to converse with you. Another piece of advice you might want to tuck away for a rainy day."

"Cocklebur, Jerusha. I believe you just compared me to a cocklebur. That's a plant Ethan considers fascinating. It can be toxic to some or medicinal to others." I kept a little half-assed grin on my face as I backed away. "Tell Ethan I'd like to have the *Rudbeckia* delivered without being hassled by the sales clerk."

"Tell him yourself. And, I'm not a clerk. I don't have any-thing to do with that side of the store. I run the carpet business. The delivery men are waiting outside for me." Jerusha whirled, balancing gracefully in those impossibly high heels, and swayed down the aisle with the flamboyance of a movie star.

Shifting my scuffed boots and glancing cautiously about me, I listened. The hammering had stopped. The workmen install-ing that Track-Back thing that Jerusha compared to the Second Coming were outside arguing with her.

About ten feet above my head, a large roll of carpet appeared to be the kingpin, keeping smaller rolls back from the edge. A pallet truck with a large forklift had been left jammed against the side of the crudely-built staircase leading up to the storage space.

The shiny loop of the handle drew me to it like a honeybee to a flower. I made quick work of it: a flip of the lever next to the handle; a shove to plant the fork further into the base of the staircase; and, finally, the *coup de foudre*, as I jacked the fork up until nails popped free and the two-by-fours of the stair groaned in delicious agony.

By circling past the employee's bathroom along the back hall, I managed to distance myself from any connection to what or what might not happen in the new Carpet and Flooring section of Fletcher's Hardware. Spotting Ethan's mother behind the cash register at the front of the store, I grabbed a couple of pie pans off the shelf and headed in that direction to cover my tracks.

"I have searched that aisle high and low for an eleven-inch, glass pie pan, Mrs. Fletcher. I've been looking for fifteen minutes and can only find these. Grandma Ethel will not be pleased if I bring the wrong size. She's put out with me for breaking her good Pyrex one." I shoved two glass pans across the counter.

"Your Grandma must have said a nine-inch pan. That's what everyone uses. It's standard. This one is exactly what she needs. I know my products," Mrs. Fletcher added. *A bit peevishly, I thought.*

"I'd trust your judgment any day, Mrs. Fletcher. You've been running this store for a long time. And very well," I added, buttering up Ethan's mother.

"Some people think they know more than others. They don't know everything about some things."

I flashed Mrs. Fletcher what I thought was a sympathetic and knowing smile without saying another word. The combines were coming into the wheat fields just as I was heading into town. Before Grandma Ethel realized I had slipped away, I needed to get back to the farm to relieve Papa in the grain truck.

CHAPTER 10

Without even realizing it, Grandma Ethel relieved me of the tinge of anxiety I was feeling about what might be happening in Fletcher's Hardware in Ellsworth.

As a kind of ceremony during harvest—even though none of the harvest crew or our field hands ate with us in the evening—the supper table groaned with slabs of fried steak and mounds of mashed potatoes. Grandma Ethel's cloudy eyes looked directly across the table at me.

"You would not believe what Bessie Tipton just told me on the telephone. Lordy mercy. I'd have stayed out of that store if I knew what a dangerous place it was. Ethel might have known and warned us, considering how often she visits that store."

Refusing to rise to her bait, I smiled genially at Grandma Ethel and speared a slab of fried steak from our own butchered steer.

"I doubt that poor girl will ever be the same. Her knee is likely to be as unstable as her eyes," Grandma Ethel appeared to be winding herself up like some quiz show host, hinting at the answer.

"Mother Ethel, will you please tell us what you're talking about. What did Mrs. Tipton say?" Mama urged as Grandma Ethel chewed her steak like a cud, placidly, the second time around, before answering.

"That Cambellite preacher's daughter, the one who's sweet on Ethan Fletcher, caught herself a world of misery this morning. All them old rolls of carpet stored up in the loft at the back of Fletcher's come down with that girl riding on the top roll like a cowgirl. Just tumbling down like London Bridge. What do you say to that, Ethel?" Grandma Ethel's squinty eyes peered into my carefully arranged, stoic face.

"No comment. That's what I say, Grandma Ethel."

"I don't like the tone of this conversation." Papa's voice had a sharp, puzzled sound as he glowered at both me and Grandma Ethel. "Did something bad happen to that new girl clerk at Fletcher's?"

"I'd say a concussion and a busted thighbone and shinbone might be considered a bad thing. If you cared about the girl. Our Ethel might be pleased to have the competition in the hospital." Grandma Ethel stuck her fork across Mama's plate to harpoon a slice of beefsteak tomato. "These tomatoes is coming on faster than I can keep up with. I could use some help canning tomorrow, Ethel. Unless you need to pay a visit to your friend in the hospital."

"Jerusha Benbow is no particular friend of mine, Grandma Ethel. I met her for the first time at Ethan's graduation. I might have seen her around the store. That's about it. Maybe I'll send her a little card." I speared a tomato and dangled it above my plate. "I'm driving the grain truck tomorrow. Thalia can help you with the canning unless her social life interferes."

I smiled encouragingly at Thalia who had been uncharacteristically quiet at mealtimes for the past week. "Thalia, can you help Grandma Ethel can tomatoes tomorrow while Papa and I drive the grain truck?"

"Huh? Oh. Whatever you want." Thalia mumbled as she pushed an untouched steak around her plate and stared into space as though nothing much was registering behind those pale, blue eyes.

I looked at Thalia quizzically. Buff 's car hadn't been in our driveway for more than a week. Come to think of it, our demanding, self-serving princess had not been herself for the past week or so. My sister flitted aimlessly in and out of the house like a lost butterfly that might be missing the great migration.

By the second week of August, an immediate obstacle to my future hobbled out of town almost as fast as she had migrated into it. Jerusha's father had a falling out with the Fletchers over hospital bills to fix the damage to his daughter's leg. Mrs. Fletcher claimed that Jerusha was not an employee. Expanding the carpet business had been her own idea, funded by her father, with Fletcher Hardware providing space for a small rental fee.

Our local justice of the peace handled misdemeanor cases like this one. Unfortunately for Preacher Benbow, the JP sang in the choir with Mrs. Fletcher and had settled the case at Wednesday night practice as they belted out "Arm of the Lord, awake! Awake!" *a cappella*. By the time "Triumphs of mercy wrought by thee" rang out slightly off-key, it was determined that ecumenism would be served if some other congregation's pulpit search committee hired the new preacher.

The preacher from Salina already had three strikes against him in the local church: he garnered only sixty percent of affirmative votes after his trial sermon; he let his daughter climb up unsteady stairs wearing outrageous stiletto heels; and, he was threatening to sue important church members who had shown his family exceptional kindness. The covenant of works—moral law itself—had been challenged, as well as Mrs. Fletcher. It simply wouldn't do.

As a Christian act, Mrs. Fletcher begrudgingly paid moving expenses for a preacher who named his unfortunate daughter after the Biblical Jerusha who had married a leper. Without a word to her son, Lona Fletcher added a custom-built greenhouse with a roof lantern to the back of the hardware store.

Those were the last days of a full-blown summer that didn't bear repeating for the Benbows, the Fletchers, or for my family. We had weeks of drought, then a deluge that brought the trees and grass back to life. Though green, the trees sagged listlessly as though regeneration were exhausting. Those trees seemed to mirror our lives.

Thalia's morning-to-night sulking set our entire household off-kilter. The Muse of Comedy never moped. Thalia had never been much of a reader, but I brought home Dumas' *The Count of Monte Christo* from the Cootenah Library for her. I figured that she might identify with Edmond Dantès, who was trapped, imprisoned, escaped and wreaked marvelous feats of revenge. Something to take her mind off herself.

Rain flooded the wheat fields so badly that we couldn't salvage much grain; Papa developed symptoms of angina; Grandma Ethel blamed Mama for using lard instead of Crisco; two of our Hereford bulls broke through the fence and got broadsided by a semi; and, Thalia spent hours watching the road for someone who never came.

Well, they did finally did come one hot late August evening. Buff and his two football cronies, Sammy Wiley and Bart Bresno, stopped by the mailbox on the far side of the wheat field near our house—probably too tanked up on choc beer to get within a yard of Grandma Ethel's sniffer.

Papa had gone to Yoder to look at a new Hereford bull that one of the Amish was willing to sell—otherwise, Thalia would never have waltzed out of the house with her midriff exposed and her raggedy shorts not even covering the cheeks of her butt.

Something was going on with Thalia besides her usual lollygagging. I'd known that for a couple of weeks. Buff no longer commandeered the front porch swing until Grandma Ethel would politely send him home. When Thalia was on the hall phone, she now ducked into the closet with it. No calls came for her, but she called someone, and often.

When Buff and his buddies pulled up by the mailbox on the main road and honked, I peeked through the curtain at Thalia traipsing down the porch stairs and through the wheat field, reluctantly, or defiantly, depending on how you judged the set of her chin.

The oddest image flashed before me of mules pulling a cultivator over the flailing body of a fair-haired child. Just at that moment, the last rays of the evening sun blazed across the stubble of the wheat field and turned Thalia's hair to molten gold.

She didn't come home until almost 5 a.m. the next morning before either Mama or Grandma Ethel were up and about. I could see Thalia hesitate at the edge of the field; then, she cut through the stubble at an angle, stopping occasionally to touch the ground, the way a mourner taps the soil on a grave to test the permanency of a new dwelling.

Slipping out the back way through the kitchen, I hurried to meet my sister, feeling somewhat complicit in what might have happened to her, though not with any real sense of guilt. Thalia had made her own bed.

One side of her mouth was swollen, as though she'd almost chewed through her own lips. Her skimpy white top hung off her body, flapping in the morning breeze like a loose-fitting sail.

"I need to get to our bathroom, Ethie. Up the back way. I don't want to be seen. Can't be seen. Ever again." The face that turned to me was not Thalia's. It looked like one of those death masks where the features have been misshapen by the weight of plaster. I detected in her eyes a faint, evasive look, as though she were tucking away something too terrible to see.

"What happened to you?" I could feel the anger behind my words, not because of my sister. Thalia courted disaster in those indecent shorts, but Papa wasn't here to defend our good name. "Why didn't Buff drive you home? What did those boys do to you?"

"I fell down. I walked home. That's all. Don't ask questions. Don't say a word to Mama or Grandma Ethel. They did nothing compared to what I'll do to them some day." Thalia's lifeless words were barely audible, but there was a purposeful look deep down in those pale eyes that I had never seen before, as though Thalia knew the answer to every question that had been asked from the beginning of time.

Later that week, Buff 's parents swooped down from Olympus with the panache of Jupiter and Maia to get their guilty quarterback Mercury out of town before Papa could take a shotgun to him—not that he ever would. Papa doesn't have an ounce of violence in his body.

Grandma Ethel does, but she just sat around with lachrymose eyes muttering about rapist quarterbacks without knowing that a halfback and fullback had been on the field. It took her a full week to get into the swing of things so that the entire football team as well as Episcopalians were complicit in what might be happening to Thalia.

When I think of Grandma Ethel at that troubled time in our family, I'm reminded of those big vats of hot, black tar being ladled onto the streets of Ellsworth. The odor of tar, like Grandma Ethel's vitriol, hung about our lives that late summer. She pulled me aside to take my hide off for using the word "fruitful," even though I was talking about our high-yielding corn crop.

"Don't you never use the "f" word within your sister's hearing."

"The 'f' word?" Grandma Ethel could occasionally surprise me.

"Fecund or fertile. Just like fruitful. You've got a mouth on you, Ethel. We don't need that kind of talk around here with all this going on."

CHAPTER 11

Not much was going on during those long evening silences in our household when we weren't listening to Arthur Godfrey or the Bell Telephone Hour. I had the faintest sense that my stock was rising as that of Princess Thalia fell.

Her face was unreadable as she brooded around the house, but I sometimes spotted what appeared to be a flash of anticipation that every car crunching down the gravel road in front of our house might be Buff, flipping that two-spoke steering wheel of his Chevy Impala, expertly missing Mama's bed of summer annuals.

Never one to dampen spirits, I felt obliged to help Thalia face reality after hearing some diverting news. "I was at the hardware store this morning when Mrs. Fletcher told me something interesting. She said that Buff has gone back east to stay with his mother's folks. Plans to finish his senior year there."

Feeling the faintest tinge of pity for my undeserving sister, I reached down to where she sat like a penitent child all wrung out with grief in Mama's favorite rocker, carelessly crumpling the pages of a library book in her lap.

I patted the top of her shining head and couldn't resist the *coup de grâce*. "'Love is blind, and lovers cannot see the pretty follies they themselves commit.' *Merchant of Venice*. Shakespeare is full of wisdom that you might find edifying, Thalia."

Without looking at me, Thalia spiraled gracefully up from the rocker and touched her hair, her bosom, and her arms as though expunging my human contact, the way a cat does. Then she thrust her library book of Dorothy Parker poems into my hand. "Scratch a lover and find a foe. You're about three hundred years behind the times, Ethie."

Except for comments on the weather or Mama's cooking or how the harvest was going, Thalia and I didn't have much to say to each other toward the end of that summer. Even Grandma Ethel, who always got a word in edgewise if not smack up alongside the listener's head, was strangely silent but never idle.

While she sat, her fingers moved faster than Madame Defarge's knitting needles, as though she might be tallying the weeks of gestation or adding an errant quarterback's name to the roll in line for the guillotine.

Mama seemed serenely detached as she watched the metal tips of Grandma's needles flashing. Then Grandma Ethel stabbed her skein of wool as though the quarterback were snarled inside: "If Hector was still alive, we wouldn't be sitting here like bumps on a log. He had a shotgun and knew when to use it. He wouldn't be put upon by town-folks. No matter how many banks they own. That boy would be making amends as we speak."

Mama responded with a gentle sadness. "Mother Ethel, I don't think we want to invite anyone by forceful means to be a part of our family. I'd rather not hear such remarks in this house."

Having rarely heard Mama speak in opposition to Grandma Ethel, I stood in the doorway in a state of shock as I watched Grandma trying on a variety of expressions—red-hot anger, ashen disapproval, and pink lubricity.

She settled for an oily response. "Well, Eula, considering your background, I would expect you to let other people run over this family. That's why the lower classes stay where they are. No gumption."

Outwardly, nothing much changed in our household except for tiny shifts in the way that Mama and Papa tried *not* to be attentive to Thalia, as though they were acting a part and the stage directions were missing. I knew that they might be realigning her for a future they hadn't expected but couldn't say the words.

As for Thalia, she tucked herself into a tight nexus of hard-edge silence and sat every evening reading *The Count of Monte Christo*. By my count, she had read it four times. I'd checked it out for her, but it was probably overdue.

"If you don't want to go to the library, I can check out something else for you. What's so fascinating about that book?"

"Revenge. The best revenge novel ever," she muttered quietly. "The Count asks: 'How did I plan this moment?' Then, he answers it: 'With pleasure.'"

Those blue eyes of Thalia's had moved past the point of pleasure into a space of reckoning where I didn't want to travel with her.

I was impatient for the seasonal movement of my life to start. I'd be off to K State at the end of the month to start my final year of a library science degree. After that, I'd be a shoo-in to take over the Cootenah Library. With her worsening arthritis, Marge Buckly couldn't heft a book higher than her waist. The weight of unshelved books would pose a hazard if the library were anywhere but in the damp and musty courthouse basement.

I liked to think of the Ancient Library of Alexandria, lost for two thousand years and entombed under the slums of a modern metropolis. Half a million priceless scrolls vanished without a trace and no librarian stamping in and out cards. With only 1,500 volumes, our little Cootenah Library couldn't hold a candle to that ancient library with its lecture halls and gardens.

In rural Kansas, we grow up thinking about culture on a manageable scale. My plan to recreate the ambiance of the Alexandrian Library that had been dedicated to the nine muses was already underway—a collection of flat images of those Greek statues. With a safety razor, I had covertly sliced photographs of the nine muses out of an art book in the university library.

The book hadn't been checked out in eight years. Public exposure of those lovely plates was overdue; they would fit nicely along the hallway. The muse Thalia would be positioned on a dark section of wall between the men's and women's bathrooms.

No garden could be accommodated in the courthouse basement, but a nice patch of bare earth sat just outside the single window level with the ground. With my encouragement, I knew that Ethan could find the same kinds of ornamental plants that grew in those ancient gardens.

The two of us could create a pale facsimile of the Library of Alexandria in the same way that we could fabricate a passable life for ourselves, even in a small Kansas town festering with obstructions to happiness.

With a sense of relief to be away from a house where no one was willing to name the problem afflicting all of us, I went back to K State the last week of August, ducking my head only when I saw anyone from Ellsworth on campus. Knowing that Papa needed my help on the farm, I occasionally caught the Trailways bus home on weekends in September and October.

Heavy autumn rains had washed out fence posts along the back canyon where we couldn't take the truck. I was comforted by the hard work that didn't require a word to be said. Papa seemed bereft of words. We finished the fence by the last weekend in October, so I reminded Papa I wouldn't be home until Thanksgiving break. "I've got two term papers due, Papa. I need to spend time in the campus library."

Papa nodded, but seemed ill-at-ease as he steered the pickup along the top side of ruts in the south pasture. "Your friend Ethan seems to be doing a right smart business with that garden addition to his folks' store. With that greenhouse and all, it should really kick into gear come spring."

The mention of Ethan made me sadder than I would have expected. The first time I saw him after the Benbows left town, I didn't mention the *Rudbeckia* that never got delivered the day of Jerusha's tumble.

Knowing how close-mouthed Ethan usually was, I didn't expect him to talk about Jerusha or the Benbow lawsuit. Nor did I expect him to talk about *Ranunculi*, but he spotted me in the parking lot and rushed out of his greenhouse, holding a small pot of flowers, shouting: "I did it, Ethie! Just as I told you I would. These are the exact color of Thalia's hair. A red-gold *ranunculus*."

For the next fifteen minutes, Ethan talked non-stop about the difference in dividing tubers versus planting *ranunculi* seeds and how alfalfa pellets, kelp meal and bone meal improve the bloom.

All the time he was talking, cradling a small clay pot sprouting yellow flowers, I kept thinking about that idiotic grass head pot Thalia made for Mama out of a coconut shell. Its big, sad, painted-on eyes disturbed me until I upended it in the trash. Seeing the exact shade of Thalia's hair in the pot that Ethan was holding sent a frisson of unease right down my spine. I could see Mrs. Fletcher eyeing us from the greenhouse door.

Remembering Jerusha's little lecture about "speaking Greek" to Ethan, I made a flimsy excuse about needing to help Papa and climbed into the pickup before Mrs. Fletcher could make it across the parking lot.

After that brief political climate that I call the Jerusha Heresy, I had noted a subtle change in the weather at Fletcher's Hardware. Mrs. Fletcher would welcome me with what I like to think of as "demi, hemi, or semi" sentences, as though she might be working her way toward accepting me.

"A practical girl like you, Ethel, would. I never imagined that she. Just shook me to the core when that father of hers."

I nodded sympathetically, knowing that Mrs. Fletcher couldn't bring herself to crank out an entire thought as it related to Jerusha or even mention her Christian name.

By the end of summer, Ethan butted the new greenhouse against Fletcher's Hardware and filled it with odd plants that never would sell to people in Kansas who liked familiar things. No one in Ellsworth would buy a plant they couldn't name. But I never said.

Whenever I managed to get a glimpse of Ethan in the store, I was effusive about the beauty of plants behind clear glass panes. I spent hours in the Cootenah Library boning up on everything related to greenhouses—from Tiberius's cucumbers to Kew Gardens.

In view of what happened next, I almost regretted all the hours I'd spent memorizing the Latin names of plants just to convince Ethan that I was hog-wild about his scheme to expand the family business into a nursery.

The idea of a nursery hit me right between the eyes when I got a ride home for the Thanksgiving holiday. Perfume from bouquets of hothouse flowers replaced the miasma of shame that had hung around our house for months. Grandma Ethel met me at the front door, her eyes flashing little sparks like a firecracker's fuse just before the gunpowder ignites.

"We didn't want to say a word until you got home, Ethel, but things is turned around here for the better. Who could have believed that they was made for each other? I been drivin' myself around the bend thinking about the ceremony. Something quiet like. But with lots of folks. Who could believe our good fortune?"

I certainly couldn't. Neither could Thalia. She looked guiltier than Lady Macbeth as she stood behind Grandma Ethel, rubbing her hands and saying nothing.

She might have been saying: "Out, damn'd spot!"

Or, she might have heard me say: "Hell is murky" in Lady Macbeth's own voice. I knew at that very moment the place where Thalia was bound and promised myself that I would do my best to speed her on her way.

But Thalia, blossoming all pink and gold with a pregnancy that she made no effort to hide, edged around Grandma Ethel and flung her arms around me. "I know that you and Ethan have never been more than friends. He told me so. Otherwise, I would have done something else before I ever . . ."

Letting her voice trail into a whisper, she moved her face so close to me that I could see nothing but eyes. Thalia's eyes were that translucent shade of blue that seemed to shine with delight unless you looked too closely. Then, they were fathomless, going farther and farther inward where something inhuman waited.

Grandma Ethel couldn't wait. She shoved herself between Thalia and me, waving her arm toward the living room, now rank

with the heavy scent of greenhouse flowers. "Ethan is plumb besot-
ted with our little girl. She's a prize all right, but we're thinking
just some nice white flowers and a small church service. Ethan's
mama is downright touchy about the church. White flowers is
important when the dress can't be . . ." Grandma Ethel's voice
dropped right off into doomsday and woke me.

Her fixation on white flowers sent my mind spinning through
the pages of every seed catalogue I'd pored over all summer long.
I remembered the York rose, the first Duke of York's emblem for
purity, for the mystical Rose of Heaven, for the virgin bride that
Thalia could never be, and a state that I was doomed to inhabit.
The York rose was that hunchback king's flower.

The notion of sisterhood takes on a life of its own in a family like ours when the twisted, self-serving desires of a younger
sister end the older sister's hope of happiness. Private dissent
never intrudes on public ceremony in a small town in Kansas.
We simply put on our masks and follow the piper.

Grandma Ethel whipped me up a bilious yellow taffeta Maid
of Honor dress that defied description. A stiff, noisy ruffle that
struck mid-ankle threatened to trip me with every reluctant
step I took down the aisle of the Baptist Church the day after
Christmas, thinking only of masks.

Papa and Mama wore their tentative, worried but relieved, masks.
Grandma Ethel plastered on her pleased-as-punch-hope-she-does
n't-deliver-at-the-altar mask. Mr. and Mrs. Fletcher might have
stepped out of a Japanese Noh drama, their voices unnaturally
shrill, their eyes a bit wild behind frozen faces.

Thalia, cleverly swathed in layers of the palest pink Crimplene,
wore a funeral mask of her own making. From the front of the
altar, I watched her stepping briskly along with Papa holding
her arm. Her perfectly beautiful blank face stared straight ahead
at nothing.

All I could think of was a photograph I'd seen of the death
mask of Keats with these words under it: "How long is this post-
humous existence of mine to go on?"

My own mask trumped everyone's. Pure-dee Max Factor. Layers of beige Crème Puff pressed powder, a great slash of blood-red where my smile should have been, and ding-dong Avon cat's eyes watching everyone watching this wedding farce.

Ethan wore no mask at all as he stood with the preacher by the altar. He was the same chalky gray that he always is, an undercoat, waiting for a color but knowing it won't come. Satisfied to be the primer.

CHAPTER 12

THALIA:

Reading Dickens' *Bleak House* the night before this absurd wedding ceremony gave me an odd sense of comfort. My fiancé Ethan Fletcher was a perfect stand-in for John Jarndyce, the legal guardian of the orphan Esther. Like Mr. Jarndyce, Ethan was older, sober, upright, and generous.

Unlike Esther, I was not a self-deprecating and grateful orphan who had experienced a cruel upbringing. I simply had the misfortune to chance upon a narcissistic clone of myself—Buff Pennington. At fifteen while I pranced along the football field sideline doing a few raunchy moves, I had no notion of something called risk. In the mid-twentieth century in rural Kansas, we might as well have been living under Victoria's reign. We turned our heads when our farm animals did obscene things.

The night after the last game of the season, the winning quarterback tucked me under his arm, gave me whiskey chasers with my beer, wedged me into the back of his car, and vowed to love me forever as he rearranged my underwear with one hand while his other hand stifled my scream.

"All of our classmates do it, Thalia," Buff offered a sly insight into the mores of Ellsworth High as I wept and worried more about bleeding on the upholstery of his Chevy Impala's back seat than the loss of my virtue. "Buck up, Thalia. You got nothing to worry about. I know when to pull out. I don't like rubbers. Blocks the sensation."

Far be it from me to do anything that might have blocked sensation for Buff. I was his steady girlfriend, invited to pool parties in his backyard, flattered by his father, and eyed curiously by his mother.

Until I missed my period. Buff's answer to a missed period was what he called a "spontaneous abortion," helped along by brutal and frequent sex. When the first waves of nausea hit me, I stayed home from school, pretending I had the flu, feeling desperate. Hiding with our old black Bakelite phone in the hall closet, I called Buff's house repeatedly.

"Buff is out with his friends, Thalia. I told him you had called, but you know boys. They have interests of their own. I'm sure he'll get back to you. In time." The ice in Mrs. Pennington's voice lowered the 100 degree temperature of the closet to near zero.

He did get back to me. Right after Papa left the county to buy a new bull. The high-pitched voice on the phone didn't sound at all like Buff. I could hear hoarse giggles and shuffling in the background.

"Sammy and Bart are coming with me. Then I'll drop them off somewhere. We're just taking a little ride out in the country. Meet us by your mailbox around 8 o'clock. I don't want to come inside. I'm not in the mood to see your mother or grandmother."

Frankly, I wasn't in the mood to see the two stooges who always hung around Buff, for reflected glory, I guess. Sammy Wiley couldn't remember a play, but managed to block by sheer size and weight. Bart Bresno sported a mouth of teeth that would have done a piranha proud. He hung onto Buff like a limpet.

"He's a genius with motors," Buff retorted when I complained that I didn't like Bart being with us so often.

After almost a week of silence from Buff, my anger was near the explosive level. The August heat didn't help. The day had been a scorcher, 110 in the shade. So, I might have put on something too skimpy considering the way that Ethie looked at me when I went out to the front porch swing to wait for Buff's Chevy to turn onto our gravel road.

Buff sat in sullen silence as his creepy friend Bart flung open the passenger's door, flipped the front seat over and crawled into the back with Sammy. The vacant expression on Sammy's face made me think of one of those monsters in Brueghel's paintings, complacent, but ready to do the Devil's bidding.

Heading east on a road that led nowhere but to leased farmland, the scent of August struck me with the sad finality of life stalled. The crops had been gathered; the fields were idle; nature was waiting for what came next.

What came next was beyond belief. A piranha had sprouted a hand that snaked around and gripped my right breast. I dug my nails into his hand and yelped. "Keep your filthy paws off me!"

Bart's vulpine smile caused me to shrink closer to Buff. My thoughts were so violent and irrational that I drew in a deep breath and touched Buff's hand on the wheel for comfort. Odd hand. Stubby with dirty nails. A David should have a harpist's hands with long, graceful fingers to caress the strings. To say words that would outlive the singer. To make the Psalms travel into the future to comfort others.

"I don't want to be in this car with those two. Take me home, Buff!" Buff slowed down but didn't turn around.

The gaping, eager jaws of Bart couldn't resist taking the limelight. "You're causing some problems for our buddy here, Thalia."

"I'm what? Have you been talking to these idiots, Buff?"

Hunching down behind the wheel, Buff had a guilty look, like some young boy who was taking his father's car out for a spin and couldn't remember how to drive. Then he turned that gorgeous, self-absorbed Greek profile for a three-quarter view of his face in my direction, and I could see right into the place where his soul should be and wasn't.

"My friends here found an answer, Thalia. Mostly, it was Bart. He knows about this kind of thing."

"Kind of thing?" I could feel the nausea leaving my throat and heading down into my gut just as Buff gunned the Chevy and spun crosswise on the gravel road.

"Getting rid of something that neither of you want." Bart's fetid breath washed over the back of my neck as I shifted toward the dashboard. Just ahead of us was the old Simpson farm, the house deserted for a quarter of a century. The early corn crop had been harvested. Dried stalks stood like rows of shabby, stunted soldiers under the soft moon.

Not a breath of wind stirred anything as Buff turned off the car and climbed outside, jiggling his car keys in front of the crotch of his 501 button-up jeans.

I noticed an artful patch just below the last button where his keys dangled. Not his mother's needlework. A skilled seamstress, careful. If I could focus on the patch, I might still be able to reach a human wearing those jeans.

"Do what you have to. Make it quick. I can't watch." Buff turned his back to me, twirling his keys like a whirly jig.

Nothing else moved. Then they did. My first thought was that I'd never seen fat Sammy move that fast on a football field. He circled the car and pulled my door open just as Bart shoved my seat forward and locked both arms around me. Sammy's eyes were dull as stones, as though whatever propelled him forward was mechanical, not volitional.

Before I could wind myself up for an ear-splitting scream, Bart stuffed a dirty handkerchief in my mouth.

Buff was next to me instantly, tugging at the rag as Sammy lifted my feet and yanked me out of the car. "You're choking her!"

"Get back, Buff. Stay out of this. It has to be against her will, or it won't work. We done talked about this. She ain't gonna say nothin' about any of us. She'd be too ashamed. Right, Thalia?"

I could hear Buff's voice, just a soft monotone of "sorry, sorry, sorry." It was Bart doing all the talking. Sammy squatted over me and tugged at my shorts as I struggled against 250 pounds of a determined fullback.

"When women are raped, the fear makes them secrete juices that kills the fetus. That's why raped women never get pregnant."

Bart's announcement was as loud as a town crier. "You go first, Sammy. I've got her legs. You could help out here, Buff."

Buff couldn't. I arched my back against something that Sammy might or might not be doing to me and could see Buff' bent over, his shoulders shaking. He could have been crying or laughing. I'd never know.

At that moment, a set of chiseled teeth nibbled along the side of my neck. The moon wandered off behind a smutty cloud leaving only one bright star in the sky. I think it might have been Venus, close to the moon that time of year.

Something too vile to imagine found its way into my body, so just like the Count of Monte Christo, I left by taking my prison mate Faria's place within the burial sack, dead to the world, escaping, and plotting my terrible vengeance.

CHAPTER 13

ETHEL:

The tornado changed my life in so many ways when it swept away a house that had sheltered four and a half generations of the Ellis family. The "half generation" was that seed planted by Buff Pennington in my careless sister's womb. I imagined it growing there, its little germ protected by the tough outer pericarp. That germ had all the potential of an embryo that could sprout roots and leaves or arms and legs.

By the time Thalia's December wedding was over, and she had marched down the aisle and off to her new home with the groom who should have been mine, that little embryo probably had a brain that was differentiating asymmetrically.

I rather hoped that its rapid eye movements inside the messy vat of Thalia's belly were helping it take in everything that my sister had done or might do to blood kin. It's best to be on guard in this life.

I've become accustomed to my life taking a backseat to Thalia's. After that Christmas wedding, I had one more semester at K State to finish my degree in Library Science so that I could nudge Marge Buckly out of her cushy job at the Cootenah Library. Did anyone in my family notice that I made the Dean's Honor Role? Did anyone in my family notice that I didn't come home the entire last semester?

Frequent phone calls from Mama, Grandma Ethel and, occasionally, Papa filled in what they considered the blanks in my life. I edited the gaps: "Thalia is experiencing a bit of edema" (Thalia's ankles were fat as Grandma Ethel's); "Ethan has hired a cleaning lady to help" (Thalia's slovenly habits were becoming a burden); "Mrs. Fletcher's church has Thalia on its prayer list" (Mrs. Fletcher's prayer group were caucusing for a good gossip); "Thalia just gave birth to the most beautiful baby boy" (Thalia's little by-blow had only one head).

Finally, in mid-May I got a call about me. "We'll all be there tomorrow for your graduation, Ethie." Papa's overly cheerful voice woke me on that dismally rainy Friday night in mid-May. "I'm driving the truck so we can bring all your things home. We're real excited, Ethie. You've done us proud."

I stretched out atop that twin bed on a lumpy, cotton mattress in a dorm room where I'd spent much of the last four years of my life and thought of Papa's words.

Though Papa wouldn't have known it, he'd used "proud" in the Latin sense—*prodesse*—to be of value. Tomorrow, I would have my day in the sun—or rain, but attention would be focused on me walking across the stage, holding my diploma, hearing the faint applause of Papa, Mama, and, maybe, Grandma Ethel. There's no way that Thalia and Ethan would bring a six-week-old infant out in public.

The stadium was packed. The mid-afternoon sun baked a herd of black-robed students sweltering in unseemly ninety-degree temperatures, restless as range cattle before a storm. Being harangued by the guest speaker about the "burden of responsibility" set my teeth on edge, so I began to scan the crowd, hoping to spot Papa's best summer straw hat with the black grosgrain ribbon.

Just as the speaker wound down to a soft urging to "think about what is important to your community," an ear-splitting wail blasted from somewhere in the bleachers behind me. Not just once. Continuously, as though the siren on a fire truck was stuck open, at full volume.

"God. That kid has healthy lungs," the boy next to me muttered as he twisted around to find the source of the noise. "Wow.

What a gorgeous mother. Maybe its sister. She looks too young to have a baby." He elbowed me and pointed toward the top of a golden head hurrying down the stadium steps followed by Ethan, Mama, and Grandma Ethel.

Only Papa watched me walk across the platform. Thalia and her baby had upstaged me once again. Inside my head, prudence waged a battle with infanticide and won, hands down. When Papa and I walked out to the stadium parking lot, I spotted my family grouped like one of those Christmas manger scenes gone awry.

Sitting on the tailgate of Papa's pickup next to Mama, Thalia bounced her squalling child like a dysfunctional yo-yo. Ethan stood nearby as grave as Joseph but with a pained expression.

The clarion call of Grandma Ethel would silence the heavenly hosts. "Nobody would listen to me when I said over and over not to bring little Lance into a crowd where he could catch all kinds of germs."

Grandma Ethel squinted her tiny eyes accusingly at Papa and me. "You know I was right, Jacob. There was no reason to drag every member of the family all the way to Manhattan to listen to speeches under a broiling sun."

"There was every reason. Ethie is the first member of our family to earn a college degree." Thalia glanced over at Ethan and flushed. "Immediate family, I meant. Blood kin. Lance may not remember the ceremony, but this is the first time he's met his aunt and his godmother."

In one smooth move, Thalia scooted off the tailgate and thrust her red-faced infant against my resistant body, pulling both my arms tightly around it and her. "You will, won't you, Ethie? Be Lance's godmother?"

Obviously, Thalia hadn't read the entire book of Dorothy Parker's poems last August when she quoted the line about "scratch a lover and find a foe" to me. In Dorothy's "Godmother," the old hag gives the "young whelp" sadness and the gift of pain.

With a belch that rattled his small body from head to toe, Lance stiffened and then relaxed, cuddling against me like a new-born pig. His round blue eyes looked up at me with a curious expression, as though I might have the answers that no one else could provide.

At that moment, I thought that I might just be the one. If the answers came with pain, so be it. After taking an Intro to Philosophy course my junior year, I became a dyed-in-the-wool Parmenidean, a follower of Parmenides, a Fifth-Century Greek philosopher, although I never shared that fact in our quasi-Methodist/Baptist household.

Nobody could see the future. I never liked looking at the past, so believing that there is no such thing as change suited me to a T. It's a captivating philosophy to believe that the universe is a set of all moments at once. The history of all of us and everything we're about simply is. Time is just an illusion. Our future isn't unfolding. That fact comforts me. I expect it may comfort little Lance when he's old enough to understand the messy way he came to be.

CHAPTER 14

THALIA:

Though Ethie never seemed very taken by children, the way she held her little nephew, on that bright, sunny day in the K State parking lot sorted out what might have been ill feelings toward me and Ethan. As Maid of Honor in our wedding two days after Christmas, I thought Ethie looked more like one of those frozen-faced runway models than a loving sister.

But then, runway models are dazzling beauties; Ethie prizes herself on accenting her plainness—ironing her already straight hair and using eye shadow as though it is rationed. Also, a runway model wouldn't be caught dead wearing one of Grandma Ethel's creations.

As she was whipping up yellow taffeta ruffles, I told Grandma that yellow was Ethie's worst color; it gave a split-pea soup cast to her skin. "Ethie really doesn't want to be in the wedding, Grandma Ethel. She said that weddings aren't her thing. The least we could do would be to let her pick what she wants to wear," I protested, already chagrined by the scope of the ceremony and the size of my waistline.

"Yellow is a happy color. All these ruffles will make folks think of the sun coming up. This wedding is a joyful event. I expect your sister to wear this dress and smile. She had plenty of time to catch Ethan if he was interested. Which he wasn't."

Grandma Ethel lisped through her new dentures, bought especially for the wedding. "We'll be on exhibit, Thalia. People in this town are always watching. Mark my words. Best foot forward. Your sister won't let us down."

Like one of those jointed mannequins with a painted-on face, Ethie lasted through the ceremony, the reception line, fruit punch, and a three-layered, buttercream frosted cake before slipping out a side door of the Baptist Church, and getting on a Trailways Bus to Manhattan.

Ethie left a brief note on the kitchen table that she had made a special arrangement with her house mother to stay in the near-empty dorm during the rest of the holiday. Being Ethie, she added a cryptic sentence: Thomas Edison said the best thinking has been done in solitude.

"If you're trying to invent a telephone!" Grandma Ethel screeched, waving the note aloft. "I was counting on Ethel to help me set up the cupboards in that house of Ethan's. There's not a single shelf that don't need oilcloth tacked down. Considering your condition, Thalia, you'd think your sister could get into the spirit of helping out a new bride instead of spending all her time bent over some books."

I didn't feel like a new bride. I felt like a consolation prize at an old-timey carnival with Grandma Ethel shouting through a speaker horn: *"Come one, come all. This sideshow features Thalia Ellis, former football queen and head cheerleader, as the main freak show attraction. See how she glows and grows. Her only sister refuses to talk to the beast."*

Ethan talked to the beast. He showed up on the front porch the week after Ethie went back to K State to begin her senior year. Cradling a pot with a reddish-gold cluster of flowers, he extended it as solemnly as if he might be one of the Biblical magi: "Ranuculus, Thalia. Persian variety. I've been trying to develop a bloom the exact color of your hair for almost a year. I think I've got it." He handed me the pot, turned on his heels and walked at a fast clip back to his pickup.

"I think he does have it," Grandma Ethel whispered in my ear, her garlicky breath sending waves of nausea up my throat. "That boy won't be put off by something as trivial as a little trouble. He'll be back, Thalia. Mark my words."

Whether Ethan Fletcher returned or not made no difference to me. Gagging ruled my life. Just thinking about Grandma Ethel's onions in white sauce could make me puke. Sorting out the gastrointestinal mess caused by an alien invasion of my body kept me weak and placid and receptive.

Thinking about what everyone in Ellsworth might be thinking about me diverted my thoughts from what I needed to think about: retribution. Somewhere I had read that revenge is a dish best eaten cold.

Coldness couldn't begin to describe my plight. I had become a sixteen-year-old glacier, dense with ice that moved under its own weight. I couldn't go back to Ellsworth High. According to the School Board, pregnancy was a communicable disease. Expectant mothers had no place contaminating the innocents gleefully fornicating behind the football stadium.

Papa said I could get a GED by studying at home. "They have a testing center over in Manhattan. I'll bet Ethie can find out the best course of study for you. Veterans been getting their GEDs. It's becoming more commonplace for people who want a diploma. They're talking about getting GED testing into the prisons," he added without any intention of wounding me.

Papa and Ethie sometimes say things with a kind of glib insouciance, as though they are fortifying themselves by a demonstrable lack of concern, distancing themselves from what makes them uncomfortable with careless words.

My physical discomfort continued for months. Between bouts of nausea, I worked my way through all of Dickens and started on Thackeray, eager to disappear into someone else's problems, someone else's small victories, someone else's life in another century.

The life-shaking offer that Ethan made in mid-November might have sprung right off a page of fiction, except for the plot, the lack of characterization, the setting, the mood, and the theme.

After that first visit when he left the pot of ranunculus that looked nothing like the color of my hair, he began dropping by once a week with flowers from his greenhouse. He'd perch stiffly on one of Grandma Ethel's wooden side chairs without eye contact while Grandma Ethel made what she liked to call "small talk." Boring. Aphids on the roses. Grubs on the hostas. I wanted to add: *Parasite growing in your granddaughter* just to liven up the conversation. But, good manners held sway. Grandma Ethel's rule: No serious topics could intrude when discourse was social.

Formality intruded late one November afternoon when Ethan showed up just after Papa had driven Grandma Ethel to a Baptist ladies quilting bee. I had caught a glimpse of Ethan's truck driving by the house to the end of the section line and back twice before he pulled into the drive.

His huge bunch of stargazer lilies sent off such potent fumes that I gagged, lunged toward the front hall bathroom, and vomited as quietly as possible. Waiting for the sound of the front door to close and a pickup to leave, I finally came back to the parlor. The lilies had disappeared. Ethan and Mama sat like graveside watchers, waiting for someone to toss in the first handful of earth. Then, like the ghost she often was, Mama slipped out of the room and Ethan was saying something to me that I couldn't quite understand.

"My Grandpa Fletcher left me his Dutch Colonial just at the far end of Blake Street. I've had good renters since he died. Gave them notice that I might need it. It has four bedrooms and two bathrooms. It was one of those ready-cut, mail-order homes. About thirty years old. The kitchen needs some work." Ethan stared down at his brown, wing-tipped shoes as though they might get up and walk out against his will.

"I know about your situation. Have known for two months. That damned old busybody Cora Buckly at the telephone exchange listens to private conversations. Nosy bitch. Told my mother. We had words." Ethan's face flushed, then turned ashen, but the tone of his voice never changed to reflect what he was obviously feeling.

He just kept reading his lines in a monotone. "You're a lot younger than me, Thalia. A beautiful girl. I used to tell Ethel what a good athlete you are when we were driving back from K State for the home games. All those back flips down the sidelines. Ethie didn't much care for football, I guess." Ethan paused, shuffled those highly polished shoes and then amazed me.

"I want to marry you. Take care of you and the child. I don't care what happened. Not my business. You set whatever conditions you deem reasonable. I just want to take care of you. I'd do anything for you. If you don't mind me being there."

The last words were mumbled so softly that I could hardly hear Ethan. I could see him though. Clearly. Brylcreem, a little dab'l do ya, glistened along a careful part in his dark hair. Two lackluster eyes stared down at me past a perfectly straight nose. His face was kindness personified. It simply lacked any liveliness.

Ethan Fletcher was just what I needed at this moment in time. He was the self-effacing Joe Gargery in *Great Expectations*, giving and asking for nothing in return. He was the modest Dr. Watson, praising the arrogant Sherlock. Ethan was offering me an exit from humiliation, from the kind of social ostracism I could expect as an unmarried mother in this upright, introverted community.

Ellsworth started hiding its sinful underbelly back when the drovers were bringing cattle up from Texas. An underground district with saloons and whores and bathtubs and barbers was concealed beneath the streets where respectable, married women pushed their baby buggies.

I might not belong under the streets of Ellsworth, but I would never be that golden girl who once pranced along them.

This shy man shuffling his shoes on Grandma Ethel's braided wool rug could get me out of this fix. I clamped my hands across my stomach and sucked in. Not exactly out of this fix. But he was offering a haven of sorts. A nice house in town away from Grandma Ethel. Any conditions I cared to impose on our relationship. His name for a child who would never resemble him.

And, best of all, a smoldering anger toward anyone who dared to gossip about me.

CHAPTER 15

ETHEL:

There's something to be said about being hired as the county librarian a month after graduating with a library of science degree from K-State. A few, well-placed complaints nudged the inevitable end of Marge Buckly's retirement, heralded by stale cookies, a card with many signatures, and a limp farewell bouquet.

The way that Marge sorted books would make Melvil Dewey turn in his grave. Carlyle's *French Revolution* perched right next to Gene-Stratton Porter's *Freckles*. As for Marge's eavesdropping sister Cora, all-digit dialing at the local telephone exchange would soon stop up her curious ears and shut her gossipy mouth.

Local gossip is tasty as sand-plum jelly, unless the Ellis name comes up; then, our hackles rise. Like those little erectile hairs along the back of a testy dog, those of us with Ellis blood grow little sensors that pick up even the slightest slur.

There's no denying that Thalia set herself up as a target for scandalmongering. But, the bad-mouthing stops between out-siders and family—that rule is intuitive in the Ellis clan. Ethan's mother, Lona Fletcher, missed that primordial gene.

Lona's cash register at Fletcher's Hardware was Broadcast Central, sitting just across the street from a concrete block build-ing housing the manual telephone switchboard that provided a perfect medium for secret-sharing. Unlike the reticent visitor in Conrad's "The Secret Sharer," Cora Buckly stored secrets like earwax, then trotted over for a bit of irrigation from Mrs. Fletcher.

On Monday morning, just before I opened the library, I was in Fletcher's Hardware rummaging through the odds and ends in office supplies for a date stamp when I overheard enough slander to put me off Lona Fletcher until the Second Coming.

"My poor boy does his own shirts, cooks meals, and has been known to change a diaper. Unheard of in my day. She's a slothful girl at best. Baked him the weirdest cake for his twenty-third birthday last week and missed the date. It's June fifth not June sixth. I don't want to speak ill of her. She just cast a kind of spell over my boy that he can't seem to slough off." Lona's harsh whisper bounced down the aisle and drummed with a sour note on my tympanic membrane.

"The girl was out to here when she got him to marry her," Cora chimed in. "Buff Pennington's mother is tight-mouthed as a clam, but I know she's relieved that her boy went to college back east. That girl was always trouble. Besides, Mrs. Pennington would never be social with that Ellis family. They're farmers, country people."

Putting the date stamp carefully back on the shelf, I took the back exit from the store and avoided the greenhouse where Ethan had lined enough bedding plants outside to stock a major botanical garden. I headed back to the courthouse.

I could grouse all day about the humid conditions in the courthouse basement, but, truthfully, my clients are happy to have open stacks, an occasional assortment of new novels, and the current *Farmer's Almanac.*

A perk of my new job sits right next to the basement library—all the county records. This Ellis farmer intended to plow through old files to see if there might be anything that Mrs. Fletcher might not want on the airwaves.

The Fletchers were law-abiding, prosperous merchants. To my knowledge, Jerusha's lawsuit over her tumble down those rickety stairs was the first whiff of scandal to touch them. I might have felt an inkling of guilt, but the slyness of those two gossipy women trumped guilt any day.

Sagging, damp, cardboard boxes lining the storage room walls were labeled and dated: Property, Probate, Court Records, Vital Statistics, and Miscellaneous. Puzzled about where to begin, I decided that the year before Ethan's birth would be a good place to start.

Because she isn't keen on calendars, Thalia had just celebrated Ethan's twenty-third birthday on June sixth. I'd get his mother's maiden name and check out her branch of the family.

I pulled out the box labeled Vital Statistics, 1930-1940. In a file marked "Marriage License Applications," I started with January of 1935, thumbing through the months clear up to December. I'd have to go back further. *Or not.* A Marriage Certificate dated December 6, 1936, proved that Cleve Fletcher saved Lona Langley considerable embarrassment by tying the knot seven months before little Ethan popped out.

Hanging the "Out to Lunch" sign on the door early, I trotted down the street to Fletcher Hardware, an ingenious but subtle plan forming in my considerable brain. Locating the rubber date stamp, I carefully turned the day, month and year, grabbed a Fulton Stamp Pad No. 0 Black, and headed toward the cash register.

"Hello, Ethel. Didn't I catch a glimpse of you earlier? You slipped out without saying a word," Mrs. Fletcher flashed me a guilty smile.

"I had to find the right size of date stamp for our library check-out cards. Marge smacked the old one so hard that two of the numerals are busted. Do you happen to have a piece of paper so I can check this one, Lona? Is it OK for me to call you Lona, now that we're kin." Putting on my hunched shoulder submissive posture, I flipped open the metal box, stamped the pad and held the date stamp aloft.

Sighing, as she rummaged under the counter for a piece of paper, Lona smacked a spotless sheet of typing paper on the counter. "We're not exactly kin, Ethel. A remote connection by marriage doesn't really mean kinship."

I pulled the sheet of paper toward me and smacked it firmly, over and over. Then, I turned it around, shoved it in front of Lona Fletcher and watched December 6, 1937, work its magic.

"Check your dictionary, Lona. I've already checked the calendar. Some girls really need to rush to the altar. I suspect Thalia isn't my *only relative* that made it in the nick of time."

CHAPTER 16

THALIA:

When I think of being saved, I remember those brush arbor revivals that set Grandma Ethel off like a Roman candle whenever some circuit-riding preacher sent out the call. An open-sided shelter built of vertical poles with bushes and tree limbs on top was supposed to keep the sun off our heads. It was a magnet for ticks, chiggers, public confessions—and, blissfully, over in a day.

Being saved is actually a revealing ordeal that goes on and on. I like to think of Ethan as my good Samaritan, not my knight in shining armor, as Grandma Ethel insists. I'm finished with knights dashing around in front of cheering crowds. Their codes of chivalry suck. The good Samaritan simply showed mercy, a quality that I should try harder to appreciate.

When Ethan offered to marry me, he meant what he said about "any terms." A chaste cheek kiss marked our agreement. I might have been no more than a favorite aunt. He continued to bring flowers and sit while Grandma Ethel talked. Two weeks before the ceremony, he took me to see his grandfather's house where we would be living in Ellsworth.

The gambrel roof of a large, white boxy house towered over its neighbors. A long, wide front porch spoke to me of shelter.

"It's not a traditional Dutch Colonial. Grandpa Fletcher added the porch. He said you can't live in Kansas in summer without a big porch. I found these nice wicker planters," Ethan adjusted a reedy box with legs. "They just need a coat of paint. Geraniums will do well or maybe lobelia if it's not too hot. Marigolds are nice, except for red spider. Anything you like, Thalia. You decide."

Shivering in a twenty-degree cold front, I tried to keep my face from freezing into a mask of incredulity as Ethan worked his way through botanical possibilities. "I'm chilled to the bone, Ethan. Can we go inside?"

Ethan's stricken face followed me past two workmen trying to shove a kitchen stove into a slot too small for it. "It's GE. All electric. They may have to take out part of a cabinet, but I thought you'd like . . ."

I didn't stay to listen. A wide staircase that went up to a landing and bent into the distance seemed to be calling me. Upstairs, immediately off the hallway, two dormer windows flooded a bedroom with sunlight, warming it, comforting me. A simple bed, dresser, desk, and bookshelves glistened with white paint. A quilted bedspread, blue as the summer sky, hung precisely one inch above the floor.

"Oh, Ethan. What a beautiful room. All of our furniture is so dark. Grandma Ethel says that if it's not mahogany, it's not good wood. These big, bare windows are wonderful. Ours are always draped." I reached for Ethan's hand in the first gesture of affection that I'd ever shown him, squeezed it gently, then dropped it quickly. He got the message.

"This was Dad's bedroom when he was growing up. I just painted the old wood furniture and got a new bedspread. Until the baby. Well, I thought you might need your own space." Those wing-tipped shoes of Ethan's were doing a buck and wing against the wooden floor as though they might just shuffle out of the room.

"My own space? Grandma Ethel doesn't believe in space. She fills every inch with furniture, covers it with her hand-crocheted doilies, and stacks whatnots on all surfaces. Then, she fills in the spaces between with prattle."

I walked over to the window and looked out at the last tracings of an early snow, wondering what I could say to this man who looked so ill-at-ease. Yet, he had been brave enough to make his wishes known to a girl who used to do backflips along a football field, a girl with hair the color of a yellow ranunculus, a girl who didn't really know who she was anymore.

I'm like a Mimic octopus, one of those strange creatures that changes into something else—from the most popular girl in school to an about-to-be married woman with a baby on the way. I remember reading that the Mimic octopus changes itself into shapes like sea snakes or jellyfish to frighten away prey. Clever octopus. Stupid me. From the window, I could see almost to the edge of Ellsworth and imagine the road past our house that led to the old Simpson farm and that field of stubble.

It was agony to think of that night—not the pain of forced sex with Sammy and Bart. The betrayal. Buff was a flesh and blood statue of David. What fifteen-year-old ninny wouldn't submit? I believed that I was in love with Buff. Everyone was. Even those two cretins, Sammy and Bart. They were willing to face criminal charges of rape to help Buff out of what he called a predicament. Or, maybe they just wanted a share of what he'd been having. Me. Used. Soon to be reused.

"Thalia is the second golden-haired angel in our family," Grandma Ethel would proclaim every time Ethie was within earshot; then, she'd point to the photograph of Papa's long-dead brother Jason on the mantel.

"A golden child in every generation. That one lost through carelessness. We almost lost this one in the silo." Grandma Ethel's blatant preference galled me. In more subtle ways, she made Papa feel like a second-best stepson—even though Jason was unknown to her and in the grave before she became Papa's stepmother.

Grandma Ethel would like nothing better than to put me on a shelf like one of those Dresden porcelain figurines she collects. How had I failed to see that I was just that kind of ornament for Buff? An object. An adornment.

A blast of winter wind rattled the panes of glass, but the thought of revenge warmed me as nothing else ever could. The treachery of Buff had tucked itself so far inside me that it would fester like unrelieved loss until I could make it right.

Ethan touched my shoulder as the loud sound of banging and muffled voices from the kitchen startled me. "I'll ask them to take a break until you've seen the house."

As Ethan started toward the bedroom door, I was struck by his gentle, unassuming manner. What I once thought of as a kind of numbing boredom now seemed to me as the epitome of graciousness. It was a quality that I found a bit unnerving.

"No. They need to finish their work. Their noise is a good sound. Show me the rest of the upstairs. Grandma Ethel told me she'd seen you moving a truckload of things from your folks' house this week."

From the set of his jaw, I had touched a sore spot. "Moved out. Shouldn't have stayed in my old room after graduation. Mother insisted. I gave in. Bad idea."

Ethan braced himself against the frame of the door, as though he might need to support the walls of this house against an onslaught. "My mother is a good woman, Thalia. She just gets these notions. All that nonsense with Jerusha Benbow. And her church. Its easier to go along with Mother than to listen to her when I don't. So, I've stopped listening to her."

If loss was a color, Ethan's lackluster, dark eyes were the exact hue of deprivation. I had no doubt about the cause. "Your mother isn't exactly over the moon about our engagement, is she?"

"Dad has been very supportive." Ethan's answer was oblique at best. "After I left the room, I heard him shouting something about stones and glass houses at Mother. I see her at the store these days. That's about it."

We walked down the hall to a large bedroom with windows overlooking the backyard. Remnants of frozen honeysuckle clung to an archway leading to a space filled with bare trees on their sides, their roots balled and burlapped.

"Need to get those into the ground before we have any more snow. I tried to buy a few acres outside of town so I can expand my landscaping business," Ethan's voice shifted up a register. "No one is selling after they filmed part of that TV Wyatt Earp series with Hugh O'Brian in Ellsworth. Folks around here think Ellsworth will be the next Hollywood."

Watching those dark eyes of Ethan glowing when he said "expand my landscaping business," I decided to tackle his problem, carry the ball so to speak. That's the way Buff always talked, as though he couldn't get out of the huddle. I tried not to hate Buff as much as I wanted to hate him. I reached for Ethan's hand, and, this time, clung to it to save myself. "Papa will give me a piece of land for your trees and plants. As much as you need."

For the first time since Ethan made his offer, I didn't feel like a freeloader. It might be possible for me to bring something to the table besides my advancing girth. Just like the Count of Monte Cristo, I would avenge myself brilliantly against Buff, Sammy, and Bart—but I needed the safe port and the camouflage of decency that Ethan could provide.

CHAPTER 17

ETHEL:

Some might think that life in a small town verges on boredom. They would do well to check out the meaning of "verge," the Seventeenth Century meaning—which is the century most of rural Kansas inhabits.

Lacking the hustle and bustle of cities, small towns incline toward the trifling, the inconsequential, the minor episodes that create the real stuff of life.

Just take a look at Jane Austen's small world: a proud man of wealth annoys the prejudiced heroine; a widow and her daughters are cast out of their stately home; a matchmaking girl creates discomfort for her friends and neighbors. Yet, Jane turns minor, village happenings into best sellers for centuries.

I have no close friends, so, I observe others with Jane's same, careful interest. By others, I mean my library clients, Mama, Papa, Grandma Ethel—and Thalia's little family. Just as I expected, it hasn't grown since the untimely arrival of Lance into that big Dutch Colonial that should have been my house.

While poking around upstairs when Thalia was setting the table for one of those little family dinners she loves to host with the food Grandma Ethel and Mama bring, I noted two things: all of Thalia's clothes are in the front-facing bedroom; all of Ethan's clothes are in the bedroom that looks out on the backyard. At the end of the hall is Lance's bedroom. Another big bedroom is used as a store room.

In the third drawer of Thalia's dresser, a diaphragm in a plastic container practically jumped out at me. No surprise. I've seen one before. Our library subscribes to the *Britannica Book of the Year Series*. I'm well-schooled through Margaret Sanger's birth control treatises. Wouldn't dream of putting books like that on the shelves. It's in my private collection. I also order the first printing, first edition of the best authors. Again, for my private collection. The county hasn't ever raised my salary, so I've had to implement my own life savings.

Thalia's weekly dinners in Ethan's lovely Dutch Colonial fill me with mixed emotions. During the three years that Lance proceeded from crawling to walking and, finally, to charging painfully into us on his tricycle, I maintained the same vacuous smile. My godmother smile. Waiting for him to be old enough to understand what I might tell him to reverse my pain.

My pain was of the nudging variety, a splinter that lies just under the skin. Watching Thalia sashaying around the dinner table with dishes that Mama and Grandma Ethel had prepared always made me think of myself in that old tale about the dog in the manger. He bared his teeth so the livestock couldn't eat the hay, but he couldn't eat it either. His anger just kept him gnashing his teeth.

Some might interpret that parable to mean that some begrudge others what they can't enjoy themselves. I like to think that the dog was warm and comfortable in the manger and delighted in chasing away creatures that might dislodge him.

Thalia had dislodged me from the moment she was born, all golden and pink, claiming Mama and Papa, excluding me. She had dislodged me from my future with Ethan the moment her own future was threatened by disgrace.

To keep my thinking from spiraling into dark notions, I force myself to remember that I am a convert of Parminides. "Justice does not loose her fetters and let anything come into being or pass away, but holds it fast."

Parminides never experienced a Kansas tornado, or he might have changed his tune. Inhabiting one of the top ten violent tornado states, Kansans are always on the watch for purplish skies, rotation of clouds, a big wall cloud, and straight-lined winds. Our local radio station might put out an alert from the National Weather Service the minute bad weather was spotted, but that was long before the Fujita scale labeled funnels as "devastating" or "incredible."

At exactly 5 p.m. on that odd day in June, I had locked the library door right in the face of Cora Buckly's protests. Her thin, waspish mouth pressed against the glass like a wasp trying to feed its larvae in a nest, letting me and everyone left in the courthouse know that her sister Marge, the former librarian, was flexible about hours.

While the sky roiled overhead with dark clouds and vicious flashes of lightening, I was safe in the bowels of the courthouse and halfway through Nabokov's novel, *Lolita.* Nothing could have pleased me more than to find my sister Thalia right there in print tempting an older man. Humbert had his flaws and, perhaps, a taste for younger girls, but Lolita tempted him beyond belief. This was a novel I wouldn't dare put on the shelf. Someone might say that I'd purchased it to expose Thalia's wiles.

Just as I was at the point where poor Humbert is begging Lolita, now seventeen, to leave her husband, a loud thumping at the library door forced me to get up, head toward the door, and give Cora Buckly a well-deserved dressing down once again about library hours.

A ghostly Thalia wavered in front of the frosted glass and shouted: "The tornado, Ethie. It went west. They say it's bad toward the west."

I swung open the door to what might have served as a tri-partite Greek chorus to a drama on some other stage. "Grandma Ethel is too claustrophobic to go into the storm cellar," Thalia's comment left too much unsaid.

"The sheriff said power poles are down on the main county road, but we can go the back way." The reasonable voice of Ethan calmed me.

"Nawful storm. Don't wanna see Aunt Ethie. Wanna go home!" The caterwauling of Lance comforted me as nothing else could have done. I just wanted to know I still had a home, so I plucked him from Ethan's arms, raced up the basement steps, circled those big back fins of the Plymouth DeSoto, crawled with Lance into the back seat and shouted: "Go West, young man, and grow up with the country!" Horace Greeley's optimism seemed necessary at such a grim moment.

As Ethan veered around debris in the road leading to our farm, I lifted Lance onto my lap and began pointing out the oddities of nature gone mad: elm trees with witches' fingers pointing skyward, a wire basket of unbroken eggs, the top of a silo flattened like a tin pancake. And nothing else. No house. No wind. No Papa. No Grandma Ethel. Just Wordsworth's "bliss of solitude" and Mama's daffodils in the front flower bed.

After checking an empty cellar, we stood as hopelessly as Rodin's bronze statues of the Burghers of Calais. Thalia brought chaos and uncertainty to heel when she announced: "There's not a scrap of hers left here, Ethan. Ethie comes home with us."

With only the clothes on my back, I moved in with them, grimly pleased to see little Lance's face furrowed like one of those stiffened and painted linen Greek theater masks. Only the young know the meaning of anticipation. It has to do with probability—nothing pleasurable about it.

After the worst tornado in the history of our county swept Mama, Papa, and Grandma Ethel away to Oz or some Baptist heaven, I intended to stay only a month or so with Thalia and Ethan—just until I could reconcile myself that not a stick nor a shingle nor one of Grandma Ethel's framed Norman Rockwells would ever be found. But then, I settled into a curious kind of comfort—like one of those hens on wooden eggs, thinking she could warm them into hatching.

Something had hatched in this fine house that Ethan's grandfather had willed to him. The day his grandparents blew away, three-year-old Lance Fletcher sat sniveling in the basement because a tornado had ruined his birthday party. I tried to think of my nephew in kindly terms, but he was a dead ringer for Buff Pennington, who had just come hobbling back to his daddy's bank, after leaving Ellsworth over three years ago.

The gossip was that he was wounded on a football field back east, kicked in the privates at a private college.

Nothing remains private in small towns. Marva Duprey, who does transcription for the local GP, spread the word: "Intratesticular hematoma. Fibrous tissue. Unlikely to sire again." Marva relies on an historical context for her gossip. By planting the word "again," she managed to rake up bitter memories.

The fact remains that Buff left my family in a state of shame and put my almost-fiancé Ethan on a low-hanging branch within easy reach of Thalia. In the Latin sense of the word, I take umbrage against Buff. He is the shadow that lurks around the corner. Thalia never mentions his name, but I recognize a sister witch.

That night when Lona Fletcher brought up his name in such a casual way at the dinner table, an image of Thalia popped into my right temporal lobe. She was dancing around the caldron like one of Macbeth's witches shouting: "For a charm of powerful trouble/Like a hell-broth boil and bubble."

Nothing appeared to be bubbling, but something was brewing behind that lovely, frozen façade of Thalia that had nothing to do with her mother-in-law's purposeful comment.

Ethan flushed with anger, but remained silent.

I've never quite sorted out how my sister snagged an obedient son like Ethan. Ethan's mother roiled the religious waters when her son married outside her church, but she was too late. She didn't have the foresight of an Episcopalian like Mrs. Pennington who got her son out of town.

Two weeks after the tornado swept our parents away, Ethan's mother stepped right into the void, reinstating those Ellis family dinners in the Dutch Colonial. There was no doubt in my mind that Lona Fletcher was tallying up the value of prime wheat land, good pasture, and three spring-fed lakes. Her worthless daughter-in-law Thalia now shared ownership of a sizable piece of farmland.

At dinner time, Lona burst uninvited through the back door with her husband in tow and said: "Cleve and me just can't get over how you girls' folks just disappeared in the storm so you couldn't even have a regular service for them. Just that little, short memorial thing without any kind of viewing of the bodies for people to remember."

I watched Lona's eyes glazing over and imagined her trying to sort the parts and pieces of Mama and Papa and Grandma Ethel from the cows and pigs and chickens that swirled up together in that violently rotating funnel two weeks earlier.

Lona plopped a big wicker basket on the kitchen counter. "I brought meatloaf and potatoes, but my yeast must be dead. The rolls didn't rise." Lona dropped little brown golf balls onto a cookie sheet. "Warming might soften them up."

"Stones," I muttered.

"You don't have to be touchy about the rolls, Ethel," Lona said in a missish tone of voice.

"Tombstones. To remember them, we put stones in Clear Creek Cemetery. That's where all of Papa's family are buried. The Ellis family has been in this county for several generations, Lona, even if they are *only* farmers." I glared at Lona, remembering her gossip.

"Grandma Ethel chose her own inscription. Bought her stone years ago with everything but the death date on it. Gray granite." Thalia eased between Lona and me. "It says: 'Absent from the body, present with the Lord.' From *Corinthians*, Grandma Ethel told me."

"It should have been reversed to say 'Body absent,'" I retorted, irritated that Thalia was trying to make nice with her mother-in-law in the kitchen.

"I chose Mama's inscription: 'Always in our hearts.'" Thalia patted my arm. "But Ethie put part of a lovely poem by Emily Dickinson on Papa's stone: 'Unable are the loved to die, for love is immortality.'"

"Our new preacher doesn't hold with poetry on gravestones. I'm sorry that I haven't had you girls over to meet him." Lona flashed one of her righteous smiles at me as she shoved a congealed mass of meatloaf into the oven. "He says the dead in our Christian cemeteries should be remembered only with Biblical inscriptions. I'll arrange a little get-together with our preacher soon."

"'I'm sorry for the Dead—today. It's such a congenial time.' Emily said that. Occasions like this always bring her to mind, Lona." I was just working myself into a fine lather of resentment when Ethan's father interrupted.

"There's a new auto repair shop going in just at the edge of town on 156. That Wiley boy, Sammy, and his friend, the Bresno boy, are leasing that old vacant building. I hear that both boys have been working in a big garage in Kansas City. Lubes, repairs, and they have a side business of arc welding—putting little spikes on those wire wheel covers for snazzy hubcaps. Weren't you in school with those boys, Thalia?"

I watched Thalia clutch the edge of a laminate counter as though this new topic of conversation had broadsided her.

Lona whacked her again. "That's not nearly as interesting as what Cora Buckly told me today. The Pennington's boy is going into the banking business with his father. Bringing that girl he married back East with him. Cora says there's some resentment from the other loan officers at the bank. The boy getting preferential treatment like that."

"Cora eavesdropping on phone lines again?" The acid in my voice stirred Ethan to action.

"Thalia, why don't you show Mother and Dad where you want them to sit. Ethie, will you can help me get the food? I think Mother's nice meatloaf may be getting over cooked."

Gripping my arm, Ethan whispered tensely as he steered me toward the kitchen. "I don't know why she would mention the Pennington name in this house. If we can get through this meal without me strangling Mother, it will be a blessing."

I patted the broad, warm hand that linked me to Ethan in a way that he may not have been able to understand. I wasn't a librarian for nothing. Carrying the cookie sheet of nasty flattened rolls to the table, I scooted the tray toward Lona and said: "I do believe these rolls are edible. Risen from the dead so to speak."

Making a show of moving Lance's chair next to Thalia, I scooted in as close as possible to Lona and said brightly: "Three copies of Miss Harper Lee's blockbuster *To Kill a Mockingbird* arrived in the library this very morning, and I said to myself. I'm going to let Lona Fletcher check out all three of them for her book group. If you can't break a few rules for relatives, what use are you to the family?"

Having already read Miss Lee's tale, I dominated the dinner conversation by emphasizing the morality of Atticus Finch and leaving out the tasty bits.

The tasty bits going through Thalia's mind during the rest of that dinner left her rigid with silence. When I brushed past her with store-bought cookies and a leaking quart of orange sherbet, I felt as though I were passing through a cold patch, as though ghosts had congregated all about her.

They had. Two days later, Thalia was at the library shortly after I unlocked the door. "Do you have any books on writing?"

"What kind of writing? We have Fowler on *Modern English Usage*. Herbert Read's *English Prose Style*. Strunk and White."

"No. I mean like cursive writing. Handwriting. I want to practice my writing," Thalia flushed with her obvious lie. "It's not very pretty."

I squinted at her skeptically. "There's the Palmer method using muscle motion. We have the old 1912 textbook somewhere around here. Palmer claimed it was faster than a typewriter, but I doubt it. You'd be well advised to learn to type better, Thalia. Just in case you need a skill."

"Calligraphy. That's what I want, Ethie. To improve my handwriting by making it different. Sort of by copying."

"We don't stock Asian books, Thalia. Here's Dr. Spock's new book on child rearing. You'd do well to find out why little Lance bit his grandmother after dinner this week. Lona looked fit to be tied when he latched on to her ankle. I rather enjoyed her expression. Capped off an evening I'd rather not repeat. Do they have to show up for dinner every week?"

I watched Thalia holding Dr. Spock an arm's length away, as though little Lance's appetite for human flesh was the least of her concerns.

Something was troubling Thalia. While the Fletchers sat with us around the dinner table, she had retreated into a dark place the moment that Mr. Fletcher mentioned the new auto repair shop.

Lona Fletcher's announcement that Buff would be returning to Ellsworth caused Thalia to batten down like a coastal resident facing an incipient hurricane.

This morning, as she charged into the library stacks, Thalia was energized. I could see something behind those pale blue eyes spinning like a slot machine multiplier.

"Do you think that retribution sets things right?" Thalia looked around at the stacks of books and whispered the question almost as though she thought all the authors might be listening.

"Like the Greek god Nemesis handing out to each one what was due? Or the Old Testament retribution of an eye for an eye?" I narrowed my eyes at Thalia trying to sort out the relationship between the question and the questioner.

"More like Nemesis, I suppose, being sure that things are evened out. A rightful kind of retribution. Purposeful and right." Thalia ran a manicured fingernail along the spines of books on the "s" shelf of fiction and turned those guileless blue eyes away from me. Every reader of fiction knows that the context and the intention preempt the words of a character.

Whatever she was up to, whatever plan was fomenting behind those glacial eyes meant that someone might be meeting the Count of Monte Christo sooner rather than later. I didn't need to look into the witches' cauldron to see what was boiling. Buff and Bart and Sammy should be quaking in their boots.

CHAPTER 18

THALIA:

Later was a word that had become my byword, a way to keep vengeance in my heart when my life with Ethan kept bad memories at bay. I made myself remember the sharpness of jagged cornstalks against my back as Sammy Wiley and Bart Bresno topped a pregnant girl who might have been Thalia Ellis.

She disappeared that evening, watching Buff turn away from her screams toward the East where he was already imagining a girl from Boston to show off in Ellsworth.

That August night, Sammy and Bart were willing to face criminal charges to help Buff out of what he called a "predicament." Or, maybe they just wanted Buff's castoff. I can't recall pain that night. I only remember how betrayal tucked itself so far inside of me that it would fester like unrelieved loss until things were made right, later, sometime later.

The word "later" held all the power of what would happen eventually, subsequently, in the course of things, and, in due time. Later meant that my anger would have time to escalate, to intensify, to surge into something so flat-out right that even Ethie might be proud of how I fix things providentially.

The idea came to me the minute that Ethan's father just happened to leave a receipt on his kitchen table from "B & W Auto Repair," hand-written and signed by Sammy Wiley. Fat, round cursive letters, with a little circle atop the 'i'. So like Sammy.

That night in the field Sammy and Bart were not simply Buff's pawns, doing what he allowed them to do. They were pinch hitters, just like me, in love with Buff. Everyone was. I remember him standing several yards away, aloof, like that statute of David, his head turned to something in the distance, toward a future that didn't include me.

What does the notion of future mean to a fifteen-year-old when the quarterback hero pulls her against him and says: "Mine." I remember only that a great wave came over me, rolling me all thick and white, dissolving me into tiny crystals of sand. What girl wouldn't have given him what he wanted, what every boy wants? If I balked, he might never say "mine" again; if he didn't, I could never reassemble my scattered self. That's what teenage love feels like. That's why we never recover from it.

Today, my recovery resides in the shelter of Ethan where I have become whole again, after a fashion. Not real, but whole, seemingly unbroken. Because Ethan makes it easy to take him for granted, I may be damaging him, chipping away at his wholeness. Ethie sees it that way. She doesn't say, but I know what she means without a word being uttered.

ETHEL:

Those interminable family dinners with Ethan's mother were enlivened only by watching her trying to make things right if only she could sort out the chronology of events that left her "nettled," as she liked to say.

For Lona Fletcher, "nettled" meant losing face in Ellsworth, knowing that everyone else knew that a cuckoo had laid its egg in her son's nest. She needed a choice piece of gossip to move past her son's defection to Thalia and whatever Lance might be doing to her new polyester pantsuit.

The miniature version of Buff painting her leg under the table with ketchup- smeared fingers jogged Lona's memory cache. "I just recalled something I heard from Mabel Talbut. It was over a year ago when she still worked in the doctor's office. About that Pennington boy."

"As I recall, Mother, Mabel was let go for talking about patients outside the office. I don't think you should be repeating idle . . . " Ethan cautioned.

"You know I never repeat idle gossip," Lona retorted. "I should have been one of those journalists. I missed my calling. Someone drops a word here, a word there, and I find an interesting connection. No harm in that," Lona asserted as she kneed Lance away.

"A cousin of one of my church ladies is a friend of the Penningtons, a social friend, invited when they have a do." She frowned and added as an afterthought. "Episcopalians tend not to mingle with the community. Incense is not what we do around here."

Thalia's eyes were glassy, like those round opaque insets that keep the curious from seeing inside a front door; Ethan attacked a slab of his mother's tough roast as though Lona, herself, were splayed out on his plate.

"You were saying, Lona. About an interesting connection." I swung my knees sideways and put on my listening expression to get Ethan's mother back on track. This weekly dinner wingding might prove interesting.

"My friend's cousin said that Boston girl Buff married had to drive all the way to Kansas City for a checkup with a doctor who deals only with female problems. It's not her." Lona's voice hissed like a gas jet just waiting for a match.

I struck it. "If she saw a doctor in Kansas City, I don't see how Mabel Talbut fits in."

"Well, you wouldn't, Ethel. You don't have that journalistic instinct. I'm the one that put two and two together. Buff played too much football. He got a urethal tear when he played at that little college back East. Infection spread to the you-know-what." Lona's mouth pursed tightly as though an invisible string was tugging on a nameless little pouch.

"Scrotum?" I asked brightly.

"We don't use words like that in front of children, Ethel." With a single motion, Lona scooped up Lance and plopped him in my lap. "All I'm saying is what Mabel told me in confidence. I deduce that the Pennington line isn't going anywhere."

She patted a red-faced Lance abstractly and looked down her long nose at Ethan. "You don't need to be glaring at me, Ethan. Has nothing to do with us. I'm just saying that one of our leading families won't be increasing the town census. Sad, really, considering."

THALIA:

Ethan rarely bristles. Even when his mother says hurtful things. My mother-in-law's tongue bludgeons, then stupefies her victims. She should study Ethie's style. Like one of those medieval torturers who could flay skin bloodlessly off a body, Ethie can rip open the heart and leave it beating guilelessly for all to see. Lona Fletcher will regret testing my sister's patience.

Ethie's expression is unreadable. She watches Ethan whittling at his steak, his face somber with shock that his mother would say Buff's name under his own roof or would speak of his sterility as the so-called fruit of his loins sits sniveling on Ethie's lap.

My mother-in-law oozes scandal like a hidden barrel of hazardous waste, slowly, lethally, as though the rusty container should have held and didn't. I could almost see the pollution streaming around the table, sending a dark flush across Ethan's face.

At that moment, a flash of light shot under the west-facing windows behind Ethan, the way it does just as the sun sets on the flat plains of Kansas. Just the slightest nod of Ethie's head alerted me that she would never suffer in silence.

Like the little boy who should have kept his thumb in the hole in the dam but didn't, Ethie shoved back her chair, picked up my squalling son and announced: "Considering the turn of the conversation and the hour, Lance needs a bedtime story. I found a beautifully illustrated copy of Grimm's *The Changeling* hidden away in the library today. Just the thing to send him to dreamland."

Or give him nightmares. When I was a child, Ethie's bedtime stories—"Rapunzel" and "The Girl Without Hands"—frightened yet intrigued me. All that chopping off of hair and hands and princes who waffled when they should have acted.

Just as she reached the landing, Ethie shouted back down: "I'll double-check the windows in the little prince's room. If it could happen to the Lindberghs, it could happen to anyone."

It could. It would, but not in the way that anyone left sitting at the dining room table might imagine. Ethan glanced at me only once, then launched into the merits of fertilizer with extra magnesium, a topic guaranteed to send his mother home early.

His mother's tittle-tattle about Buff's possible sterility didn't have quite the impact on me that she had imagined. A narcissist like Buff would be perfectly happy replicating himself once. Too many versions would clutter his playing field. Now, there would be no other little Penningtons.

"I'll buy little Lance a book of Hurlbert's Bible stories. I don't think those old fairy tales Ethie reads to him are appropriate for children." Lona interrupted my train of thought, trying to get back on her own track.

The girls in Grimm's fairy tales always fascinated me because they seemed to be flirting with evil. Rapunzel lures the prince to her tower by singing; the handless girl steals pears from a royal garden. There is something to be said about flirting with evil, wondering if it rubs off, if you are inhaling it like asbestos fibers so that the days of your life are chopped off with every breath.

"Really, Mother. Hurlbert's gruesome stories with all those graphic illustrations? Joseph's brothers throwing him in a pit to die; Abraham holding a flame to torch Isaac on a pile of wood." Ethan shook his head. "They gave me nightmares. I should have read more fairy tales, Mother."

Ethan spoke with winsome regret. He never talked much about his childhood, but his very determined mother couldn't have made it an easy one for him. At moments like this, I prize Ethan, the way he gently undercuts his mother without doing any real damage to her, the kind of harm our Grandma Ethel inflicted on our mother and Ethie.

When Ethan is at the hardware store, working in his nursery, I picture him, steadfast, reasonable, playful with a child who isn't his, and wish he'd come home early so I could show him my gratitude. Then, he comes home, and I wonder if my life will be so disgustingly normal that I'll be forced to leave it.

At that point, I return to *The Count of Monte Christo.* Ethie says it's too battered to return to the library. No matter. I've committed his acts of revenge to memory. The planning of revenge sustained the Count in prison. My plan might just preserve me into old age.

CHAPTER 19

THALIA:

"I'm here to pick up my mother's leg of lamb for Easter. I hope it's ready." The faint edge of irritation in the voice near my shoulder at the meat counter trapped me in front of a glistening slab of liver. Like Prometheus waiting for the eagle, I could sense the sharp claws, the probing beak even before the pain.

The predator struck in an unexpected way. Moving under a will of its own, my grocery cart spun into a Greek statue dressed in a silvery gray suit.

"Well, aren't you a fine little fellow. I knew we'd run into each other sooner or later. He is a beauty, Thalia." Buff glowed with confidence as he gripped my cart with one hand and cupped Lance's face with the other. "We need to talk. Not here. Some place where I can see the boy," he murmured as he whispered in Lance's ear.

Almost irrationally, I trembled and edged backward. The barrier between this man and me was thick as coal dust, grimy and bitter with resentment.

"Mrs. Pennington's leg of lamb, sir." The crackle of butcher's paper being slid across the counter startled me. "I put it on her bill like she said. Anything for you, Mrs. Fletcher?" Just as the butcher turned aside from his bloody table, the late-afternoon sun flashed through the plate glass window and sent shafts of light through Lance's blond hair.

At that moment, an image of that old sepia photograph of my father and his long-lost twin Jason came to mind. The bloody meat cleaver on the butcher's block, the shining disks that sliced through Jason's small body, and the hand on Lance's head formed a collage.

One that spoke. "I can fish. He gonna show me how. Nice man." The guileless expression on my son's face as he smiled up at Buff pushed me into action. I gave a negative nod to the butcher, snatched Lance out of the cart, and hissed like a cornered cat: "City park. By the swings. Three o'clock tomorrow."

ETHEL:

Thalia forgot to get the pork chops again. Sometimes, I close the library early when it's my turn to cook dinner on Tuesdays and Thursdays. I put the "Inventory in Process" sign on the door, so that any of those prying county commissioners know I'm looking after the taxpayers' collection.

When I got to Ethan's house—I never think of the Dutch Colonial as belonging to Thalia, since my claim is stronger than hers—Thalia was on the front porch with Lance. With a peach-tree limb, some string, and a childish paper cutout of a fish, she'd rigged up a fishing pole for Lance.

"I'm teaching Lance to fish," she said brightly, tossing the string into the rose bushes.

"No! Man gonna take me. Not you." Lance sat pouting on the stoop, the way he often does when things aren't going his way. "That man! He said."

"I can't imagine what's gotten into this child. He missed his nap again. I made you a perfectly good fishing pole, Lance. You play with it or quit complaining. Your Aunt Ethie and I don't want to look at an unhappy face."

Thalia turned her glorious red-gold hair toward the setting sun and stretched her arms wide and upward as though she were replicating the Winged Victory of Samothrace, more magnificent with her own head attached.

I'd never say so aloud, but Thalia is shot through with light, the way that really gorgeous people appear to be. I guess the gods choose them, bless them with physical beauty, and then sit up on Mt. Olympus to see what a mess they can make for themselves and others. When I say Thalia is shot through with light, I don't mean she is transparent. I'd like to believe that, but she's complex.

Thalia is always self-obsessed, but not like that sick sod Narcissus who couldn't get over himself. After the evening that she went out with Buff and his buddies and came home alone, Thalia turned inward to a place where no one else can go. I'd say that she is absorbed by something more grave than sorrow. No. Something more hard-edged than grief.

"Remember that old Psalm Grandma Ethel used to quote about vengeance, Ethie? When someone pissed her off? 'He will bathe his feet in the blood of the wicked.' I looked through the Bible trying to find that particular Psalm. No matter. I don't think God spends much time punishing the wicked to insure justice."

That stopped me in my tracks. Again, I had to consider the relationship between what a sentence means and what the person who is uttering it intends. Behind those disturbing, glassy eyes of Thalia lay purpose, so finely honed that it could slice through to the bone.

"Grandma Ethel used the Bible selectively to justify her own little vendettas. I don't think our neighbor's pigs in her garden constituted a felony," I said flippantly.

I'd seen that hurt expression on Thalia's face too many times. It offended me in some deep, visceral way, as though I had failed her again with doubt, even though no doubt was expressed. I would make small amends.

"Here's what I believe, Thalia. We're just an infinitesimal speck in this galaxy of gas and stars and dark matter. So if someone mistreats us and we can be a mote in his eye, I'd say pluck it out. Not the mote. The eye."

Thinking about the missing pork chops that Thalia was supposed to bring from the butcher's today and Grandma Ellis's fury over those hogs in her garden, I swung the front door screen aside and patted Thalia's shoulder abstractedly. "The Olympian gods have much more interesting ways of getting even than the Old Testament god. You should read the *Iliad*, Thalia."

THALIA:

I have read the *Iliad*. What does Ethie think I do all day? I've worked my way through every book from Ethan's humanities course at K State. When I read the Greek plays or Homer, at times, I almost feel akin to one of those Olympian gods looking down on small lives, moving people like pieces on a chessboard. I see patterns in the *Iliad*.

The pawns are moved first; then comes Achilles or Hector. Someone larger, the real target, the one who veers off the track. The one who makes a fatal mistake. Believes he can claim a child he never wanted or trust a girl he has wronged.

Tomorrow at 3 p.m., a pattern will begin to unfold. I like to think in terms of a pattern rather than a scheme. A pattern can be a motif, something as benign as the way an Aran sweater is knitted with honeycomb or basket designs—unless the knitter adds unique stitches to identify the sailor after the sea has claimed him and washed away all the identifiable parts.

Just a fishing trip. Part of a design. Fabricating a crime that they don't know they're committing. It starts with the gentle push of a swing holding a golden-haired, laughing boy.

"I knew you'd come around to my way of thinking, Thalia. We were special. You and me. There's no reason that Lance can't have some kind of relationship with me." As Buff shoved the swing rhythmically, his shoulders flexed the fabric of his gray suit jacket without disturbing the elegantly tailored line of it at all.

"It needs to be done on the QT. My position, you know. The wife and all. And old rock-solid Ethan. Don't want to stir up the rumor mill." Buff flashed the kind of naked, wicked smile I could imagine on Grand Inquisitor Torquemada's face just as he expelled the Jews from Spain.

"A short fishing trip you said, Buff. At your father's cabin near Kanopolis Lake. No more than a few hours. Lance needs a nap in the cabin right after lunch. See that he's back here before Ethan gets home from work. Your car can't be seen at my house. Better send Sammy and Bart to pick up Lance. An auto repair truck in the drive won't interest the neighbors. Wednesday at 9 o'clock. Lance will be waiting on the front porch."

"This can work, Thalia. We can do it!" The sudden enthusiasm in Buff's voice took me back four years to the scrimmage line. I could hear him barking orders with confidence as I waved my pompoms and pranced along the sidelines like a circus pony.

"The boys and me have been talking about doing some fishing. A little early for walleye, but we'll be sure the little guy here catches something. I'd better get back to the bank. Made a phony excuse to leave."

Just as he turned away, Buff tried to pull on a mask of regret, to line his handsome face with furrows. "You're a good sport, Thalia. If my mother hadn't been so pushy, we might have . . . well. What's done is done." Without another word, he walked back toward where he had hidden his car near the line of cedars.

I fought an impulse to shout out: "You got it wrong again, Buff. Lady Macbeth says: 'What's done cannot be undone.' And, her hands are very bloody."

CHAPTER 20

THALIA:

To prepare Lance for a fishing trip with strangers might prove a bit traumatic to a boy not quite four years old, I told him bedtime stories about lakes full of fish where little boys should never go without holding the hands of nice men. These little boys never talked to anyone about trying to catch a fish. It needed to be a secret from the fish or they wouldn't take the bait.

Ever since Ethan's father left the S&B Auto Repair bill on the kitchen counter, the night he talked about the mechanical skills of Sammy and Bart, I had been practicing my penmanship with the fervor of a cloistered monk. At first, Sammy's loopy letters were difficult to emulate. The demand itself wouldn't pass muster if the readability level exceeded the third grade.

Mrs. Thalia Fletcher

Your boy is safe for now. Bring 50 thousand dollers to Horsethief Canyon turnoff tonight. Right trail. 100 yards to roten stump. No looking back. Boy will be OK if you bring cash. No tricks. Yours truely.

ETHEL:

I've been keeping a weather eye on Thalia all week. A good sailor knows to stay windward of obstacles ahead. A Kansas wheat farmer senses a change in the weather. Papa always said that he could smell brimstone in the wind that brought torrential rains just as the wheat ripened so that we couldn't get the combines or trucks into the field.

Now, Thalia and I go halves with our neighbor who takes care of the Ellis fields. Not a single brick or board of our home remained after the tornado. Just a bit of the foundation and Mama's flowerbed.

I may have established my reputation as the town librarian, but I'm a wheat farmer at heart. I miss our old homestead. Homestead has a nice ring to it. From the Old English meaning: place of one's dwelling. That dwelling can't be as the sister-in-law, living in Ethan's Dutch Colonial for the rest of my life.

When the tornado blew our folks away, somewhere past imagining, I hung on for dear life to Thalia's offer of a home with her, Ethan, and Lance. I wouldn't be underfoot like Grandma Ethel always was. I would just wade along the stream of our collective lives without getting my feet wet.

Solicitous and understanding whenever Ethan tired of Thalia's temperament, I would be St. Flora to victims of betrayal. That would be me, Ethan, and little Lance who didn't ask to be the cuckoo's egg.

In the space of almost a year since I moved into Ethan's house, I have learned something about the peculiar nature of love. As cruel and capricious as a spring storm, that old shape-shifter, love, thickens my tongue so that I can no longer name it. I can feel it though.

Thalia's notion of love has passed from a lukewarm sense of gratitude for Ethan to the certainty of enduring affection. She demonstrates it with soft-footed trips to his bedroom late in the night. For Ethan, love and bewitchment are synonymous terms. Therefore, he exists on a precipice.

From the day I came home to find Thalia casting a paper fish into the rosebushes to entertain Lance, something changed. Like an Agatha Christie mystery, intrigue wrapped itself around every object and every action.

I walked in unexpectedly two times and saw Thalia tucking a lined tablet into a kitchen drawer. After she went upstairs, I examined it. The word "thousand" humped across the page over and over like an example of bad penmanship. And, there was an unexplainable object tucked into the back of Thalia's wardrobe—a small orange life vest.

Lance's obsession with drawing the Christian fish symbol all over the wallpaper of his room unsettled me, as though he were somehow complicit in what was yet to happen.

Had I been easily agitated, Lona Fletcher would have prompted me into an act of crime at our Sunday night dinner. Her meatloaf defied description.

"I added eggplant and turnips since I was a wee bit short of ground beef," Lona said as she plopped a rounded lump of something that appeared to have a purplish spine erupting from its smashed body. "I'll pop it in the oven for twenty more minutes or so. Give us girls time for a pre-prandial chat. Something I heard about one of the Penningtons."

She flung one hand toward the door as though swatting flies. "Ethan, go help your father get the freezer out of the pickup. His knees are bad today. Take it around back. Homemade ice cream. Sweetened condensed milk. No eggs. Just the way you like it."

I watched Ethan struggling with an old wooden ice cream freezer, spilling ice and rock salt as he lugged it around the side of the house toward the back porch.

His face might have been flushed with exertion or the mention of the Pennington name. Like a master puppeteer, Ethan's mother had tried multiple ways to keep her son on a string. Lately, she mentioned the Penningtons at every opportunity.

From where I stood in the kitchen, I could see Ethan setting the freezer in a galvanized tub on the back stoop, throwing an old quilt over it, then wrapping an arm about his father to help him up the stairs, and smiling at something his father said. Like a *tableau vivant* depicting absolute affection, father and son were stopped there in the afternoon sun.

The curve of Ethan's back, that tentative and careful smile, his inability to hold a grudge for more than a minute—even against his shrew of a mother—reminded me once again of my deep feelings for Thalia's husband.

It wasn't exactly love. I'd never been struck by love, the way those bolts of lightening snap out of those great cumulonimbus clouds that hang in the west over our wheat fields. The kind of love that terrorizes its victims. I'd never succumb to that state.

I would simply prize Ethan all of his live-long days, until his knees ground bone on bone with arthritis like his father, or his heart sputtered with clogged valves like Papa's old tractor.

Like Jane Eyre, maybe I needed a damaged Mr. Rochester before I could speak up for myself, claim what belonged to me.

"Before the boys come inside, I wanted to let you girls know that there's been rumors about embezzlement at the Pennington bank. I have it from a reputable source that the bank examiners were here two days in a row last week." Lona Fletcher's pustule of a mouth oozed out the first bit of gossip before she could hit her stride over her meatloaf at dinner.

"Bank examiners routinely audit banks. It's a requirement, Lona. Doesn't mean there's a problem," I added, to put a cork in her mouth.

"There is if one of the officers who shall be nameless has been seen in Kansas City with some unsavory types. Mafia. Gambling problems they say," Lona added knowingly.

"Who says, Mother?" Ethan's voice had an edge to it. He moved across the room and swooped up Lance.

"People. People who have good reason to know. Keep their accounts at the Pennington's bank." Lona took on a defensive stance. "I should say they *did* keep them there."

"Well, we don't, Mother, but more than half of this county does. As business owners, we should never feed the gossip mill. Bad for everyone's business. Now, when is that special meatloaf going to be ready? Your little grandson here wants to get to the ice cream. Right Lance? Your grandmother makes the best ice cream in the world."

I watched Ethan gently tickling Lance, boosting him into his highchair, ruffling his hair, ignoring his mother, and never meeting Thalia's eyes. He wanted her so fiercely that he claimed her little hatchling as his own—moreover, he forced his mother as "grandmother" to claim what she couldn't abide.

CHAPTER 21

ETHEL:

The dull, grinding noise of the Cootenah Library phone at 9:45 a.m. Wednesday morning irritated me. Having just received a box of books from a retired high school math teacher, I was debating the numbering hierarchy of geometry texts—and wondering why I bothered labeling books that would never be removed from the shelf.

"You'd better come home, Ethie. We have a crisis. Lance is gone. We don't know where." Ethan's voice resonated in my ear, gravelly, the way that sand grates against an out-going wave.

"He was on the front porch. Wasn't there when Thalia checked at 9:30. Someone left a ransom note under a brick. Thalia just found it. Orrie's here."

Ethan's voice had an unusual ragged quality that worried me more than an odd ransom note.

As I pulled Papa's old 1955 Chevy up to the curb alongside the blocked drive, the glaring sun colored the trio on the front porch like a medieval triptych of Mary and her guardian saints, minus a baby Jesus.

Thalia's face was painted white with calcined bone; Ethan's blue work shirt glimmered with an azurite hue; the cheeks of Deputy Orrie Davis flushed cinnabar, a sign that he might be seconds away from coronary thrombosis.

"I know it's worrisome, Miz Fletcher, but we need to search the neighborhood first. We don't call the FBI until it's a last resort. I can't remember the last time that . . . ." Orrie looked hopefully in my direction and waved a piece of paper. "This note looks like some kind prank to me. Criminals don't stick ransom notes out in plain sight of anyone driving by."

I snatched the note from Orrie and noted that the big, round, perfectly-formed zero in "50" and the character "O" in "thousand" were identical in size and shape.

"That's evidence, Miss Ellis. I'd think you'd know that." Orrie grabbed it out of my hand and stuffed it in the front pocket of his polyester pilled shirt.

I did, and I needed to get into a kitchen drawer to hide a lined tablet covered with little circles of all sizes and shapes. My sister would never be mistaken for the Napoleon of crime with the trail she might be leaving behind. I could hardly believe that Thalia would forget her forgery tools in the kitchen drawer, so near the crime scene, even in the spirit of verisimilitude.

"Possible crime scene inside, Miss Ellis. Can't have traffic!" Orrie screeched as I hustled into the house.

"I know, Orrie. Bathroom. Can't wait. I won't touch a thing." I could hear Orrie spewing behind me like a bottle of coke on a warm day. Going straight to the kitchen, I eased the drawer open, stuffed a tablet and a handful of 2B pencils into my tote bag, flushed the half-bath toilet, and clumped noisily back out to the front porch.

I tapped my wristwatch as though it might be Dick Tracy's two-way radio and said: "It's almost ten o'clock, Orrie. Who's looking for my nephew? Why isn't the police chief or the sheriff here?"

"They're both down with flu, Ethie," Thalia chimed in a voice that was hardly that of a traumatized mother. "I told Orrie he needed to get a search organized. He should ask the neighbors if they saw anyone around here." She paused and added helpfully, "A truck. Or any men," Thalia added lamely as she fiddled with the knot of a scarf around her neck.

Her face might have been paler than usual. She sniffled a bit and twisted her fingers nervously. It came to me faster than that dim-witted Dr. Watson. This Sherlockian sister of mine was dropping clues faster than Moriarty.

I stepped right into Dr. Watson's shoes: "Has anyone recently paid special attention to Lance, Thalia? Made over him?"

Right on clue, Thalia turned those half-shuttered eyes away from Ethan and widened them in mock surprise. "I had completely forgotten, Ethie. At the meat market last week, I turned around to see Buff Pennington whispering something in Lance's ear." She reached for Ethan's hand. "I was that surprised. I haven't laid eyes on him since we were in high school."

"You don't mean the banker's son, Buff? Best quarterback Ellsworth had in years. Threw that ball like a bullet. That game against Beloit was just about the best." Orrie glared at Thalia. "You can't be thinking that he had anything to do with . . . the banker's son?" Orrie struggled to sort his sport heroes from criminals.

"Of course not." Thalia let the "not" drop into an alto range, trying to suggest indignity at the thought, while leaving something in question. "It's just very strange that later that day my little boy said some nice man promised to take him fishing."

She released Ethan's hand, sidled close to me, dropped into an Adirondack chair on the front porch, trembling as though a 6.7 earthquake had just hit the Dutch Colonial. "I didn't think a thing about it until just now."

She hesitated dramatically. "I did think it was very strange that Buff didn't say a word to me. We were in school together. That's odd, isn't it, Ethie. Not speaking like that. Very odd."

Before Thalia destroyed any credibility she might have had with this moron of a deputy, Watson needed to step forth.

"Not so odd, Thalia. We don't socialize with the Penningtons. I doubt that you do either, Orrie. You're Church of Christ like Ethan's folks, aren't you? Episcopalian bankers don't exactly hobnob with regular people like us." *I could sort out the class structure in Ellsworth by religious affiliation quicker than Grandma Ethel.*

As Orrie Davis snapped his little notebook closed and arched his chest, it was all I could do not to launch into that old hymn

"Blest Be the Tie that Binds." Orrie Davis clearly understood the next line: "the fellowship of kindred minds."

This neighborhood was full of kindred minds.

"They having some trouble over there, deputy?" Raylene Thomas shouted from behind a waist-high rail of the next-door bungalow. Raylene had owed $34.25 on overdue books since 1947; after five warning letters, I had to cancel her library card.

I stepped forward to make amends of sorts if Raylene could help, but Thalia grabbed my arm and hissed: "Let Orrie talk to her. We'll just let things take their course and never be sorry. F. Scott Fitzgerald said that."

Fitzgerald also said that girls were beautiful little fools. I'm sure that he meant girls like Thalia, but at the moment, I was compelled to pick up the crumbs Thalia was dropping so that we would end up in the witch's oven together.

"A truck was in your drive this morning, but it didn't stay long. Writing on the side. Had really strange pointed hub caps. I figured you might have a dead battery and needed a jump." Raylene's usual puzzled expression settled in. "Folks around here just call a neighbor, so I did wonder."

Orrie whipped out his notebook again, bristling with self-importance, licked the tip of his pencil, and pushed through the rose bed next to Raylean's porch rail. "Tell me exactly what, Miz Thomas. What time. Who was in the vehicle. What happened."

"I don't spy on my neighbors, Orrie. That's my New Dawn climber you got your big boots on. You broke off a new growth branch," Raylean swung a thin, blue-veined leg over the porch rail, straddled it, and kicked at the deputy with her floppy house slipper.

A flushed Orrie retaliated by fingering his holster while dodging her foot and stomping on another rose bush.

"We need your help, Raylene. I'll replace your roses. Lance has gone missing. Please tell us what you saw," the soft urging of Ethan seemed to calm both Raylene and Orrie.

"Not much. Not who was in it. When I heard a door slam, I looked out the window, thinking it might be my milk delivery.

He missed me yesterday. Old people like me that don't drive shouldn't have to . . ."

"The little boy, Miz Thomas. Did you see anyone take him?" Orrie's screech of frustration unnerved everyone but Raylene as she narrowed her eyes with a sly kind of expression.

"Roses, did you say, Ethan? For what this deputy you called out here has damaged? I think he also bruised my Lady of Shalott with those big clompers of his." Raylene swung her other leg up on the rail and dropped three feet down to her rose bed with startling adroitness; she squinted at Orrie as though trying to bring him into focus.

"I did not see a child. I did not see who was driving. But there was more than one person in the front seat. Don't know who. Didn't have my glasses on. You can get out of my rose bed now, Orrie. Ethan says he'll take care of the damage." With the trace of a rather fatalistic smile, Raylene nodded toward Thalia and added: "Did you check the creek over there? They say children are attracted to water. I don't know. Never had any."

Ethan spun around and grabbed the deputy's arm: "Lance has been talking about fishing. We need to check that creek. Now!" Ethan sprinted across the street, heading toward a narrow ravine about fifty yards behind a row of houses.

Protesting, Orrie trotted half-heartedly behind him. "We need an organized search, Ethan. Not go off half-cocked. Wait up, Ethan. Not the way it's done . . ."

As we watched the heads of Ethan and Orrie bobbing along the side of the ravine and then disappearing near the footbridge, Raylene clutched the front of her oddly checkered buff and brown robe, walked up onto the porch, and scraped one soggy house shoe against the slanted brace of Thalia's Adirondack chair, leaving clumps of mulch on the porch.

She announced: "That deputy is one brick short of a load. Your librarian sister could teach him a thing or two about enforcement, Thalia. She sets a fine and takes away library cards on her own say-so. Judge and jury."

Thalia and I watched Raylene stalking slowly down the sidewalk, her neck disappearing into the thoracic vertebrae of her upper back like a determined tortoise. When she reached the edge of her porch, she turned and pointed a bony finger at Thalia. "Those letters on the truck were S and B. Tell Ethan one climber and one floribunda will do nicely to make amends."

"Do you remember the summer that I read *The Count of Monte Christo* over and over, Ethie?" Thalia adjusted her knock-off Hermes scarf, stretched out one long leg, pointed the toe of her shoe, and flipped the leavings of mulch off the porch.

"Almost five years ago. Why wouldn't I remember that summer?" I tried to keep the testiness out of my voice. *That summer changed my life, Thalia's life, and Ethan's life. And here was Thalia lounging on the front porch, watching me being insulted by her neighbor, and not really agitated about her missing child.*

"Shouldn't you be doing something about Lance, Thalia? You're sitting out here like some lady of leisure while Ethan and Orrie are mucking around in that creek. Considering what people think *might* be happening, isn't that stupid?"

"That's the point I was making, Ethie, about *The Count of Monte Christo*. Dumas reminds the reader that all human wisdom is contained in three words: wait and hope. I told you a few minutes ago that we need to let things take their course. Lance will be OK. Others may not be."

Thalia looped her scarf up across the bottom of her face like a medieval executioner and stared down the block toward Ethan and the deputy.

CHAPTER 22

After Ethie's quick phone call to the sheriff on his sick bed, I watched Ethan striding back toward the house, his hands dangling uselessly, and the words "quiet desperation" struck me with a force I hadn't anticipated.

Images from old photographs filled the space between Ethan and me: Dorothea Lange's dustbowl "Migrant Mother," her eyes locked in despair; the disbelieving faces of Polish Jews by the train tracks bound for Auschwitz; the shocked faces of American soldiers at the gates of concentration camps.

Why is it, I asked myself, that revenge must spread its rancor? My targets were Buff and Sammy and Bart—not Ethan. Yet, here he was, moving up the steps, reaching toward me, struggling to get past a web he couldn't see.

"There's no trace of Lance," Ethan's voice was almost a whisper. Then, it wasn't. "Either the sheriff or the police chief needs to get here and help find our boy or I'm calling the FBI."

"Sheriff Gates won't like that, Ethan. We don't want them federal boys horning in on our patch here. There could be leads we ain't followed yet." Orrie studied the tracks his muddy boots had made across the porch as though they might reveal a suspect.

Ethie blocked Orrie from taking another muddy step. "Raylene gave us a lead after you went down to the creek. The truck in the drive had S and B on the door. S and B Auto Repair. I've already called the Sheriff. He's on his way to the repair shop. He wants you to hustle on down there, Orrie."

Struggling to get out of that awkwardly shaped Adirondack chair that my mother- in-law gave us as a house-warming gift in the dead of winter, I was just about to toss Buff's name into the mix when I felt Ethie's fingers digging into my collarbone.

She whirled to face Orrie and screeched: "Horsethief Canyon is out by Kanopolis Lake. That's where the note said to leave ransom money tonight. I think the Penningtons have a cabin out there."

As he stared down at Ethie, Orrie countered: "So do dozens of people in Ellsworth, Miss Ellis. That's why the note is a prank. Kidnappers don't leave specific directions right off the bat. They do more like a scavenger hunt. Go here and find another note. Then go somewhere to find the next note. That keeps anybody from tracking them. No easy trail. We got us a coincidence here. Some kid sees an opportunity for a good joke. A little boy just happens to wander off. A coincidence."

Orrie pulled the crumpled note out of his pocket, squinted at it, and stuffed it back. "We don't bother bankers and the like if we don't have to. We especially don't bother the FBI. We handle our own enforcement with our own people."

With a snort of disbelief, Orrie stepped off the porch, but took a final jab at Ethie. "You been reading too many of them mysteries in your library, Miss Ellis. We're dealing with a coincidence here."

If words could kayo, Orrie would be down for the ten-second count. Ethie's sharp words hammered Orrie as he hurried to his car. "Coincidence? Ransom note. Missing child. Federal criminal code 18 U.S.C. 1201. Felony offense. What else do you need to call the FBI, Orrie?"

Just as Orrie reached for the door handle of his car, Ethie's hand grabbed it first. "The FBI in Kansas City has 73 agents and 43 support staff. Read that in the *Kansas City Star*. If you and Sheriff Gates don't find Lance by noon, I will personally drive to Kansas City and ask every one of them how a felony can be just a coincidence."

As we watched Orrie backing over Ethan's spreading juniper along the drive, I marveled once again at how Ethie could spew out facts like an encyclopedia.

She leaned close to me so that Ethan couldn't hear and whispered: "I don't think we want to involve the FBI. They probably specialize in forgeries. We'll just help Orrie and the Sheriff sort out the happenstance of two auto mechanics and a banker's son getting up to no good. You need to portray the stricken mother, Thalia. Don't appear to be too helpful."

Wrapping her arm around me solicitously, Ethie eased me toward the front door. "It's probably best if Thalia lies down on the couch for a spell, Ethan. I would never suggest this under normal circumstances, but you might want to pay a casual visit to the bank to see if Buff knows where his friends might be. He and Bart and Sammy were thick as thieves in high school."

I didn't want to sink down on the couch like a consumptive, but I had to admire Ethie's oblique management of my revenge plot. Announcing that those three "were thick as thieves in high school" brought back the memory of that night in a field of dried cornstalks and total disillusionment. Bile rose in my throat, tasting sweetly of retribution.

ETHEL:

The Greeks portrayed the muse Thalia with the mask of comedy in her hand. The drama that she had just engineered to make her son disappear might need one of those *deus ex machina* contraptions with a god aboard to descend to the stage of Ellsworth, Kansas. We might be well on our way to the production of a tragedy if I didn't step in and take charge.

Frankly, I see myself as an observer, participating in Thalia's life only as she has forced me into it. Thalia dabbles in danger, holding her life confidently and lightly as though assured a blue-ribbon destiny. Remembering her as a young child, scaling the side of that silo full of grain, I can imagine her willfully plunging into a reservoir of golden wheat, her sense of buoyancy prevailing over prudence.

Papa might have blamed me for my silence that day. He never said. Just before it happened, he was praising me as I expertly shifted the tractor's gears. Then, that flag of Thalia's dress high up on the silo caught his eye and his heart.

I recall bracing myself in the little door at the top of the silo, watching Papa crawling along a two by four he'd placed on top of the wheat, frantically groping for something just out of reach.

Then, Thalia's yellow hair floated to the surface on that ocean of wheat that had shifted in hue to the color of sand. At that instant, I was struck by the image of Papa's golden-haired twin Jason being furrowed into the dark soil of Kansas. It seemed that both the land of Kansas and the crops it bore were thirsty for golden children. Or careless children.

When she reached puberty, risk became Thalia's playmate: flirting with the high school jocks; pleading for Grandma Ethel to hem her skirts above her knees; prancing along the sidelines of the football field; and, doing three backward flips when one would have exposed her bottom to the world.

The fact that I was six years older than Thalia settled a weight on my shoulders that didn't seem to be shared by Papa, Mama, or even Grandma Ethel—until my sister managed to stop the Annual Homecoming Parade with her elbow.

Regardless of how many front and back flips punctuated by disgraceful splits that Thalia could manage, she was still in junior high and banned from the cheerleading squad until she was a freshman in high school.

Rules and refusals sent Thalia into a paroxysm of slammed doors. "I'm better than those other girls. Not one of those cheerleaders can do a back flip. Especially not off something moving."

It wasn't her smart mouth at the breakfast table that morning of the parade that set me on edge, but the determined gleam in her eyes flashed brighter than a lighthouse.

I'd been reading about those Fresnel lenses in old lighthouses. The concentric rings of glass prisms could bend light for 26 miles to warn ships off rocky shores. That Frenchman Fresnel might have figured out the aberration of light to make it bend at his will.

When Thalia got that glint in her eyes, no one could change her mind. I tried. "Thalia says she isn't going to the parade with us today; we need to be heedful of what might be going on in her head," I warned at the breakfast table that morning.

Our family always joined the rest of the Ellsworth population lining the streets to watch the marching band tiptoeing around piles of steaming horse manure, the football team and cheerleaders on a flatbed truck, and an assortment of crepe-paper strewn floats depicting the downfall of the rival team.

"What's going on in her head is pure-dee disappointment," Grandma Ethel stared me down. "A pretty girl like her with all that talent for flipping around should be at the head of the parade, football queen."

"Thalia is thirteen years old, Grandma Ethel. Children can't be football queens. She needs to bide her time," I added testily, knowing full well that my time for wearing that crown had never come and never would. Like Papa, I was the child in the shadows, hiding sensibly on the porch, avoiding lunging mules and sharp harrows.

"She'll look like a queen in that outfit I stitched up for her. We were up half the night, quiet as a couple of mice. You'll be downright surprised. Not saying another word." Little folds of skin tucked themselves around Grandma Ethel's squinty eyes, as though they were concealing a great secret in an unlikely place.

After twenty-two horses, floats roped with streamers of crinkly crepe paper, the high school band slaughtering Sousa marches, cheerleaders hopping around waving pennants that spelled out "Bearcats," and a dozen bicycles, the homecoming parade appeared to be petering out.

Mama complained of the heat, but Papa couldn't get Grandma Ethel to budge. "There's something coming you've got to see," she announced just a car horn blasted.

From a side street two blocks away, we could see a Chrysler Imperial nudging its way ahead of the boy scout troop. Someone was standing on the roof of the car waving red pompoms. Then she wasn't standing. As the car neared, we could see Thalia stretched stem to stern atop that Chrysler, the crotch of her red panties touching the roof, her fluttery skirt leaving nothing to the imagination.

Cheers were going up along the street as Thalia maintained the longest split in history atop a moving car. As the car neared where we were standing with Papa gap-jawed and Mama red with shame, Grandma Ethel announced: "I doubt that Pennington boy has his driver's license. I do hope he's careful with our girl. She's something else. A regular acrobat!"

Amid all the shouts and laughter, Grandma Ethel's loud voice spurred Thalia to action. One toe and one heel moved effortlessly as Thalia rose like a phoenix, took a step forward and catapulted into a front flip onto the hood of the car.

Just at that moment, Buff hit the brakes; Thalia bounced off the right fender and rolled against the curb. Buff scooted down in the driver's seat as the car came to a shuddering halt with no one apparently behind the wheel; Mama screamed; Grandma Ethel bellowed; and, Papa scooped up his flushed-face daughter who was doing her own shouting: "I told you not to hit the brakes, Buff. It would have been a perfect landing just behind the hood ornament."

Struggling out of Papa's grip and cradling her left arm, Thalia leaned into the open car window and uttered what I didn't know at the time to be prophetic words: "We had about five minutes of fame. It was worth my broken arm. Your mother is coming down the street looking fit to be tied. I doubt that she'll ever be entertained by me."

As we left the emergency room two hours later and headed home, Thalia begged Papa to take us all to the homecoming game that night. "We never miss a home game. People will notice if we're not there."

I had to set her straight. "You've humiliated this family, Thalia. Made a public display of yourself in the parade. Upset Mama. She cried the whole time you were getting that cast on."

"Well I, for one, say we go if Thalia is up to it." Grandma Ethel stroked Thalia's curls and glared at me.

"Last I knew of it, anyone can be in the parade—walking, riding a horse, or a car. It wasn't Thalia's fault that boy hit the brakes. You can't blame her for somebody else's mistake. Whether you like it or not, Ethie, your sister was born to be in the spotlight."

As the entire football team autographed the L-shaped cast that went from her hand to her armpit, Thalia took the olecranon fracture of her elbow in stride. I just hunkered down and hoped that Ethan Fletcher and his parents didn't think ill of the Ellis family for showing itself disgracefully again in public that same day.

When I think back to that night at the football stadium, I'm annoyed again by remembering the laughter and small eruptions of applause as we climbed up three rows of bleachers to our seats. Just as Grandma Ethel proclaimed, Thalia was in the spotlight. Too young. Making a fool of herself. But, there she was.

Astronomers know that events occur in time and space that can't be explained by physics—a kind of singular warping where things are sucked into black holes and spewed out in another form. I'm no astrophysicist, suggesting that Thalia has galactic import, but, even as a child, she had a puzzling impact on our small world.

From the moment that Thalia made her appearance, our well-settled family went off-kilter. Papa, Mama and I had shared the burden of our farm life just like a Russian troika—three horses harnessed abreast, hauling the millstone of Grandma Ethel.

"Envy makes the bones rot. *Proverbs*," Grandma Ethel whispered to me over Thalia's head anytime I tried to correct my sister when she was young enough to listen. I wasn't jealous. Who could envy incandescence? That would be like Papa putting away the old photograph of his shining twin Jason because he couldn't match his luster.

I might have been vexed, but usually I was just exasperated because my attempts to curb Thalia's excesses drove a wedge between Papa and me. It wasn't Thalia's fault. It was Grandma Ethel, the snarling watchdog, ready to snap, eager to get her teeth into the golden child, ready to bark at me, the girl in the shadows.

Thinking about darkness, several years ago, when Thalia went on her first real date with Buff, I had a dream about Leda and the swan. Since I had never been inside a real art museum, I often checked out those big, clunky art books from the university library to bring home on weekends.

Rubens' hefty nude Leda, clutching the swan between her hungry thighs, frightened me as no other art work ever has. I knew the mythology behind the work. The chief god Zeus lusts after the beautiful Leda, takes the form of a swan, and seduces or rapes her.

In my dream, Thalia was the head on Leda's body. Buff was a struggling swan, his handsome face narrowing into a grotesque feathered thing with a sharp bill.

I couldn't tell Papa or Mama about such a dream. I had already expressed my disapproval that Thalia at barely fifteen was allowed to date. That evening when Buff swirled up the gravel road toward our house in his Chevy Bel Air, I was almost blinded by the wings that seemed to lift and fold back on that hood ornament. Zeus had come to call, and not one welcoming face on the front porch of our farmhouse recognized him.

Zeus might have come back again in the skin of that tornado that sucked Papa, Mama, Grandma Ethel, and all our worldly goods up its black snout. Neither Grandma Ethel's Baptist god nor Mama's Methodist god would be so careless of their charges.

CHAPTER 23

ETHEL:

Standing outside, waiting to hear what Sheriff Gates and his deputy Orrie with his below average IQ might have worked out with the hints I had dropped, I looked into the house through the window from the porch and could see Thalia stretched out on the couch in the living room; at that moment, the image of Rubens' painting blocked my view. Zeus as a swan seemed vulnerable, nestling the arch of his throat against Leda's naked body. Her muscular, right arm could snap his neck like a straw.

At that moment, I felt an odd sense of connectedness to my sister. Peel off that layer of beauty, and the same muscles lie right beneath our skin: *frontalis, nasalis, risorius.* The Victorian writer George Meredith would have seen right through us. "Each sucked a secret and each wore a mask."

Lately, I've come to acknowledge that kinship fetters my sister and me in an undeniable way. Thalia appears to have honed a sharp edge onto the concept of retaliation.

She didn't spend the first trimester of her pregnancy reading *The Count of Monte Cristo* for entertainment. I'm certain that Thalia's blueprint for retribution involves plots of abduction, imprudence, and vengeance with a dose of public shame for the guilty.

THALIA:

When I heard Ethan's truck pulling up the slanted drive, I positioned myself on the couch like Mimi in *La Boheme*, just this side of consumptive death. If Ethan grabbed my hand and burst into Rodopho's song *"Che gelida manina"*—what a cold little hand—I wouldn't have been surprised. The fact that he shot out of here to follow Ethie's suggestion to check on the whereabouts of Buff gave me a considerable jolt.

From the moment Ethan proposed almost five years ago, holding that odd little bunch of yellow flowers, he has never, ever mentioned my erstwhile lover, the father of my son, by name. When his mother brings up the Pennington name, Ethan flushes and changes the subject.

I would have spared Ethan the humiliation of going to the bank to look for Buff, but I knew that he wouldn't find him there. Sheriff Gates and his deputy wouldn't find Sammy and Bart at S&B Auto Repair shop either.

Watching the Sheriff's car pulling up behind Ethan's truck in the drive as Ethie vaulted down the front steps, I knew how a playwright must feel when the director commandeers the scene.

Rarely has Ethie taken the spotlight off me. Grandma Ethel would have wrested it out of her hands if she had tried. Well, there was that moment at my wedding when Ethie marched down the aisle in that hideous ruffled yellow thing that Grandma Ethel purposefully made her wear to detract from my bulbous growth. Those were bad weeks and months.

I knew that in her heart my sister had claimed Ethan. She never said, but that Thanksgiving weekend when she came home from K State and we told her about the engagement, she planted a dozen white York roses around that cistern by the well. The York rose is the symbol of the Virgin Mary, herself—innocent and pure.

Certain that the roses were Ethie's notion of a metaphor for something she wasn't saying, I could only hope that another Hundred Years' War wasn't in the offing. With an early spring, the roses sent their canes in all directions, concealing that eyesore cistern and a useless well.

After being rescued from that old well, Grandma Ethel dropped a few hints that Ethie had purposefully laid a trap with the roses as camouflage.

Ethie has always camouflaged her feelings as she goes through the motions of doing what is expected of her. She came home for my wedding at Christmas and unflinchingly wore the ghastly dress that turned her face the color of split pea soup. Then, she stayed in Manhattan the entire spring semester of her last year in college, taking calls from Mama and Papa at the phone alcove in the hall of her dorm. Not from me.

After being told that she couldn't come to the phone six times, I gave up. At that point in my life, I needed my sister to shore me up with her trenchant comments, not Grandma Ethel's tiresome visits with all those pink and blue booties popping off her knitting needles like portents of multiple embryos.

Pumping herself back and forth in Ethan's prized Thonet bentwood rocker, Grandma Ethel wallowed on the wrong side of half-truths. "We have such a restful life with Ethie away at school. Your Mama would be talking non-stop about this new baby if she hadn't gotten out of the practice of saying what she thinks. I don't miss my namesake's sharp tongue one iota."

I missed Ethie's sharp tongue more than I could ever say. She had a way of getting to the core of things, like Dorothy Parker. As we stood in the nave of the church at my wedding, waiting for the music that would horrify Ethan's Church of Christ mother, Grandma Ethel rearranged my veil yet again and announced to no one in particular: "I always knew solid and true love would find our beautiful girl."

"And love is a thing that can never go wrong, and I am Marie of Romania." Dorothy's words popped out of Ethie's mouth just as the pianist embarked on "Love divine, all loves excelling" and my sister struck out down the aisle, tawny ruffles falling behind her as though she might be scything a field of wheat.

As I stood vacant-eyed in front of a Baptist preacher, all I could think about was that I was marrying a man I didn't know, a man who rightfully should have married my sister, and I was taking her place in an unfamiliar world.

At sixteen, with an unmentionable thumping around in that pumpkin belly of mine, I moved into my own bedroom in Ethan's big Dutch Colonial where I spent hours contemplating my pitiful self and wondering how to make conversation with someone who talked about plants every waking hour.

By the eighth month of my pregnancy, I got into the same habit. "I feel like one of those flowers that close up at night, a poppy or a tulip. They just fold into themselves when it gets dark. Now, it stays dark for me in the daytime, Ethan. My own sister won't talk to me." Those words spewed out of me like a gas jet where Ethan stood, boiling soup that I couldn't eat over electric coils.

"Poppies and tulips conserve energy when they close up at night, Thalia. I suspect that your body is just protecting the baby, sheltering it. I don't know much about babies, but when ours gets here, I intend to learn," Ethan smiled, shyly at first, then with such a hopeful, open expression that I forgot I didn't want to know him.

"We can take the baby with your family to Ethie's graduation. She'll be an aunt then. Ethie is a sensible person. She'll always do the right thing by you, Thalia." Ethan's sonorous edict settled my anxiety as nothing else had for months.

That day of her graduation, when Ethie spotted Papa, Mama, Ethan and me with a squalling baby among the spectators, she blanched. All the color drained right out of her face beneath that black mortarboard. It didn't return until I thrust a six-week-old baby into her arms and asked her to be the godmother.

Initially, she seemed agitated, holding the little bundle of Lance like a spherical projectile, her eyes scanning the area for the cannon. Then Lance wrapped his tiny fingers around her thumb, and I saw something so deep in her eyes that she couldn't name it. Kinship. That's what I saw.

The veil dropped quickly as she handed Lance back to me, but I saw it there. At the end of the day, I knew that whatever I had to do to make myself whole again would be done with my sister's help.

Chapter 24

Ethel:

Ethan bounded up the front porch steps, paused just in front of the glass panel in the door, and rearranged his face blandly, as though preparing to discuss the merits of organic fertilizer instead of the whereabouts of little Lance.

He stood rigidly by Thalia as though hesitant to speak. "I don't make a very good detective, Thalia. When I told Mr. Pennington why we need to find Buff and his friends, he clammed up. He said his son is in Kansas City on bank business today. He acted like he'd never heard of Sammy and Bart. Or you. Turned his back on me."

In the dimness of the room with all the blinds closed, Thalia lifted her head warily, like a small crepuscular creature. Then, she raked her fingers through a mass of blond curls and flashed a winsome smile toward Ethan. "I'm sorry you've had to deal with unpleasantness. I never knew Mr. Pennington would be so rude. We don't bank there, but he was disrespectful. He needs to be set right."

My sister Thalia might have stepped out of that old black and white Shirley Temple tearjerker where a dimpled child casts a spell on her grumpy Confederate grandfather. All three of us in this room knew that the grouchy grandfather was down at the bank, not a century away. Lance's kinship was not a topic for discussion. Ever. Changing the topic is a skill I've mastered during those infernal dinners with Ethan's mother.

"Back to something curious in the note," I interrupted sharply, as though we'd been discussing poor penmanship or unreasonable demands.

"Don't you think it's coincidental that the ransom money is to be left on a trail near Kanopolis Lake, and the fact that the Penningtons own a cabin at the Lake?" The beige princess phone on the hall table pealed out an answer as Ethan snatched it up.

"Say what? They hung a sign? You and Orrie? No. I'm coming too. Just in case. Well. Maybe so. OK. OK. Good idea." Ethan put the phone down carefully.

"The Sheriff said that S&B Auto Repair has a "Gone Fishing" sign posted in the window. He and Orrie are going to drive out to the Lake just to have a chat with Sammy and Bart if they can find them. We need to know why they were parked in our drive this morning or what they might have seen. Orrie says trout are biting at the riverside outlet. He and the Sheriff will go there. I'll try the other end of the lake. You and Ethie should stay here, Thalia."

When Thalia stood up abruptly from the couch and stepped toward Ethan, I knew that I could end this charade with a single word. It was a dangerous thing that Thalia was doing: fabricating a felony and trying to implicate three people in a crime they don't know they're committing. The repercussions could lay waste to our family.

I longed to jump into the truck with Ethan, to ride silently alongside him, just as I had during the years when we were driving back and forth to K State, when no ghost of Thalia rode with us.

I wanted to hear him naming the roadside plants like a monk in an ancient abbey, ticking off medicinal uses. "Butterfly milkweed, *asclepias tuberosa*, the root was used for pleurisy; purple coneflower—the *Echinacea* family—was used for slow-healing wounds."

It would take acres of purple coneflower to heal me. I'm like one of those parasites, a nematode, a slow-growing tapeworm that has moved into its host's body, participating in a life that is not its own.

Just feeding and feeding. I must remember to put in my will that I do not want a blanket of odorless, refrigerated roses on my casket. Purple coneflower will do nicely.

As Ethan stepped briskly down the porch steps, I wanted to tell him that he could save time by taking the Venango Road turnoff toward the Pennington cabin.

Time wasn't really an issue. Stumbling unexpectedly upon three fishermen and a small boy could be a problem. I pulled Thalia next to me, and shouted: "We'll be here by the phone, Ethan. Waiting for news."

As we watched Ethan's pickup tearing too fast down a residential street, Thalia's comment startled me. "Ever think about how justice comes about, Ethie? How men have dreamed up ways to torture the accused, prolonging death by partial hanging, and then disemboweling and quartering; how they held up the chopped-off heads so that the brain in its final throes could register the anger of the crowd. I've been reading about the Tudor period in history. Mobs flocked to those public spectacles. They didn't seem to mind the blood splatters."

I watched Thalia moving regally over to the couch and settling down with a queenly wave, the hand vertical with a slight twist at the wrist. "The worst offense back then was treason," she said. "It still is."

In response to my quizzical look, Thalia added softly: "The first meaning of treason in the dictionary is betrayal. However things work out, Ethie, fair-mindedness hasn't been my concern since Buff, Sammy, and Bart entertained me in a cornfield that night."

Staring at my sister, I hoped that she wasn't coming unhinged at this critical moment when her only role needed to be that of a frightened, grieving mother, with no thought of revenge, whatever her cause for retribution might be.

"Ellsworth, Kansas, is hardly the Tudor empire, Thalia. We don't have city gates for displaying heads. Too bad, though. Here comes Ethan's mother. She looks like a Court spy. And, she's carrying gifts."

"Thalia, you must be out of your mind with worry about little Lance. No one called me." Lona looked accusingly at me. "I had to hear about my own family's trouble from Orrie Davis's cousin. Once-removed," she added snidely.

"Never mind. I brought muffins from the bakery. Only a day old. And a nice shirt for Lance that I forgot to give him for his last birthday. It might not fit. But, again, it might. Hope against hope that he'll be able to wear it."

As Lona filled up all the space with obtuse statements, I harked back to a torture that I read about in Tudor times. The victim was wrapped in chains and lowered into a giant vat of boiling water, inch by inch. Envisioning Lona reddening at 212 Fahrenheit was the best thought I'd had all day.

"Should be a rolling boil." *The words must have come from me.*

"A rolling what? You're not making any sense, Ethie. Both you and Thalia should be out combing this neighborhood. Everyone knows to suspect neighbors first. Criminals of the first order can live right next door without us knowing."

Lona sniffed self-righteously as she snapped off dead blossoms from her Christmas cactus gift that Thalia purposefully over-watered.

"We could make a citizen's arrest of Raylene Thomas next door. She owes the library $34.25. A criminal of the first order if I ever saw one," I choked back a snicker.

"Mother Fletcher, Ethie is just trying to lighten up things. We've had a terrible shock. Ethan wants us to stay here by the phone. He and Sheriff Gates are following up on some clues. Could I get you a cup of coffee?" Thalia flexed her knees against the couch, as though getting up was an effort and the offer of coffee half-hearted.

"Accusing a good Christian woman like Raylene is hardly my idea of levity," Lona glared at me. "What clues exactly are we talking about?" Lona's eyes narrowed, as they often did when she looked at Thalia, as though my sister might be a "criminal of the first order."

Before Thalia could say a word, I stuck Sherlock's oar in the water: logic, deduction, and a few facts might save Thalia from incriminating herself.

"Raylene saw a truck in the drive this morning. Sheriff Gates is following up on that information to deduce if the driver of the truck saw anything. The deputy and Ethan have already searched the creek over there. Lance has talked about fishing constantly for a week. We don't know why he suddenly became fixated on fishing, since he's never been fishing. The creek water's low. He's not there," I said with absolute confidence. "He's been taken. We know that for sure."

After leaving not an inch of space for a response, I plastered on a worried face, gripped Lona's arm, and moved her toward the front door. "You could be most helpful, Lona, if you would let your friends and customers know that Lance has gone missing and to report anything suspicious. Thalia is simply too distraught to talk about it. No one would be better than you at getting the word out."

There. A double whammy. With Lona telling everyone in sight about Lance's abduction, there would be no way for the guilty to hide a crime they didn't know they were committing. We wouldn't want Lance showing up without a police escort.

THALIA:

There's something I've kept hidden away for more reasons than I can explain. When that tornado swished up Mama, Papa, Grandma Ethel, and every stick and stone of our family home that terrible day a year ago, I grieved with Ethie over the fact that only shining jars of peaches and sand plum jelly were left in a dirt cellar to mark lifetimes of labor. Every object that someone had once prized disappeared.

Once my Great-Great Grandfather Nestor Ellis built his farmhouse in 1877, not a single stick of furniture nor a bibelot of any kind ever left by the front or back door. Hoarders by necessity, farmers save every bit of barbed wire, chunks of galvanized troughs, nails, and broken tools for reuse.

Farmers' parlors show neighbors how well they work their land. When they could afford furniture, my ancestors must have been partial to the Arts and Crafts period. Large, squared off Eastlake pieces—an ebonized cabinet with carved griffons, an over- sized library table with water rings, and a vanity dressing table with a cracked rose marble top—had been moved to the attic.

When Grandma Ethel saved Grandpa Hector from a lifetime of grief, she moved lock, stock and barrel into the house with her own mother's Victorian furniture and banished furnishings that she didn't like to the attic. Her dark furniture with spindly legs and fringes where no fringes should go lined our walls and interrupted all traffic patterns.

From hints that Mama dropped when no one was listening, it appears that Grandma Ethel *caused* Grandpa Hector a lifetime of grief. Taking his two-year-old twin son Jason to ride behind him with razor-sharp cultivator plates in tow might have been an error in Grandpa Hector's judgment. Taking on Grandma Ethel provided him perpetual penance.

For Grandma Ethel, a Greek drama was in the making right in the middle of Kansas. Coming upon a grieving widower with a motherless two-year-old twin of the victim at the gravesite, Grandma Ethel could put the prophetess Cassandra in the shade with her predictions of what God surely intended. Not Olympic gods. A Baptist God.

Within a month of little Jason's funeral, Grandma Ethel's preacher father had blessed the union of his spinster daughter to Grandpa Hector. Moving all of her mother's furniture into Hector Ellis's farmhouse cemented the union. Firm, padded upholstery that would tighten the sphincters of anyone prone to relaxation ruled the parlor. Nothing was soft in our house. If a chair had a fabric back or arm, stiffly crocheted antimacassars ruled it.

I don't remember Grandpa Hector. I was a baby when he died, but Ethie told me he sat in an old wooden chair in the yard muttering "Jason, Jason, Jason" until the sun set and Grandma Ethel lured him inside with the promise that he could hold the photograph of his lost son if he didn't put his "greasy head on a good chair."

The only "good chair" in this house was the old Morris leather rocker with carved claw feet that Grandpa Hector's first wife brought to the house as a marriage gift. Papa said his real mother Rebecca must have imagined rocking her babies in that chair, but when he and his twin Jason were born, she never got up from her birthing bed. That rocker sat by the fireplace, the only stick of furniture that Grandpa Hector's replacement bride Ethel was not allowed to move.

The attic held treasures of the past that troubled Grandma Ethel, but she was too tight-fisted to dispose of anything that the Ellis family had saved. When Ethie and I managed to escape Grandma Ethel's sharp eyes, we would spend hours in the attic before summer set in. With no ventilation, not even a mouse could stand the heat, but we suffered just to touch the lives of all those Ellis ancestors that Grandma Ethel disparaged.

Sifting through the jumble of mementos in old trunks, we found that our staunch Republican forebears hoarded political tokens as though their candidates might rise from the grave for another run. Ethie would hold up the buttons and say: "It's a history lesson in presidential self-confidence, Thalia. Harding's button says "Best Ever"; Coolidge ran as the "Rock of Ages"; only Hoover lost the courage of conviction with "Play Safe with Hoover."

When Ethie realized I wasn't listening, she'd just shake her head resignedly and mutter. "Papa and Mama switched to Democrats with Roosevelt. You just vote Democratic, Thalia. That's a good way to irritate Grandma Ethel."

The trunks held lots of things that might irritate Grandma Ethel. Fragments of a cream satin and lace wedding dress that had belonged to Great-Grandmother Rebecca lay in an old, cardboard box. Silverfish had been at the delicate clusters of fabric flowers so that they sifted like pale ash through our fingers.

Moth-eaten woolen underwear revealed a nest of tiny, pink, blind-eyed mice. Ethie found a whalebone corset that could be tied at seventeen inches; and, best of all, there were piles of tintypes, faces fading into invisibility, faces that we couldn't recognize but somehow were us, waiting in that attic in a musty old trunk, waiting to be discovered, to be remembered.

I'm thinking of those faces now and how odd it was that Grandma Ethel had been the one to save only one treasure by giving it to me, sneaking it into my house a week before the tornado struck. I'm surprised Papa didn't miss it, that prized photograph of him and his twin Jason. I remember how often Grandma Ethel took it off the fireplace mantel, smacked it with a feather duster, and admonished Papa: "Jacob, as I told Hector a hundred times or more, this photograph is a reminder to guard special children. Our Thalia is one of those kind of children. Not ordinary. Special. Hair as bright as a field of dandelions. You can't be careless with her."

Grandma Ethel's little pursed mouth spewed out my undeserved praises, cautioned Papa for something he never did, always made Ethie feel less valued, and reminded all of us that we were smack dab in the middle of the fourth generation—and at considerable risk.

I can hear her now: "As Moses says in *Exodus*, God visits the iniquity of the fathers upon children up to the third and fourth generation. Women in the Ellis family started dying too young when Nestor Ellis built this house. I figure that's the first generation—in Biblical terms. Just saying. Better pay attention to family curses."

When my sister was old enough and "had too much sass in her," as Grandma Ethel reminded us, Ethie would wind Grandma Ethel up like her eight-day Halifax banjo clock, an ugly, pendulous thing Grandma hung in the place of the Maxfield Parrish print of two sun-kissed girls on a red rock that Mama cut out of *Collier's* and had nicely framed.

"Moses didn't say that. No one knows who wrote *Exodus*. Unknown scribes. It comes from both oral and written traditions. All those curses were just superstitions. Why do you upset Mama with that kind of talk?" Being labeled a "smart-mouth" by Grandma Ethel didn't stop Ethie at all. She could rattle off curses with the best of them.

"Those Old Testament curses don't hold a candle to some curses. What about those Hapsburgs—even if you don't study history, Grandma Ethel, you'd know about Marie Antoinette. She was a Hapsburg. Her ancestors slaughtered all the ravens in their castle, so that any time one of them died, a raven would appear. When that guillotine came down, whoosh, Marie's head went flying across the square in Paris with ravens holding it aloft."

"Well. I never. Jacob, you need to do something about your oldest daughter. She's getting loonier than a peach-orchard boar."

But Papa would just laugh, and that would send Ethie down another line of curses. "Maybe this house is like King Tut's tomb. First Lord Carnarvon died of an infected mosquito bite. As curses go, that's a weak sister—no reflection on you, Thalia." Ethie winked broadly across the table. "Lots of people connected to that tomb died. Might have been a deadly fungus, like that growing in your wallpaper paste, Grandma Ethel. Might have been Tut himself, mad because they scraped his mummy to get the gold off."

I never told Ethie about Grandma Ethel giving me that old photograph of Papa and Jason. It seemed to me that if ever there was a curse on our house, it came right out of Grandma Ethel's mouth. Retelling that old sad story about Papa's two-year-old twin being plowed into the soil of Kansas seemed to energize Grandma Ethel while it sapped the vigor from Papa.

Grandma Ethel should have joined the volunteer firefighters in Ellsworth. If she sensed so much as a spark of vivacity in either Ethie or Mama, she did her utmost to squelch it. I put the memory of the golden-haired Jason in my bottom dresser drawer where sunlight would never find it.

CHAPTER 25

ETHEL:

A wailing siren brought Thalia and me to the front window where we stood in silence, fearful of opening the door. The deputy wheeled an oddly striped pickup into the drive, spun around, and backed part-way up the wide, steep incline so that he managed to block half of the driveway.

Lethal spikes protruded from wire wheel covers, like scythe blades on chariots used by ancient Persians. Bart Bresco's saturnine face twisted with anger from the passenger's seat.

Sheriff Gates pulled his black Ford Galaxy carefully alongside the pickup, avoiding the sharply spiked hubcaps. Michelangelo's head of David beside him in the front seat seemed a bit porky along the jowls, paler than marble, and hopping mad.

Trying for an insouciant expression, Sammy Wiley hunkered down in the back seat, his globular cheeks so puffy that his eyes sunk back into his face. Those eyes were dark and beady, like a glass-eyed teddy bear. A bad-tempered bear.

Ethan eased his car behind the Sheriff's, grabbed a bundle from the front seat, held a beaming Lance over his head, and sprinted toward the porch.

Thalia pushed past me with an air of urgency, swung open the front door, and announced just under the continuing blast of the siren: "I am the Count of Monte Christo. Savages. All three of them. I win."

She swept through the front door, bounded down the porch steps, swooped up Lance into her arms, and took slow, measured steps to reach Sheriff Gates's car so that she could speak directly to Buff with the Sheriff between them.

As soon as the siren was silenced, in a calm, almost melodic voice, she asked Buff: "Why would you steal a child that belongs to me?" She pointed one thin forefinger toward Sammy, crouching in the backseat, and then over to Bart, sitting beside the deputy. "Why would you and your friends demand ransom for my son?"

If white marble changing to red was any indication of stress, Buff Pennington was just this side of a major myocardial infarction. Sheriff Gates put a restraining arm across his chest. "Stay where you are, Buff. I'll ask the questions."

Except for an unseasonable red nose, Sheriff Gates looked much as he always did. Brown jacket, brown lace-up shoes, nondescript baseball cap. Like any good detective, Sheriff Gates intended to blend into the background, innocuous, his expression neutral, his voice flat, waiting, with no discernible movement, like one of those Venus Flytraps. Waiting for someone to make the wrong statement.

Just as Thalia was about to oblige, Ethan stepped behind her, wrapped protective arms about her and Lance, and answered. "We found these three at the Pennington's cabin on the Lake. They've been telling lies upon lies. They don't appear to have hurt Lance. The Sheriff wants to ask you some questions. You don't have to answer, Thalia."

Thalia set Lance down gently, turned away, and walked up three steps to the porch where she stood, still clutching her son against her body. As a breeze lifted strands of golden hair about a face marred by something tragic, my sister looked exactly like that statue of Niobe in the Uffizi. That brooding face encompasses all the sorrows sent by the gods to mothers of lost children.

Motioning to Buff to stay in the car, Sheriff Gates pulled a small notepad out of his top pocket. "I just need to ascertain, Mrs. Fletcher, if you did meet Mr. Pennington in a clandestine location and agree that he could take your son on a fishing trip." Sheriff Gates drawled out "clandestine" as though the word were corrosive.

He pulled a roll of antacid tablets from his shirt pocket, peeled back the wrapper and popped two in his mouth. With the slam of a pickup door, the deputy shouldered next to the Sheriff. "Bart says that he and Sammy were helping Buff show your little boy a good time. It was prearranged."

"Like the ransom note? Like the kidnapping?" My intent with those questions was to get that imbecile Orrie back on track. I propped myself next to Thalia on the porch; she was strong as an ox in spite of her thinness. Just before I could whisper instructions to her, she turned a gimlet eye on the Sheriff.

"I haven't talked to Buff Pennington in a *clandestine* location since I was in high school. I can't imagine why he and his friends would take our little boy and try to get money from us. Isn't kidnapping a Class A felony, Sheriff? Why aren't these men in jail?"

Thalia's words were harsh but her voice smooth as honey just before chaos erupted.

"You bloody, lying bitch! What are you playing at? I've got rights! I'll get a lawyer!" Buff slammed out of the Sheriff's car and made it to the first porch step when Orrie tackled him.

At that very moment, a pickup with painted flames along its sides roared into action. As I watched Bart slam it into gear and peel down the driveway, heading left on the street, Ethan announced: "That's a dead end. If you want to get him, Sheriff, he'll have to come back up the street this way."

"He got my fishing pole! It's in the back!" A screaming Lance broke away from Thalia's grip and charged down the drive toward the street.

The ear-piercing "O" that came from Thalia as she lunged after Lance echoed like Othello's cry of "O blood, blood, blood."

If you asked me what happened next, I couldn't describe it. Not in my worst nightmare. The street was as long as a silo is tall. From the far, dark end of it came flickering, red flames.

The pickup's wheels flashed with hundreds of shining daggers. Ethan flung himself sideways at a fair-haired child, falling with him clutched tightly against his chest just at the edge of the curb.

Thalia sailed into eternity all by herself, her golden hair looping the shining blades that went on forever until they faded to red.

With Dumas's words "Wait and hope" on a small rose granite stone, Ethan and I tucked Thalia into the soil of Kansas in Clear Creek Cemetery next to where Mama and Papa would be if the tornado ever saw fit to drop them back where they belonged. We borrowed a Methodist preacher to cover all the bases in an afterlife.

Ethan contacted every nursery within a two-hundred mile radius to buy all the yellow ranunculus in stock so that the Ellis plot could compete with the sun, his way of dealing with darkness.

My way was to sporadically attend the separate trials of Buff, Sammy, and Bart. As a sequestered witness, I was only allowed in the courtroom to testify and watch Thalia's foes briefly, with the interest of an entomologist, assessing just how to pin and mount the perpetrators.

Wearing a suit that probably took four fittings on Savile Row broke the first rule of law in Ellsworth. With one of those Bullmastiff expressions that take in the territory and find it wanting, Buff's lawyer broke the second rule of law. Members of the jury in their Sunday best from J.C. Penny's come prepared to listen and think and judge—not to be told what they ought to think.

That Boston lawyer hoped they'd think that Thalia had carried a torch for her old high school boyfriend so long that "unrequited love" had "unhinged her," causing her to report a kindness to her son as a kidnapping. The photograph of Thalia's "unhinged head" cinched a guilty verdict in half a day.

Our little community would have tried and found wanting the accused before the trials started. Gossip across backyard fences, overuse of telephones, though cautiously as though lines were tapped, brought pieces of information, rumor, and hearsay together like a prized patchwork quilt. Snippets of information trickled down to me in the basement of the library from the courtroom on the second floor. Being sequestered as a witness in our little town doesn't mean that you are not privy to the tenor and tone of all testimony.

With all those objections from the Boston lawyer, the jury's confidence in the facts allowed and disallowed gave way to the need for inside information. From an on- scene source. Me. The grieving sister. The snippets of information I sent forth fired anxious speculation about what three grown men intended to do with a young child.

No out-of-state lawyer could hope to redraw an amphigoric picture built on repressed fears and small-town speculation. No juror could be sequestered away from the telegraph wires of gesture and innuendo that knit a small town in crisis.

Nothing was thinly veiled in the allusions that whispered among the on-lookers at those trials: Buff's barren Boston wife prompted the kidnapping. Sammy Wiley's father was suspected of poisoning the neighbor's dog. Bart Bresno's folks lived on the edge of town in squalor. Not even a decent roof on their shack. Just tarpaper and corrugated tin. No pride of place.

Thalia Ellis Fletcher was untouchable, the likes of which might not be seen in Ellsworth for decades to come. Not even a hint of the Soiled Dove Plea that I feared the DA might be forced to use. Thalia embodied the beauty of a screen star, the grace of a ballerina, and the selflessness of a mother sacrificing her own life to save her child. Desolate prairie towns need their myths. Boston lawyers would do well to remember that.

Buff won't serve twenty years, but he'll never show his face in Ellsworth again. The prosecutor managed to sneak in a word about bank embezzlement and the ransom note, but the judge disallowed it.

A vehicular homicide charge against Bart, along with kid-napping and intent to hold for ransom charge against Sammy, gave those two boys a few years to think about whether a night with my sister in a cornfield under a cold moon might have been more trouble than it was worth.

When I recall Thalia's last anguished cry of "O," I search for meaning. Do you know that there are over 2,000 O's in Shakespeare's plays? Many of his characters shout out an "O" as though to awaken others to a great possibility. The innocent Miranda says "O wonder" and "O brave new world." Hamlet cries out to heaven: "O God, God, how weary, stale, flat and unprofitable seem to me all the uses of this world."

After considerable reflection, I believe that Thalia's long, piercing "O" as she plunged toward death might have opened the door to another meaning. I think that Thalia was sending me a message, the words of Mark Antony to the dead body of his adored Caesar: "O, pardon me, thou bleeding piece of earth."

I think about that scene where Antony sits all alone on the stage and speaks those words to a stabbed Caesar, "thou bleeding piece of earth." Antony seems a kind of demi-god, a shrewd contriver, masterfully achieving revenge against those who killed his Caesar.

For Antony "thou bleeding piece of earth" is a dead body. For Grandpa Hector, for Papa, for Thalia, and for me, that "bleeding piece of earth" is that Kansas wheat field that embraced the broken child Jason and all his golden hair.

After the ambulance had taken Thalia away, I walked along the street, eyeing the slab of concrete, flipping dirt on carmine splotches, determined not to let a drop of Ellis blood be left for gawkers.

CHAPTER 26

ETHEL:

Librarians must sort and classify. It's a daily pattern that can also apply to a disruption of our lives. Thalia, temporarily, became too big for her life; she outgrew it the way that children do their best Sunday shoes before they are scuffed. She crashed into her own life and sideswiped those around her.

That dream with Thalia looped around the swan like Leda in Rubens' painting came back the night after my sister's graveside service. This time, Thalia and the swan perched on the side of a great, frozen glacier ready to calve into the sea. As the monstrous chunk of ice splintered into the ocean with Thalia atop it, I tried to scream "Enough!" In my dream, the sound of ice was stifled.

I awoke the next morning, feeling like a member of a Greek chorus, trying to sort out a tragedy, hoping to make sense out of the dream or Thalia's end. Like a glacier that moves under its own weight, Thalia reached the boundary of her destiny. Now, she could become our own myth: a beautiful child-wife; a sacrificing mother; and, my eternally young sister.

Standing here two weeks later, staring out of Ethan's front window onto a street with too many memories, I felt as though I had come to the edge of my world and that it might suddenly begin calving, just like the glacier in my dream, dropping the flat fields of Kansas into a vast, cold ocean.

"Bad luck has fallen on us, Ethel." Lona Fletcher's voice startled me as I turned to see an almost euphoric expression on her face. "I came through the back way. The screen was unlatched. I brought some of my nice meatloaf for your dinner tonight. And cupcakes for little Lance. Sweets can soften almost any blow."

Without an invitation, Lona plopped down in Ethan's favorite chair, fluffed yards of a hideous gold and olive floral skirt around her bony knees and gave me one of her piercing looks: "It all comes down to choices, Ethel. Matthew tells us to enter at the straight gate for wide is the way that leads to destruction. There's been talk."

She lowered her voice. "They say that once the grief subsides, a single woman shouldn't live under the roof of her widowed brother-in-law. It's not seemly. I pay little mind to them, Ethel, but I have worked out a daycare solution for Lance. Methodist Church. Only daycare in town. No other choice."

"No choice about what, Mother?" Carrying Lance, Ethan had come inside through the back door.

"I'm just chatting with Ethel about something she might want to consider. I brought over a meatloaf and cupcakes for you, Lance." She put on her I-don't-want-to- be-a-grandmother-face, and flashed a half-hearted smile at him.

"What might Ethie want to consider, Mother?" Ethan moved closer to his mother and set Lance down on her lap.

"You're crushing my new skirt, dear. Go play in your room. Grownup talk here."

Lance folded his legs yoga-fashion, dropped to the floor, and eyed the green cupcakes on the table as though they were toxic.

"You can't keep spoiling this boy, Ethan. He never does what I tell him. Those Methodists will sort him out."

"Mother, you're speaking Greek. First, what should Ethie consider? And, what do Methodists have to do with Lance?"

Lona stood and braced herself against the back of the chair, ready to make a speedy exit if necessary. "I have come in the spirit of *Corinthians* to comfort those in tribulation. I thought Ethel would appreciate a little heads-up before the gossip mill gets going, and Lance needs to be in day care. He can't hang around the store or Ethel's library all day. He needs other children. So, I arranged for him to be in the Methodist Day Care Center."

"What gossip?" The soft, well-modulated question belied the angry flush on Ethan's face.

Never one to be hoisted on my own petard, as the Bard would advise, I settled the incipient feud between Ethan and his mother right then and there. "I am moving out of this house, Lona. Within two weeks, I'll be living at our old home place."

"Your house is gone, Ethie." Ethan eyed me with caution, as though gauging the possibility of early dementia.

"Remember that old bungalow on the McGill quarter that Papa bought? Ditch McGill ordered that house in 1933 from Sears. My Grandpa Hector and Papa helped him put it together. Papa gave it to me years ago. I've had a new foundation poured exactly where our old farmhouse sat; the bungalow has been moved and bolted down. Plumbing and electrical work are being done as we speak. Do you think that will gag the gossipmongers, Lona?"

Ethan's mother didn't miss a beat. I could almost see the wheels turning in her pea-sized brain. "I question whether you should move back to the farm, Ethel, until things are settled. As I recall, your folks left the farm to both you and Thalia. As the widower, I believe Ethan inherits Thalia's half by law."

"Mother." The low-pitched drone of Ethan's voice sounded like a crop-duster, flying low and about to drop noxious chemicals. "You insult me. You insult Ethie. You insult Thalia's memory. You don't deserve an answer, but I'm going to give one. Then, I'll ask you to leave. After their folks were lost in the tornado, Ethie, Thalia, and I met with the lawyer. Thalia wanted Ethie to have the farm. Ethie wouldn't agree. So, Thalia put her half in Lance's name." Without another glance at his mother, Ethan picked up Lance and headed upstairs.

After dumping Lona's gelatinous meatloaf and bilious cupcakes, I put together a nice salad to go with these tasteless fish fingers that Lance loves. When Ethan pulled up his chair without a word, I had to break the ice that had turned the Dutch Colonial into a glacier of his mother's making. "I didn't say anything to you, Ethan, about moving to that old house, but I'm a wheat farmer at heart. I don't intend to give up the librarian's job. I need to live on the farm. It makes sense for all of us."

With cast-down eyes, Ethan shoved lettuce around his plate, then looked at me for what seemed minutes before speaking. "Reading history has always been a hobby of mine, Ethie. Some generals wage intelligent warfare to damage the enemy while their own troops stay safe. I think that Thalia was a good general. No more fish until you eat your salad, son."

So, Ethan knew more than either Thalia or I realized. Her attack was clever. Her maneuver was disastrous. I thought she was taking only minor risks, using her child as bait, to banish Buff, Sammy, and Bart from all of our lives. But the gods were not appeased. They always have a trick up their sleeves. Ready to snare a beautiful heroine with a flaw. Jealous of beauty.

"Would you like to take a drive out to the farm, Ethan? See what's going on with my house? Give me your ideas about landscaping? Only one old jagged elm survived the tornado. Want to take a little ride, Lance? We can get back before it's dark."

Ditch McGill's bungalow parked itself on the new foundation as casually as a strumpet claiming her own city block. With no barn to tower over it, no jumble of outbuildings to crowd against it, the repositioned bungalow glowed with sovereignty. It belonged exactly where it was.

"Catalpa, Honey Locust, maybe Sycamore. That flat area just behind the kitchen would be perfect for a greenhouse, Ethie. Look, Lance. Look! A baby rabbit just came out from that old stump over there." Ethan put Lance down and pointed toward the stump.

"You could set off that unusual triangular part of the roof over the porch with a different color of paint. Maybe widen the porch. Larger windows. A great view with all those old Osage Orange trees gone." Ethan had been so doleful since that terrible day of Thalia's death. At this moment, he appeared to be under the spell of possibilities.

Cupping both hands and peering through them, Ethan resembled an early day artist looking through a *camera obscura* to outline his subject. "Maybe *Quercus macrocarpa* just on that little rise by the left. No. Too tall. *Palustris*."

"I do like oak trees, Ethan. They're a solid kind of tree. All those old elms were diseased. That tornado did us a favor by uprooting them. Odd that it knocked over the cottonwood trees that Ditch planted next to this house just at the edge of the section line, but it didn't touch the house. I guess the house was meant to be. Sears called it their 'Crescent' model. Crescent comes from the Latin word *crescere*. It means to grow, like the waxing crescent moon over there." I pointed to the faintest sliver of moon visible in the fading light, just beyond where our barn once stood.

Embarrassed that I was being downright silly about an old wreck of a house, I bent over to examine what appeared to be green shoots of daffodils in Mama's old flowerbed.

Ethan perched on a set of temporary steps leading to the front door and gazed off toward an orange glow in the west. "I can help you with this project, Ethie, if you'll let me. My mother is wrong. No one would say a word about you staying where you are. Lance would miss you. *I* would miss you. Maybe it's too soon to think about a decision like this."

For once in her busybody life, Ethan's mother was right. After the drama of Thalia's death subsided, the crows would come to pick over the pieces of her life. Her dull-as-dishwater sister and her grieving widower under the same roof, day in and day out, would spark speculation, then a bit of hearsay, then all-out muckraking. That was the way of small towns. Keeps our oral history alive for generations.

Lance trotted across the yard and wedged himself between Ethan's knees, trying to peer under the edge of the house. "No bunnies, Aunt Ethie. They've gone off to bed somewhere. Maybe under this old house. I never, ever got to hold a bunny. You could help me catch one. I just know you could."

I snapped to attention at the sound of that high-pitched, petulant voice. It was Thalia's childish voice asking me for the impossible and assuring me that I could meet her demand. *I finally could.* "Bunnies, chickens, baby pigs, maybe your own pony when you get older. You can come visit, and I'll teach you how to be a farmer."

Ethan scooted across the two-by-four, makeshift steps. "Sit down, Ethie. It's so pleasant out here in the early summer with no ambient light at night. Look, Lance, you can see the faintest trace of the Milky Way. Do you know that 400 billion stars are in that small patch of the sky?"

I sat next to Ethan, not too close, just close enough to smell Old Spice.

"Is that where Mama went after she chased that truck, Aunt Ethie? Grandma Fletcher told me good people go up to heaven. I told her Mama was good, but she said not always. Is she up there with the stars, Aunt Ethie?" The small face with Thalia's eyes asked the impossible question.

Thalia's absence was a resonant blank. Tonight, only the land itself bristled with consequence.

The black holes in that velvet night sky are pulling so hard that light cannot get out of them, their gravity devouring every star that comes in their path—so that the center of the star simply collapses in upon itself. Just like my supernovae sister. It was time to give a little boy an answer, just as I said at the end of my high school graduation speech: "Getting the right answer is everything."

I pulled Lance within the circle of my arms and pointed toward the north forty where his Great-Uncle Jason met death: "Look at the field of wheat turning golden under that crescent moon. A very wise man named Mr. Thoreau said that 'Heaven is under our feet as well as over our heads.' I think your mother is up there with the stars and down here watching you on this good Kansas earth."

Ethan scooped up Lance with one arm and offered his right hand to help me up. "Thalia left a book of George Meredith's poems open on her desk. She'd made a question mark by one poem, so I read it. At first, it seemed to be a stilted, rather silly poem about country people and the pleasures of rural life. I can't get this one line in the middle of the poem out of my head: 'May-fly pleasures of a mind at ease.' I thought about the short life of the order *Ephemeroptera*, the May fly, and feared that Thalia had a premonition about her life. I don't find that very bearable."

At that moment, with Ethan still holding my hand, a breeze swept over the ripening wheat in the north forty, bringing an odor of summer that was so familiar I had to fight back tears. I couldn't fight back the words: "No, Ethan, that line 'May-fly pleasures of a mind at ease' is about solace, about consolation—a great pleasure, no matter how brief."

Lance's head bobbed sleepily over Ethan's shoulder as we walked toward the car, his golden hair luffing like a sail going into the wind. Among the radiant stars overhead, I could make out the constellation of Libra between Scorpius and Virgo and felt strangely comforted that the scales of justice, harmony, and balance hung right over our heads.

The End

A CHRISTMAS VISIT

On December 23rd in1942, just as the First Armored Division augured troubling times for Rommel as it pushed into North Africa, my great-grandmother, Annie Letitia Knight, appeared on our doorstep of our Montgomery Ward five-room house with her elephant-hide valise and announced: "One night only. You'll take me to the bus stop on Christmas Eve. I'm heading to Fort Worth."

Annie Letitia Knight, my mother's maternal grandmother, discharged the same vibrations as the Ghost of Christmas Past as she logged family sins of both commission and omission with the regularity of decades of a rosary. Her announcement of "one night only" erased the frozen smile from our mother's face and careened my sister and me into giggles of relief that this cantankerous old woman wouldn't spoil the best day of the year.

My great-grandmother rarely visited her relatives in our southern Oklahoma town. Like kerosene on live coals, she fired fury where strong-minded women learn to curb their tongues to preserve familial comity. When my mild-tempered grandfather described his mother-in-law as a carping harridan, my grandmother would remind him—too often, I thought—that Grandmother Knight was plagued her entire life by a "deep sadness."

Envisioning Orestes hotfooting it down the road with the Furies in pursuit, I had asked my mother about this chronic affliction. A genial person herself, Mother seemed puzzled by vexation: "I think a couple of her babies might have died at birth. That would have caused deep sadness. No one ever said for sure. None of my aunts and uncles on Mama's side seemed to want her around. Poor old thing."

With an iron-fisted grip on my sister's and my scrawny arms, Mother shoved us toward our great-grandmother. "Be hospitable. Get Grandmother Knight's valise. She'll share your bedroom."

The Ghost of Christmas past with all its dissolving parts had suddenly sprouted a pair of legs with flesh-colored cotton stockings drooping in layers atop black, lace-up oxfords and was marching decisively toward the bedroom I shared with my sister to claim the twin bed closest to the gas heater.

As she waded through the living room debris of wrappings and twice-used ribbons, Grandmother Knight nodded toward our bargain fir tree, its bad side pressed into the corner of the room, its good side festooned with tiers of tinsel icicles ironed into dripping submission. A string of one-go-out-all-go-out-lights waited in abeyance for Christmas morning.

"Tacky little thing. I'd go cut a big native cedar before I'd settle for that," she said.

Grandmother Knight stopped and sniffed like a birddog scenting a covey. "Odorless. Store-bought thing. Probably been cut since the Fourth of July. When I was a child, we had birds made of blown glass. From Germany. Before we got crosswise with them. Again."

She sighed with resignation, as though the lack of imported ornaments and the renewed war effort made a burdensome connection. Tromping over our hand-decorated butcher paper, she patted Mother's shoulder sympathetically. "I'll have a little rest before dinner. One of those chickens I saw in the pen out back would be tasty. Fried. If it wouldn't be too much trouble." Those seven words summed up her character.

Not too much trouble for my worn-out mother with four children in nine years and a holiday season that wired them and exhausted her. We watched our mother close in on a cornered chicken and wring its neck with one deft flip of the wrist so that blood splatters formed a festive pattern of Christmas red on the snow bank by the chicken pen. Before Mother had gutted, plucked and singed the bird, Grandmother Knight was stretched out on my peach chenille bedspread with her shoes still on.

Just in time for dinner, Grandmother Knight had shed two layers of sweaters and taken pride of place in our father's chair at the table. Her swatch of cream-colored hair lay coiled on her neck like a dead albino python. Her puckered mouth opened and closed like one of those small cloth sacks of tobacco with a drawstring as she sorted the world.

"Rationed sugar. No bananas. Oranges scarce. No metal for toy soldiers. China doll factories closed for the war. Over a foreign place like Hawaii. FDR was just hankering to get into it. Smoking those big stogies with Churchill. Mark my word. Nazis from the East and Japs from the West. They'll be no place to hide and food shortages."

Through spectacles as thick as the bottom of a glass obscuring pale blue eyes clouded with cataracts, Grandmother Knight managed to spot and spear both breasts and the pulley bone of a chicken meant to feed six.

My father eased silently over to the Zenith radio and found Bing Crosby crooning "White Christmas." At "merry and bright," Grandmother Knight shoved back her chair, dangled a well-gnawed pulley bone in my face and said: "Make a wish," as she snapped off the short end. "I win. Time for bed, girls. I need to be at the bus depot early in the morning."

Like the Ghost of Christmas Future, Grandmother Knight swathed herself in a voluminous white cotton gown, snatched a blanket off my sister's bed, and muttered: "You'll be warm together. I'm always cold. Chilblains. Go to sleep now."

We couldn't. The rasping noise of scratching coming from my bed sent us into a spate of sniggers and elbow jabs.

"Patsy Ruth. Peggy Lee. Go to sleep right now or your mother will find two strangled daughters in the morning." That little pursed mouth of Grandmother Knight whispered to us in a voice that didn't seem the least threatening.

Reassured, my sister braved the lion. "Mother reads us to sleep at night during Christmas. You could tell us a story. Or tell us about Great-Grandfather Knight. Thomas Jefferson Knight." He was a cipher, a man in a photo sporting a great handlebar mustache. He had passed on long before we could remember him. I piped up: "Or about your children, your babies." Despite my sister's elbow planted in my ribs, I wanted to hear about the lost children that might have caused that deep sadness.

Grandmother Knight breathed a long, trembling sigh of resignation. "All right. I'll tell you something I've never told anyone. If you tell, I'll come back and walk on your faces at night with my ghostly feet. But it won't be about Thomas. Doubting Thomas. He doubted he was good enough for me." She sniffed. "Then he doubted I was good enough for him."

She scooted up in bed. In the pale reflection of the single bulb porch light outside the window, she looked almost girlish with her long braid of hair stretched across the pillow. "You ask about my children. Thomas made me a baby machine. One after the other." Her voice was guttural as she barked out the names: "Lily, Belle, Ethel, Elmer, Luther, Mattie, Lorena. None present, but all accounted for."

"This story is about a man named Django. Spelled with a D. The gypsy way. Romanys they were. Camped down by the Brazos in that fall of 1897. He played "Turkey in the Straw" on the fiddle at our harvest dance. Fingers moving like the wings of butterflies. Hair like feathers from a Cochin rooster. So black, it gleamed purple in the night. His eyes were as blue as the summer sky." She paused and gasped as though remembering might wear her out. "He danced two waltzes and a polka with me before Papa dragged me home. I was only fifteen but full-grown."

She turned in the narrow bed to face us, her eyes wide and watchful. "He could climb the trellis by my upstairs bedroom with no noise. Django showed me what beginning means. The wagons left long before Christmas so no connection would be made. His mother was all for us. I was to be ready before sunrise on December 24th with that selfsame bag packed." She pointed toward the elephant-hide valise by the foot of the bed.

"He never came. I stayed in my room by the window all day and all night, saying I was sick. On Christmas Day, his mother came to the edge of the porch, and I walked to her slowly, making my ears go deaf so I would not hear the word influenza."

Grandmother Knight slumped back down on the bed. "Such an infinitesimal thing is in that word. It stuck in the back of my throat like blackstrap molasses and formed a deep sadness that will not go away."

Stiff as swaddled mummies, my sister and I lay in silence, dreaming of endings until the sun rose. We demanded to go to the bus depot with Grandmother Knight.

Just before she planted a shoe with a puddling stocking on the first step of the bus, we each placed a soft kiss on her crepey cheek. It was all we could do for our great-grandmother who had shared a deep sadness with the taste of blackstrap molasses.

ARKANSAS MIRACLES

1947

Those long, hot summers in Southern Oklahoma tempered us, as children, to develop a low-key resilience to anything that might change the pattern of boundless days ahead of us. The small tyrannies of teachers were behind us for the summer. We left behind the rancid odors of old school rooms and textbooks, including *The Wonderworks of Science*, a book guaranteed to crush the spirit of any aspiring scientist.

With summer came the annual visit to our father's parents and sister, who lived on matching, hardscrabble cotton farms outside of Dardanelle, Arkansas.

Tucked into a hillside of Loblolly pines, our grandparents' house sported a high, wide, welcoming porch and a yard where hollyhocks flourished. Before the Rural Electric Association brought in a strand of electric wire to power the single light bulb in the house, daybreak began with a rooster's crow and night fell with a burst of fireflies.

Across fields of cotton, languid against dry summers, stood our Aunt Birdie's house, Sears Roebuck model #147: her incentive to marry Uncle Hugh. Except for the front-porch swing, the house had a forbidding air about it. The bright ochre of Colonial Yellow paint dulled under a glaze of grayish dust from acres of poorly drained Roellen soil. Perpetual ruts cut by Uncle Hugh's wagon and team of mules marred the front yard. No flowering shrub or brave line of irises challenged the bungalow's bleak lines.

Ozel Jr., Aunt Birdie, Grandmother Emma Cox, Richard, Mildred, Grandfather William Harrison Cox, Peggy and Patsy.

Our jolly Aunt Birdie had married a taciturn man, Hugh, a man ill-suited to welcome relatives or engage in polite conversation. When he uttered a sound, it was likely to be one of disgruntlement.

The first memory of Uncle Hugh settled indelibly when I was eight years old, hanging on the side of a corral, admiring his gleaming, russet mules. "Do you think I could ride one, Uncle Hugh?" I shouted above the noise of his hammer against the wagon wheel. "I'm a good rider. This one likes me." I pawed the muzzle of the curious mule with no name.

"No. Go away, you little brat. I'm working. I don't have time for you."

Tick-tock. Tick-tock. I would never have time for Uncle Hugh. Any time I might devote to him would be spent in sweet revenge.

Uncle Hugh observed country ways, showing no obvious disrespect to his in-laws. As long as my old-before-her-time Grandmother Cox lived just across the field from her daughter, her son-in-law Hugh dropped his muddy boots by the back door. He left the table silently, with no compliment to the cook. He wore his good felt hat to church when the roads weren't too muddy for travel.

Then, ovarian cancer moved my grandmother along, so fast that her slightly bowed legs could only follow willingly. With the loss of his wife of fifty years, my grandfather had not the faintest notion of how to do "women's work." He walked across the cotton field every morning and every evening to sit at his daughter's table.

For relatives accustomed to Uncle Hugh, his slights to my grandfather might have appeared miniscule. I watched him spear a drumstick onto my grandfather's plate, while he eased two chicken breasts onto his own. I saw him elbow my grandfather more than once. To call this frail old man, Old Man, within his hearing, especially a father-in-law, broke the rules of civility as I knew them.

To ease his sister's burden of caring for my grandfather, my father collected him every summer at the end of May and returned him to Arkansas in August, sporting new suspenders and a nicked, close-shaven face.

Driving at a steady forty-five for over three hundred miles to Dardanelle took the better part of a day, so one fine morning after school was out for the summer, my father announced: "You girls will come with me to get your grandfather. We'll stay with Aunt Birdie. She wants to see you."

We liked Aunt Birdie. A large, buxom woman with a booming voice, her face resembled the men on my father's side of the family: high foreheads, straight noses, solid chins, the kind of faces that make imposing death masks. From our cast-off clothes, Aunt

Birdie stitched bright tulip designs into quilts as gifts for us. She baked oatmeal cookies and, on her rare visits, crept around the house at night turning off rotating floor fans to "save electricity."

Reluctant to go, but unwilling to miss seeing Aunt Birdie, my sister and I packed our new ukulele and braced ourselves for a confrontation with Uncle Hugh. We had both mastered the three fingerpicking techniques needed for "Old MacDonald Had a Farm" and "I've Been Working on the Railroad." Our unpolished version of "Billy Boy" needed a bit of work.

After traveling miles through Oklahoma and across the border into Arkansas, we awoke when the car's tires bumped across dried ruts in Aunt Birdie's front yard.

Waving both arms like windmills, she hurried down the steps and crushed us against her damp apron bib. A faint odor of sour milk hung about her welcoming arms, as though staleness had become unnoticed. "The separator faucet broke. I tried all day to fix it. Hugh's lying down for a spell. One of the mules stepped on his foot two days ago. He can't put weight like normal. He's been brooding about it."

She pointed toward the porch swing. "You girls rest right there. We'll go across the field to see Papa after you've had some cool buttermilk. Or just plain milk if you'd rather."

I nudged my sister. Just behind the swing, the front bedroom window opened onto the front porch. Somewhere in that room lay the brooding Uncle Hugh. He was in for a real treat.

Old MacDonald's farm originally had only dogs, mules, and cows. Our version added an entire zoo with unusual sounds for the Gila Monster.

When our father and his sister started out across the field to find Grandpa Cox, we claimed road fatigue so that we could continue to serenade Uncle Hugh. If "I've Been Working on the Railroad" didn't rile him, "Billy Boy" certainly would. The window went down with a loud thump. Our music continued, cranked up until our vocal cords clenched in agony. We left early the next morning with our grandfather in tow and not so much as a parting wave from Uncle Hugh.

We didn't return to Arkansas for two years, although my grandfather continued to spend his summers with us, under the mimosa tree with the neighbor he called Old Man Johnson. Wearing identical, lace-up, black boots, they aimed sociably at coffee can spittoons. They rarely engaged in any conversation beyond noting the heat of the day.

The call came from Arkansas late one evening that our grandfather was drawing his last ragged breath. As my family packed into our Placid Green Pontiac Chieftain for the trip to Dardanelle, I tried to remember this grandfather who occupied such a small space in my life.

He was a counter, par excellence. Once, he announced to my mother: "Mildred, do you know how many doorknobs are in this house?" When a train flashed by not a quarter of a mile away, he lifted one arm in salute: "There's twenty-five boxcars, one caboose and an engine on that train."

Beyond the fact that he had fathered five children and lost one of them, Maxine, at the age of three, I knew less about my grandfather than about his father, my great-grandfather who fought in the Civil War. According to his obituary, he "languished in Rock Island," a fearsome Yankee prison.

My mother, who came from a family of near-rabid conversationalists, explained the peculiar silence that hung about Grandfather Cox as "an affliction from being kicked in the head by a mule." His grand mal seizure at the dinner table sent us outside with no notion that we might have been observing latent damage from a mule's hoof—or something more genetically sinister.

One memory haunts me. The summer before he died, I was at the piano playing an old Civil War song, "Aura Lee," (later conscripted by Elvis Presley as "Love Me Tender") when I felt a hand on my shoulder. Startled to find my grandfather behind me, I stopped and whirled toward him. "Play on," he said, softly. Then, he began singing "As the blackbird in the spring 'neath the willow tree," the words of "Aura Lee" in a baritone, as though the notes had closed in on themselves but the words hung, shimmering in a time long past, "praising Aura Lee."

Just as we arrived at Aunt Birdie's late in the afternoon for my grandfather's funeral, set for the next day, Uncle Hugh bounded down the front porch steps, too full of good will to be recognizable. Almost before we were settled into a row of hard-backed chairs, brought in for mourners, Uncle Hugh commanded our attention. "It was my turn to sit with Father Cox, so I will tell you about the miracle."

I blinked in disbelief. A small miracle was occurring before me. The "old man" was now "Father Cox."

Uncle Hugh continued: "Birdie and Father Cox's brother, Homer, sat with him all day. I spelled them after I ate the dinner that the church ladies so thoughtfully brought over, being as how Birdie's had to neglect chores these last few days." Uncle Hugh cocked his head toward the screen door, as though listening for the sound of Greeks bearing gifts.

"He was breathing real raspy, but that had been going on most of the day. I eased my chair close to the bed," he smiled companionably at us. "We put him in the spare bedroom, knowing that the end was close at hand. Not that close I thought, seeing his high color and no fever all day."

Like an evangelical preacher who knows the tricks of timing, Uncle Hugh paused and reached over to pat our sobbing Aunt Birdie on the shoulder. "Father Cox seemed to be trying to speak. I thought he might crave a dipper of fresh well water and was getting up to accommodate, when he said as plain as day: "They're here. They've come for me."

This time, there was no falsifying the emotion that Uncle Hugh was feeling. His eyes flushed with tears. They ran down his cheeks with the force of an unchecked spigot. "Then, I seen them. All golden and white. Mostly, I heard their wings."

In a hushed voice, he whispered: "Father Cox tried to push himself up. His eyes was closed, but he felt the Holy Spirit. It was all around us. Then, he let out a sound. Not so much like a groan but a great Amen."

In a quivering voice, he added, "I was meant to witness that miracle. It could have been Birdie or Homer witnessing it, but it was me."

The silence in the room gave me time to consider miracles. We were all Methodists, not Catholics who believe that plaster saints weep and listen to prayers.

Unless they happened a couple of thousand years ago, Methodists aren't keen about miracles. Oh, they like to hear about Lazarus popping up out of his winding sheet. And the blind man seeing gives Methodists a nice, fuzzy feeling. They never talk about water being turned into wine. Methodists are teetotallers, with grape juice for communion wine.

During that long evening before the funeral, half a dozen neighbors stopped by to hear the same story. By bedtime, I could have told it better. My angels would wear haloes. They would boost my grandfather into a chariot finer than the Romans drove and hoist him through the roof that gaped open like the Red Sea. He would send back that same little salute he gave to passing trains. And the angels would sing "Aura Lee" in perfect harmony with perfect pitch.

Mount Pisgah Methodist Church could soak up five gallons of paint and still keep its weathered appearance. The Arkansas winds and drought had sucked every drop of moisture out of that gray, hand-hewn, shingle siding.

A few post-war cars held pride of place in a parking area filled with rusting pickups and long-in-the-tooth automobiles. Two wagons angled off to the side of the church, their mule teams munching new grass.

Wearing our best Sunday sweater sets and plaid wool skirts, my sister and I marched ahead of our family, as Uncle Hugh beckoned us to front pews decorated with little purple velvet signs marked "Reserved."

The odor of camphor filled the church, as good black dresses and wool suits sent up fumes from old trunks and wardrobes. Yellow swaths of forsythia and reticent branches of dogwood did their level best to hide the collapsible metal stand supporting a plain, wooden casket. Small bunches of daffodils in fruit jars crowded around the pulpit. All of these flowers had been gathered from woods and fields this morning. No thick blanket of store-bought flowers with their stale, hothouse scent wafted over the coffin.

This little community of church women knew how to send off one of their own, the way a plain man of the fields would want to go, with early spring blooms, picked by hand, free for the taking.

A tiny woman, with something that resembled a tortured bird nesting on the side of her black straw hat, crept in by the side door and settled in front of an old Ludden and Bates upright piano situated on the far side of the pulpit. The pianist slipped her fingers along some keys that were flat and some that were sharp with a kind of expertise that mends broken notes without a piano tuner.

"Farther Along" rang out with the kind of assurance that the old hymn provides. It was the only song I ever heard my father sing. The promise that we'll "know all about it" and "understand why" must have been riveting to a boy growing up on a small, cotton farm in Arkansas.

A collective intake of breath announced the graying preacher, entering from the side door. So bent over with Kelso's Hunchback, the man faced the casket as though in prayer, lifted one hand and gently caressed the top of it. From somewhere in his chest, a deep, rumbling voice announced: "My new assistant, Reverend Hall, will say the words for Brother William Harrison Cox today." Then he stepped over to a chair beside the piano and nodded in the direction of the side door.

My gasp could have woken the dead. Lord Byron walked right out of Richard Westall's painting to the pulpit. His neck-length, raven locks framed a pale face. The eyes were so deep-set and expressive that they might have been plucked right out of Michelangelo's David, along with the nose.

"Come my friends Tis not too late to seek a newer world."

Well, that got me dead center. The flat-topped and pompadoured boys in my school, their jeans belted high and cuffs rolled, talked endlessly about carburetors and had mastered the play called Quarterback Sneak. Romantic poetry provided me a retreat from a troubling teenage world. When the words from Tennyson's "Ulysses" came pouring out in a perfect baritone range—A flat below middle C to A flat above middle C—I fell in love.

That kind of glorious sexual tension that the Romantic poets describe but never name struck me like fire from flint. Then my sister's elbow intruded.

"You're gaping," she whispered. "Might draw flies."

My sister could read me like a book. She knew that I wasn't pondering "Psalms." And I knew exactly what "hot enough to draw flies" meant, even though my sister would never say the entire phrase.

Closing my eyes, I tried to remember my tall, silver-haired grandfather inside that dark, cramped coffin. He had been born when Grant was president, before women could vote. He never raised his hand against his children and had reared four of them to respectable adulthood. He planted honeysuckle vines around his outhouse for "concealment." He could number boxcars faster than the train could pull them.

A fresh spring wind whispered through cracks in the shingles of that church as though a host of angels might be gathering to form an escort to Ard Cemetery where he would lie beside his wife Emma and his daughter Maxine.

An intense sense of sadness settled on me as I thought about missed chances, lost opportunities, the way that we should touch and hold dear our own flesh and blood, know their sorrows and their joys as well as we know our own. An enormous space widened between me and that man in the coffin.

> "For tho' from out our bourne of Time and Place,
> The flood may bear me far,
> I hope to see my Pilot face to face
> When I have crost the bar."

Lord Byron spoke with Tennyson's voice directly to me about the barrier between life and death. The fierce sense of regret I was experiencing became a gentler emotion known as rue. And, I whispered words from the same poem: "And may there be no moaning of the bar/When I put out to sea."

Weeks later, back in Southern Oklahoma, having left the phantom Byron in the hinterlands of Arkansas, I remembered that the preacher began the eulogy for my grandfather with Tennyson's poem "Ulysses." The great adventurer reflects on the end of his life when he says: "I am a part of all that I have met."

With the arrogance of the young, I had seen only the neutral and gray of my grandfather's life—the missing part was spent beneath the teardrop-shaped Mount Nebo, among white oak and black hickory and loblolly pines stretching up to the heavens. I imagine my grandfather, although silent and introspective in his lonely, old age, caught up in one, last, fine dream with Ulysses: "It may be we shall touch the Happy Isles."

Peggy Gardner
May 2017

THE LAST REAL COWBOY

PEGGY GARDNER

THE LAST REAL
COWBOY

On the front page sidebar of the November 11, 1982, issue, the weekly *Wolfe Flats Messenger* announced: "Our old-timey cowboy, our own Wild West icon, Willie Joy, who toured Europe with wild-west shows in his youth, wandered off from the Springtime Nursing Home early this week and has not been found, even after extensive combing of the grounds. A source at the Nursing Home revealed that Mr. Joy was doleful in spirit. Sheriff Bobo Tucker asks the community to be on the alert for an elderly man believed to be wearing a short robe and cowboy boots."

Goodbye, Old Paint

At the time they transferred him from the Wolfe Flats Hospital to the Springtime Nursing Home, Willie knew his days were numbered—and not by the stroke that had paralyzed his left side, leaving him to the mercy of younger men who had not known him in his prime. In those days, no one would have shuffled him away from his own firm cot in the shed at the back of Sheller's ranch house without a fight.

This Springtime place smelled of death, an edgy odor, worse than in the hospital where the scent of dying was masked by bleach. No. This place smelled of putrefaction—not the rich, loamy odor of rotten wood in the dense stands of hickory and pecan along the Red River—but acrid and sour as old men's breath.

One whiff of this place sent him searching for escape routes. Not an easy undertaking. Guarding the front door was Melba Whittaker's big-breasted daughter, Melbina, her left mammary sporting a tag marked "Receptionist."

"Now, Willie, you just need to make yourself feel at home here. The Sheller boys can't take care of you no more. That stroke fixed things for you." He could have sworn that the face of Melbina lit up brighter than a Christmas tree with the thought of a stroke having such power. Melba's joyful pessimism had been passed down to her daughter, whose bovine face carried the same lugubrious expression into this second generation.

Melbina nailed it. The stroke had fixed things for him. He couldn't manage the push bars on exit doors from his wheelchair. He was caged as surely as the Fiji ape man he had once seen in a carnival that came to Wolfe Flats. Bent and hairy, scuttling around his cage, grabbing cigarette butts that sailed through the bars, the creature had locked onto Willie's eyes with such a knowing look that the shared shame was palpable. Long ago, but still in his dreams. Now, he had become that caged man.

At Springtime, Willie was assigned to a table with a vacant-eyed man drooling sporadically like one of those rusty, disconnected windmills that continue to heave and drip when the wind moves the blades. The opaque glaze filming his eyes identified him as Ventnor Rose, the town's blacksmith, a local legend because of his distain for face shields to guard against his forge's spray of charged sparks.

The duo across from him might once have been the Smith twins had not their glorious red-blond hair been replaced by something like the leavings in a cotton boll, their skulls splotched in places like skinned rabbits. They were uniform, still twin-like in their decomposition.

Ventnor and the Smith girls were the children of his youth, but they seemed to be alien life forms, bobbing and nodding companionably over doughy white bread and Thursday's antithetical "veggie meatloaf."

Willie pushed the food around his plate methodically to avoid the nurse aide's unseemly attention to his intake. Delaying tactics. Not fitting for man or beast. A fox would gnaw off his foot to escape a trap and bleed to death somewhere private. Aged or injured horses would be put down with a single shot. Quickly so they wouldn't suffer. Willie remembered that his mother had been a delayer, curling in on herself like a sapless leaf, forcing her children to listen to her coughing matches with death.

Her final silence had been a relief. Willie, at ten, staring down at the waxen face of his mother in a rough wood coffin, thought that she had managed to share what lay beyond the grave with her expression of an ill-painted china doll, stiff and eternally dissatisfied with what she found there, just as she had been in life.

Now, sitting across the table from Ventnor, watching him mashing rolled pellets of white bread between ill-fitting dentures and staring into the pellucid blue of the twins' eyes that once sparkled with what the boys called "double devilment," Willie knew that this place called Springtime held more terrors than a coffin. Death oozed under the doors, thick and yellowish as the inmates' horny toenails, sapping what had been resplendent in his friends, preparing them for a very long wait.

As he waited for the spell between shifts when the day staff hustled out and the night employees malingered in the break room, Willie stayed alert, watchful. Stealing a crutch was the easy part. Getting the dragging weight of his left leg to ambulate over to the closet where they had hidden his boots was the hard part. The right boot slid on. The left one cocked out at a peculiar angle.

Ventnor, his bunkmate, "roommate" they called them here as though they were residents in a college dormitory with free wills and splendid lives awaiting them, might have grinned over at him as he finally busted the window latch. Or, as they said of smiling babies, Ventnor probably had an episode of gas brought on by too much white bread.

Staring at his own pale legs dangling out of the window from beneath the flimsy robe, Willie thought of that ungrateful little puppet Pinocchio—a lump of wood carved lovingly into a boy who would be offered everything his father could manage. His own father, Lazlo Jaworski, took a boy and tried to make him into a puppet to earn its own keep.

Willie's feet hit the gravel below the window. He steadied himself on Ventnor's crutch. Broncs had broken his legs twice and his arm once, but he had kept up his end of the chores. Surely, he could manage with a bum leg and useless arm. Just how long he could manage was the question.

The chilly November breeze snapped the robe about his bony knees, sending an icy flush up the side of his body that could still feel something. He grimaced at the thought that brief pain could be a pleasure.

The giant silver moon squatted just over his head as he hobbled into the nearby grove of chinaberry trees without so much as a backward glance at the grey hump of the nursing home. Willie knew that its windows pierced the night with little slits of light like the eyes of a greedy dragon sitting on its hoard of tarnished lives.

No busted up man could walk so far. No November night had been so cold. No other place could fire the imagination of an old cowboy who had worn out his welcome in this world. The wooden haunches of the old Tucker Ferry rose like a disembodied Colossus of Rhodes, straddling the Red River.

This was the place of his childhood. Late-flowering sunflowers hunkered timelessly along the banks of the river, glassy in the moonlight, like those dusty wreathes of artificial flowers old women stick on graves on Memorial Day, collect, and recycle the next year.

The grove of native pecans formed a shield against the early morning light, offering up their exposed roots as a backrest. A few yards away, some scattered stones marked the foundation of the house of his Chickasaw friends. Lester and Sadie Anatoby were long gone down the Jesus Road where a golden-haired, smiling phantom welcomed them into some other world. They had left him so alone in this one.

Only a mile down the river, he might find debris from his Polish parents' lean-to. Willie felt a tinge of sadness for their diminished lives in a new world away from all that was familiar. That's why the Anatoby home place became dearer, the very air dense with memories of two Chickasaws who were easy with the land, belonged to the land, taught him to love the land and loved him through the teaching.

Feeling as lumpy as the exposed roots, Willie dropped down just as the morning sun sliced along the edge of the river. sending little splinters of light into the willow break like it always did.

At that moment, Willie felt a surge of greediness for the life he had lived, as though hanging on would mean it had been important. The ridges of tree roots angled toward the river, comforting his back as he settled between them. Dim rays of the morning sun filtered between the thick, leafless grove of trees, making odd little shadows on his bare, twisted leg.

Being too useless to work was like no other pain. A coneflower poultice or a board to shore up his leg couldn't relieve the sadness.

Sadie Anatoby had cures for every kind of ailment. She had been the mother that Willie's Polish mother either would not or could not be. Like the puppeteer Giuseppe, Sadie's husband, Lester, had molded a wooden lump of a boy into a man who could whisper horses into submission and slap a brand on a squalling calf so that its pain was measured in the fraction of a second. A stamp iron made an ugly wound if you held it too long; then the flies settled into the flesh.

Willie settled between stiff rivers of tree roots and rolled his right shoulder into the leafy mulch. All those nights of sleeping rough taught him that leaf mulch made a fine mattress under the stars. There had been some nights too rare for setting his mind on them now.

Willie angled the crutch across his chest like protective armor and set about remembering his life, something he had no time to do when he was full of life. He thought of himself as a gangly seventeen-year-old, sickened by the loss of Katie when he signed on to ride broncs with the 101 Ranch. That was before the fiasco in England well-nigh bankrupted the 101. The War ended Wild West shows in Europe, but the 101 Ranch was a going concern. Always plenty of work for a good hand.

All that punishment on the broncs didn't bear remembering. The horses could remember, passing the sense of danger from generation to generation, rearing and lunging against the chutes, their eyes rolling with the terror of confinement and fear of straps. Willie carried his own bucking strap, covered with extra sheepskin—he wouldn't use one of those bare leather straps.

When he was twelve, before he got any size to him, his pa had hired him out to neighbors to break their two-year-olds. The other men would rope the horse, pull it white-eyed and lunging to the snubbing post, toss a rope without a slip knot around its neck, throw the rope over its withers, then wind the rope around a hind foot and jerk the horse to the ground. Using a bandana for a blindfold, they'd cinch on a saddle, ease Willie onto it, flip off the bandana, release the snubbing post rope and wait for the explosion.

Always, Willie hung on until a trembling and lathered horse stood spraddled and dispirited. Limping home with the muscles and ligaments in his groin on fire, Willie could not look back into the glazed eyes of the horse; neither could he look at the greed in his pa's eyes when he handed him the dollar per horse before heading off to Sadie's for a mashed pumpkin poultice and Lester's solace.

"You 'n that saddle ain't much weight, boy. It's the cinch that devils the horse. And them spurs. You don't use 'em, so you ain't purposeful. Most of our neighbors is in too big a hurry. They'll end up with a horse that spooks at a rabbit. Serves 'em right. Greed don't pay in the end." Lester's mouth would thin into a narrow, tight line, dark with the stains of tobacco juice and unspoken anger at Willie's father.

Willie drew in a deep, ragged breath as he adjusted his back against the tree roots. The dense, fragrant scent of cedars draping over the river, blue with fall berries, reminded him of Sadie boiling the berries to ease Lester's rheumatism. She said folks called them red cedars, but they were really junipers with the power to keep away bad spirits

"Not all bad spirits," Willie muttered to no one in particular as he looked hard at the low-hanging moon, suddenly thinking of Caliban in that play, *The Tempest*; Caliban believed that Stephano had dropped out of the moon.

Willie scowled up at the moon. He felt a sudden chill. He needed to remember his life as it happened. Claudius Buth with his yellow Custer wigs and love of Shakespeare kept popping into his thoughts. Claudius had a gentle spirit and a granddaughter named Miranda with bewildered eyes. Both of them came later. He wanted to recollect things clockwise so that time would make more sense.

A bad spirit that all of the juniper berries in Oklahoma could not dispel had arrived on Willie's sixteenth birthday in the form of one Tansey Yellowbird, a Blackfoot distant cousin of Sadie's, who raked spurs so deeply into the sides of broncs that the healed marks left permanent furrows to mark ownership, just as the settlers' plows had combed the prairies into submission.

Willie shifted his back so that the tree roots molded into him, claiming him. It was a comforting feeling. Thoughts of Tansey riled him, the way he just showed up at the Anatoby house that winter, hair split down the middle like an old-time warrior, teeth flashing at Katie Linton as though he had already sampled her and meant to make a meal.

I'm A-Leavin' Cheyenne

Willie remembered suffering three years of worry until Sadie sent him a letter in care of the 101 Ranch. She had written: "This from Lester. Kinfolk in Twin Falls say they seen Tansey with Katie down along the Snake. She does porely. Lester says we owe you the telling. Don't get hurt for her. Sadie."

Willie recalled the sharp pain in his heart. Saving Katie once might have made her grateful, but she didn't say. After he delivered Katie to her pursed-mouth father, who grudgingly opened his door but offered no thanks, Willie had gone back to Ponca to work on the Miller spread.

Not a year had passed before Katie Yellowbird married a tinker named Grover over by Madill. She wrote Willie a single postcard with a naked word for everyone in the Ponca City Post Office to ponder. It said: "Settled."

Craning his neck for a look-see down toward the riverbank, Willie watched a mist fine as a spider web wafting into the cusp of morning. In this very spot, all those years ago, an unsettled Katie Linton had thumped out a song on her cigar box guitar, her voice sweet and surprising in the pale morning light. Hearing her was like coming upon a wild honey tree, knowing the sting is part of the sweetness.

"When I die, take my saddle from the wall . . . turn my face to the West . . . ride the prairie that we love best."

Willie smiled to himself at the thought of Katie; he stretched his neck around to look up the river to see if anything of his father's old shack remained to help him extend his memory as far back as his mother's womb.

When the sunken-eyed Jaworski family hunkered down in hunger on the banks of the Red River that separated Indian Territory from Texas in mid-summer of 1899, Lazlo Jaworski agonized over three things.

Did the Chickasaw with dirty beaded moccasins and one shifty eye have legitimate ownership under the General Allotment Act to trade forty acres for the sack of gilt kopeks? Would the turnip seed sprout in such sandy soil for a late fall crop to stave off starvation? Was the hump under Anna's apron a son or another girl with a weak constitution?

When Lester Anatoby marked a fat "X" and crossed it with a half-moon as his sign on a paper that conveyed a fee-simple title for a worthless piece of sandy bottomland to a foreigner by the name of something that sounded like Joy, he tossed a pair of stiffening rabbits into the bargain.

Watching the two little girls hanging onto their mother's skirts with thin, scabby fingers, their eyes listless with the fatigue of hunger, Lester added, "River water's yourn to use for a garden or settin' trot lines clear up t'other bank. Us Chickasaws claim over to the high water mark on the south side of the River. Some say that's Texas. It ain't."

With enough water, turnips would flourish in almost any soil. By early November, Lazlo Jaworski humped a mountain of the purple-tinted goose-egg crop into a half-dug root cellar and covered it with straw. The Jaworskis, their chickens, and their cow survived their first Indian Territory winter on gaseous, half-rotted turnips. The taint of turnips permeated the milk they drank, the eggs they ate, and the air they breathed.

Willie Joy slid feet-first into the tail end of the Nineteenth Century during a bitter winter storm after his mother had endured two days and one night of wracking labor. The rigid animal skins that hung across a small front window and the door of the dugout did little to subdue the force of winds blasting up the roiling Red River.

Lazlo Joy, who had shed his Polish name a couple of months earlier and his tolerance for his wife's pain after two days of watching her thrash about, scowled down at his small daughters as though they were part of a female conspiracy to discomfit men.

Tow-headed bookends with dark circles under their eyes, his daughters wedged themselves against their mother, watching him accusingly. Those eyes forced Lazlo out of the dugout onto his mule for a trip through belly-high snowdrifts to pound on the lean-to of Lester Anatoby.

Asking an Indian for help galled Lazlo, especially one who had outfoxed him and had used his kopeks to build a barn and enlarge his lean-to. Shamed him in the eyes of his wife who reminded him that the Anatobys didn't live in a "*piwnica,*" using the word for cellar as though it left a bad taste in her mouth. She followed it with the old proverb about the rich man getting his ice in summer and the poor man in winter.

The rich, gamey odor of well-cured venison stewing atop a pot-bellied stove radiating with heat struck Lazlo dumb. The crack in the door widened. Colorful blankets and woven rugs covered the walls. The Polish word for "savages" stuck in Lazlo's craw and froze in his gut before it could rise to his lips.

"It's our neighbor come out in this terrible storm." Sadie's smile was tentative, a worried expression replacing it as she tried to interpret the thick, angry silence of her immigrant neighbor blocking the door.

"Yore missus?" Sadie swung the door wide and beckoned Lazlo inside, translating his greedy glance around the room as shock from such bitter weather.

"Here. Hickory coffee to warm you." She thrust a scalding tin cup into his hand.

"We'd best be off before it gets any darker." She grabbed a Hudson Bay blanket fashioned into a poncho and a leather bag. "If I ain't back in two hours, bring some of that stew for the little gals." She nodded toward Lester. "I'll sit on the mule. Mr. Joy can walk." A barren woman herself, Sadie Anatoby compensated for her bad luck by serving as midwife to Chickasaw women in a twenty-mile radius of this so-called trust patent patch of land that the government had issued to her husband.

Plunging through drifts of snow, as Sadie dug her heels into it, the mule made it back to the dugout in record time. Somewhere behind her, Sadie could hear Mr. Joy speaking in an unknown tongue as he struggled behind the mule, clutching its tail to stay in its tracks.

The Joy's dugout squatted before them like a half-frozen animal, anemic puffs of smoke trailing up from a chimney unable to draw a full breath. Only a foreigner, and a fool at that, would set the front door of his dugout facing the river.

In summer, they could sleep out and get full benefit of the breeze off the river and enjoy the shade from the pecan grove. Lester had tried to warn this stubborn man when he saw him staking out the dugout too close to the riverbank. In winter, the wind blasted down the river to pelt the hovel mercilessly.

Never had Sadie seen such squalor as when she pushed against a makeshift door into the dugout. Rotten turnips, chicken shit, and the metallic odor of new blood caused her to stop, gasp, and clench her jaw stoically.

A heaving woman with wet strings of hair clinging to her face and no sound coming from her mouth formed the center of a triptych. On either side of the slab of wood that served as her cot knelt two pale children with eyes wide and empty, as though fear had already visited, done its worst, and departed.

"Hide the chilluns' faces and cover them ears!" Sadie gently steered the girls toward their father, propped her legs on either side of the woman's knees, and shoved against the lumpy stomach in what appeared to be one smooth and connected movement.

Within minutes, a pair of tiny feet, a knee crooked at an impossible angle, an over-sized head, and two arms reaching for the lost heaven of a safe womb washed into the world in a rivulet of bloody fluids.

"Will he live?" were the first faint words coming from a throat trying to form words in an unfamiliar language with vocal cords tortured beyond imagining.

Sadie's wide brown face, punctuated with small dimples, grinned artlessly down at the foreign woman who was now her sister, as were all the women she tended and exclaimed: "Willie is a good name for a big boy. I like him."

Everyone liked Willie Joy. No one really loved him except for Sadie and Lester. And Katie Linton in her own way.

His mother harbored a faintly submerged resentment that her back had never recovered from such a tortuous birthing process. His taciturn father blamed Willie for his wife's reluctance to take him back into her bed.

At the least, their small brother's happy disposition should have endeared him to his sisters, but the silent screams of their mother haunted their dreams. Behind the innocent face of that blue-eyed baby boy lurked a monster that had delivered their mother into more pain than bore remembering.

Growing up in a household where the only signs of affection were little knots of Polish cookies on special occasions and a brusque "OK, boy" from his father did not sour Willie's view of his world. Willie was a natural optimist, born on the cusp of a new century near a raggle-taggle frontier town in a Territory bursting with the vitality of free will and its sidekick lawlessness.

However, the price of living with the constant disillusionment of his Old-World father took a toll on Willie, making him wary. His father could find little in the new world to please him beyond the endless drudgery of pushing a plow and swinging a hoe.

As soon as Willie was old enough to distinguish between a green shoot of corn and a weed, his small hands puffed with fat blisters from spring planting until fall harvest. In the cold months, when the only work was feeding the animals, breaking ice, and scrabbling along the river to look for kindling, Willie could escape to the Anatoby lean-to which had taken on airs as a framed house with its extended shingled shed roof. Lester had guided Willie's hands as he taught him how to cut the shingles with a froe and a drawknife.

"Our boy's here!" Sadie's screech would announce a halt to whatever they were doing to greet Willie in the Chickasaw way. Work stopped. Food appeared on the table. Talk began.

Although Sadie and Lester had taken the Jesus Road years before, they talked about tribal ways as though those customs had been shelved for the new religion but would surely be accommodated somewhere along that road.

The road Willie's father traveled festered with bad decisions about crops, anger at his more successful neighbors, and resentment that the New World treated him no better than the Old World. Both worlds were under surveillance of a capricious God who had it in for Poles. It was only from Sadie and Lester that Willie learned that the world away from his father's miserly, ill-kept farm could be a radiant, generous place in which to grow and learn.

Lester taught Willie how to find the deep hollows in the banks of the Red River where the wise, old catfish hid until they were fat as pigs. He showed how him to plunge both fists into their gaping mouths and flop over and over with them until both boy and fish were exhausted and panting on a sand bar.

Willie learned caution from Lester—how to spot a copperhead before it strikes, why a horse doesn't tolerate surprises, and when the flowering nettles sting.

Sadie took him to dig out the bulbous cattail roots to flavor stews and showed him how to peel the skin off a squirrel before he could count to ten.

Strings of catfish and "extry" sacks of cornmeal eased some of the simmering resentment that festered in Lazlo Joy when he saw Willie hand-in-hand with the savage who was so philanthropic. That boy of his kept him beholden to an aborigine. He could punish the boy to help the rightness of things.

Willie's father had belted him soundly from the first day that he had toddled off to the Anatoby house when he was only two years old—and weekly thereafter, just to remind him that authority belonged to the father, in the Biblical sense.

An Isaac sprawled helplessly on Mt. Moriah waiting for the knife of Abraham came to mind whenever Lazlo saw his son smiling up at Lester Anatoby. The Old Testament world held sway in Lazlo's world.

Old Paint's a Good Pony

One bright fall day, the world shifted just slightly on its axis. "I need to borry Willie." Lester Anatoby's request was low-key, as though he might be asking to borrow a cup of sugar. Lazlo looked past his Indian neighbor at the fine, buckskin mare, with a bedroll behind her saddle and a coffeepot hanging above her withers, and gave a sour grunt.

Willie's sixth birthday was two months away when Lester had knocked on the dugout at daybreak one late fall morning and asked to borry the boy for a week to look at some horses.

Willie's mother whispered to her husband that the loan of a son to a man who had none of his own seemed a Christian act. With hens that refused to sit on fertile eggs and potatoes spotted with black mold, Anna Joy knew they had to rely on the charity of the Anatobys during the hard winter months ahead.

Perched behind Lester on a buckskin mare whose sugar-foot trot was the envy of the community, Willie dared not ask a single question. The idea of being borrowed was rich with possibilities.

"We're headin' northwest. Meetin' up with some Kiowas in a couple of days. They happened on a bunch of wild mustangs over by Fort Sill and need to get rid of 'em."

Willie's sharp intake of breath would have gone unnoticed by a less-perceptive man. Lester pulled one of Willie's hands off the cantle of the saddle and examined his thumbs. "We'll put some lard on them blisters tonight. You ain't likely to fall off this horse. Jus lean 'ginst me, and take a nap. We got a long ways to go before we make camp."

Willie wasn't fearful that he would fall off the mare. Even if he did, she probably wouldn't step on him. He was afraid of Kiowas.

Sadie's childhood memories brought the dark deeds of Kiowas into the light of day. The best time for stories happened as she dug the tender roots of cattails out of marshes near the river. "Fifty years or more since they took them white women captive. Us old ones 'member that bad time when the agents tried to blame all the tribes. It wuz Kiowas. Alays wuz."

Willie had wanted to ask Sadie what the Kiowas did with the white women, but he didn't dare. Sadie liked giving answers when it suited her. She didn't like questions unless she posed them first.

If Willie stayed quiet and helped dig roots out of the thick mud, Sadie would usually remember where she had stopped in a story.

"My mam tole me they rounded up them Kiowas like they wuz mangy coyotes. Some of the old men have big scars on their ankles from stayin' so long in hackles."

Sadie had smiled over at the fresh, fistful of crisp rhizomes that Willie had peeled away from the sharp cattail blades and nodded encouragingly.

"Kiowas over around Chickasha and Mountain View took the Jesus Road when them missionaries came to live amongst them. They wuz that hungry. Kiowas still do the old ghost dances in secret places, but the ghost dance chiefs lost power a long time ago. I'd keep a good distance from Kiowas if I wuz you." Sadie's mouth was grim with the last pronouncement that day.

Willie didn't forget. At five, he knew how to count to one hundred in Polish and English. He knew the names of poisonous snakes, and he knew that when Sadie passed on a warning he should pay attention.

Following a trail through tall-grass prairie, the mare set a steady pace. Granite knobs of mountains popped up in the distance. Kiowas could be hiding in wait for them any place in this unfamiliar country. Lester hummed some odd discordant notes that lulled Willie into brief naps until they stirred up a wild turkey or an occasional deer.

Just as the sun cast streams of gold across the prairie before it fell off the edge of the world, Lester made camp by a spring bubbling up through a gyp rock outcropping. "Them's called artesian wells. They pop up all over this part of the country from the pressure underneath. What I wouldn't give to be able to see down there."

Lester cupped his hands. " It's good to drink but don't overdo. The gyp gives you the runs."

It was cold. Willie ducked his head into the heart of the fountain. This was a magic place where water ran bright and glassy out of the ground. It didn't have to settle in a bucket until the red clay sank to the bottom like the river water at home.

"You baptizing yoreself, boy?"

Lester's words made no sense.

"I don't know that word 'baptizing.'" Willie ducked his head as though he had committed some breach of etiquette that he didn't understand.

"I was makin' a joke. It's what we do when we accept Jesus as our Savior. The preacher ducks us into water to take away all our sins. Yore Ma told me that she and yore Pa hold to the Catholic faith. They ain't no priests in the Territory last I heard."

Willie looked down and shuffled his feet. Changing their last name had not made the Joys any less foreign.

Lester pulled Willie against him and wiped his damp head against his sleeve. "Jesus loves us all, Willie. He don't care about whether you duck in water or get it sprinkled on your head like Methodists. He just wants us to love everythin' about our life and not never be afraid at the end 'cause there lies heaven."

Lester flushed and turned away. Church talk sometimes embarrassed him. Seeing the bruises on this young boy infuriated him. Who was he to warn a child about not fearing the end? This child lived with fear of his father, but Willie was the kind of boy who would always keep bad things to himself. Lester would honor that.

By nightfall, Willie forgot to be afraid of Kiowas or the belting he'd get when he got back because he had neglected his work, even though his father had given Lester permission to borrow him. Tumbled into a bedroll, breathing the smoky scent of Lester's greasy buckskin jacket, watching the blue-black skies punctuated with millions of stars, and rolling the bitter grounds of coffee around in his mouth just as the sun came up meant that Willie had already gone to heaven.

The second day, Lester spotted a range cow with an oversized bag. "Coyote probably got her calf. We'll just rope her down and get some milk. Cream should be coming on good." Lester tied the cow's head to the stump of a mesquite and milked a glass jar full. Then he screwed the lid on tight.

"When the cream rises, we'll put the jar in my saddle bag. It'll churn while we ride. Sweet butter for them bacon grease biscuits come sunrise."

Two days later, just as they circled a flat-topped mesa, a distant cloud of dust in the crisp fall afternoon announced a herd of horses just before two streams of multi-colored mares with half-grown foals split around Lester's mare and headed blindly into a makeshift corral disguised with brush and tumbleweeds.

The Kiowas whooping along behind them looked no different than every other cowboy Willie had ever seen, with their double-yoked dirty shirts and shotgun chaps honed to a fine glaze.

The horses were different. The whites of their eyes flared like new moons. Yellow teeth flashed toward the riders pushing them into the corral.

Lester dismounted, pulled Willie off the back of the mare, and sat him straddling one of the rickety logs of the corral. Like a flock of frightened birds, the horses swerved in unison, one way, then another, popping off the sides of the corral as though they would test the structure until it toppled.

The soft whistle of one of the Kiowas broke across the shrieks of frightened horses. They continued to plunge back and forth but now in a uniform pattern as the old man made the chirring sounds of a nightjar as he circled slowly just inside the corral.

"That's Tonemah. He's an old chief who became a deacon in the missionary church. He leads the ghost dancers when the time is right. He knows more about wild horses than any man. I seen him lean clear down and bite the ear of one when it wouldn't stop pitchin' with him."

Lester moved around the outer circle of the corral, pulled a sack of tobacco out of his shirt pocket and dangled it toward Tonemah. A toothless grin split the face of a man who seemed almost waif-like in an oversized hat and coarse wool pants sizes too large.

"Lester! Who thet young feller?" Tonemah reached over the top rail for the tobacco and touched Willie's chin with the same movement. The caress of a hand with bone-hard calluses moved lightening-swift as Willie felt himself being swooped up from the top rail and settled onto a set of shoulders sharp as metal spikes.

"Let's pick you a pony to ketch a pretty gal's eye. You got a gal?"

Tonemah didn't seem to expect an answer. He was like Sadie. He knew the answers. He might have known that some day Willie would be hopelessly in love with Katie Yellowbird, but she wasn't named Yellowbird then. That came later. Willie didn't answer Tonemah, but he saw the pony of his dreams.

It hid behind the gleaming chestnuts, bright bays, and mottled pintos. The small, barrel-chested mare couldn't hide from him. Its odd, stippled coat had all the shades of a female house finch: brown, cream, tan, and gray.

Tonemah saw him eying the small mare. "That one, boy?" He nodded. "See how she moves to the inside, quietlike, never stirrin' up t'others? She's a right smart horse. Wolves would never get her. Even if she's away from the herd, she blends right in with prairie grass."

Tonemah boosted Willie back onto the top rail, stooped through the crossed logs, and pulled Lester aside. They might have been long-term friends, just stopping for a chaw and a chat, the small cloth bag going from hand to hand as the wild horses milled around inside the corral.

Tonemah beckoned two of the men over. "Lester's gonna take four of them ponies off our hands. He done skint me on the price, so they's nothin' to do but see how quick they settle so he and his boy can be on their way."

Lester moved his mare over by a mesquite bush, lifted the girth, and pulled off the saddle. "There's some shade here, Willie. It'll take some time for the boys to get halters on the horses."

Willie watched while two of the cowboys cornered a bony pinto yearling, trailing a lasso gently along the length of his body and roaring with laughter as the horse kicked and reared. "Need to cut this one when you get him home. He'll calm down after you've et his balls."

Willie knew about castration. It's what his papa did to bull calves with his pocket knife. He didn't think Lester would be so cruel to a horse. Lester tried to settle Willie under the shade, but Willie couldn't let go of his hand. Lester nodded at him. "Feared of Kiowas? Sadie put them ole stories in your head? It was Apaches mostly causin' trouble."

Lester had seen them himself near Fort Davis on the other side of the Pecos River up by Horsehead Crossing years ago. Apaches with bolts of cloth, ransacked from the bloody ruins of a settler's house, the bolts tied to their horses' tails, unfurling across the prairie like long, colored flags, pleasing to the eye, not to the spirit. Best not to tell the boy.

He squatted down by Willie under a mesquite and pointed toward the Kiowas standing on the rungs of a small chute, knives flashing as they were doing something to the mares. "They cut the manes and tails off the old mares to make hackamores and ropes. It don't hurt 'em, Willy. See that old stud on top that far mesa? He's waitin' for his mares. The Kiowas only keep the young horses."

Three days later, with four wild mustangs trotting in a surprisingly calm state behind Lester's mare, they arrived just in time to see Sadie grab the head of the rooster that had flogged Willie more than once. With a flick of her wrist, she flung his body into a high arc and watched dispassionately as the headless fowl flopped and bled, leaving an erratic pattern of bright blood pooling in the sandy yard.

"Yore pa's been over twice since you left. Coyotes or foxes broke into that hen house of your ma's. He borryed some wire to fix it. Got all the chickens unless some are roostin' up in the trees. Hens are stupid critters. Don't have the sense to fly to safety. Not like this old rooster here."

She lifted an inert mass with a bloody ring on iridescent feathers where a head should have been. "I been after him for months, ever since he went for Willie. He looked t'other way when he saw you comin' up the road with the horses."

Sadie walked around the four mustangs, keeping her distance. "That little dappled mare looks the right size for Willie."

Willie kept his head down, his chin tucked into his chest not daring to wish. On the way home, Lester had occasionally talked about how to train horses. Most of the time, he was trying to keep them calm as they plunged and shuddered when a quail flew up, the way horses do to share their nervousness.

"I'm gonna sell them two skittish ones to pay for t'others," Lester had announced, flinging an arm in the direction of four horses that seemed equally skittish, including a dappled mare with eyes warm as molasses.

"You boys must be wore out. Them horses look done in. I saved some carrots for your pony, Willie." Sadie held out two small, limp roots.

Willie looked up at Sadie, trying to keep an expression of hope from flashing across his face. The Jaworskis-cum-Joys did not wish for anything beyond timely rain.

"It wuz gonna be a surprise, Sadie. After we et that rooster. You never could keep a secret." Lester thumped Willie on the back and cackled as though the two of them had just been outwitted.

Lester swung the gate to the corral wide and moved all four mustangs with his own mare inside. "They trust my mare. If anything skeert 'em now, they'd tear off to Ft. Sill in four different directions. Offer them carrots to yore little mare. See her watchin' you? A good pony knows where it belongs."

Where the pony that Willie called Bird belonged was at the Anatoby place. Sadie, Lester and Willie all agreed without saying a word that Bird was their secret. Willie would help Lester gentle her. Willie would ride her on the far side of the Anatoby farm, so that his father would never see him.

Willie looked into the eyes of Sadie and Lester and knew the baptism of love. It was called conspiracy.

The big, black iron wash tub was steaming. Sadie walked over and plunged the rooster into the boiling water, once, and then again. "Got to get a good scald or the skin comes off with the feathers. I'm gonna bile him with dumplins. He's too tough to fry. Lester, you can take a pot to the Joys when you take Willie home. Them sisters of Willie need some meat on their bones. They alays look thin as rails."

HE PACES WHEN HE CAN

When a new, one-room school opened midway between town and the river, Willie walked the five miles, grateful for the days when his father didn't send him to the fields.

Although his parents spoke Polish at home, Willie never let on that he was anything but American. He would like to be Chickasaw like his friends. He could pass with his face and hands. His pale legs and white belly betrayed him as something he didn't want to be. Mostly he didn't want to be a skinflint like his father.

"Priests taught boys for free in my country. I'm not paying a kopec for that woman teacher, not a sack of cornmeal, not a turnip," Lazlo had snarled at Sadie when she asked about Willie's schooling. So, Lester paid Willie's school dues with loads of firewood. The teacher stayed with the parents of other students, but she wouldn't consider a dugout or a Chickasaw's lean-to as acceptable lodging.

Willie's father grew enough corn on the bottomland for a few cows, hogs, a mule, and turkeys—if they had the good sense not to drown in a downpour. Willie and his sisters lined their shoes with old newspapers in winter, relished the taste of cornmeal mush with bacon fat, and heard the story of the first terrible turnip winter until it took on an air of mythology.

The only mythology that intrigued Willie had nothing to do with hardships, or homeless Poles crossing the Atlantic Ocean in the sewage of steerage. At Lester Anatoby's table, he could hear about how Chickasaw braves tamed wild mustangs by whispering secret words into their ears and by looking so deeply into their eyes that a man's spirit and a horse's spirit were one.

By the time he was ten years old, Willie could read and write at a sixth-grade level that surpassed Lazlo Joy's literacy level by three grades. Fieldwork kept Willie away much of the school year, but his father had been willing to let Willie attend school when the work slacked off until that one fine November day when he was almost twelve.

"*Dosc!*" shouted his father as Willie started off at a trot down the deep ruts of the road that led away from their house. The old dugout formed a kind of half-cellar for storing potatoes and onions. Willie and his father had built a two-room, lean-to that was colder in winter and hotter in summer than their old cave.

Willie turned as a deer might, unsettled by an unfamiliar noise, but prepared to dart ahead when the second shout of "*Dosc!*" stopped him.

The Polish word for "enough" sounded harsher than the next words, "You done school. I need you." The phrasing of the words was purposefully neutral and in English, as though a force outside of his grim-faced father had passed down an edict that was impersonal, but final.

Willie never returned to that classroom where Katie Linton lit up the space. She was one year younger than him and one grade higher in a room that held fifteen students in grades one through six. Although Katie Linton looked like one of those angels on the Methodist Church paper fans, she would yank up her skirts and show her bloomers the minute the teacher's back was turned.

The teacher turned around too quickly one day.

Willie loved Katie from that very moment as she sashayed up to the bitter-lipped teacher who extended a thick, wooden ruler toward a delicate offending hand. The class stared, open-mouthed, as the whacks of wood on that shell-like palm of Katie's splintered the silence. Her small shoulders trembled, like a defenseless animal overpowered by a predator.

Against his will, Willie felt himself rising to his feet, his back stiffening with resolve. Flinching with each blow of the ruler, Katie shot him a warning glance, opening then closing only one of her dazzling blue eyes. Then, she lifted her perfectly angelic orb of a face toward the ceiling of the schoolroom and let out an unearthly scream. Not once, but three times and tumbled silently into a fluff of skirts and petticoats with about a yard of bare legs on exhibit.

The ruler spun out of control. The schoolteacher's face went from livid to ashen in the space of seconds. "Water! Water! She's fainted!"

No actress could have managed a finer display of near death. Willie and two more boys lifted her gingerly, as though they were retrieving Ophelia's corpse from the water.

"Here! Here! My desk. Gently. I barely touched her. Never have I . . ." The tremulous words of the teacher did not rouse Katie. Her breathing was shallow and ragged.

After a few minutes of being draped across the teacher's desk, Katie came to her senses, gradually, spacing out her recovery as though she might be auditioning for the role of Mimi, her consumption advanced, but an aria in the offing.

"Air. I need Willie to take me outside. Alone!" she spoke imperially. The teacher stood back and motioned Willie to her desk.

Hobbling against him and squeezing his arm hard, Katie staggered down the school's front steps, angled off toward a grove of trees, and slipped behind a big oak.

"Skeert that old-maid hellcat!" Katie hissed. "Did you see her face when I fell on the floor?"

Willie shuffled his feet and looked down. He had been admiring those muscular legs with bloomers and a fringe of lace capping Katie Linton's knees.

"You were ready to stop her. I saw it when you stood up, but there wasn't no need to get in trouble on my account." Katie sniffed self-righteously. "My pa will give her a talking to. He don't hold with *violence* toward children."

The way Katie spun out "violence" made the word sound like some kind of hymn. That's the kind of voice Katie had, even as a young girl, turning the harshest words into a melody.

Willie angled the crutch against a tree root to push himself up just a tad so he could clear his head for thinking about Katie. Seeing her almost every day at school ended just before his twelfth birthday. Not only did he work his father's fields, but during planting and harvesting, Willie was farmed out to neighbors from sun-up to sun-down. Breaking horses was just a sideline.

As the weeks and months spun out with hardly anything but changing seasons to mark their passing, Willie held on to the comfort of his Chickasaw friends. No matter how tired he was at the end of a day, Willie always checked on Sadie and Lester.

Consumption had checked in on his mother three years earlier. Except for a regretful glance at her daughters, Anna Jaworski appeared more than willing to travel with her colony of mycobacterium to a place that smelled better than turnips and sour milk.

For six months after their mother's death, Willie's sisters stayed home from school, hoeing, canning, and piecing, avoiding their father who sometimes eyed them with an odd expression.

They were tall, lean girls with bitter lips and long memories. Then, the Methodist preacher's wife invited them to live with her family so they could go to the town school and pay their way by helping with chores. The next year they moved to Atoka. Willie and his father got two postcards and a letter. Then, it was as if the Joy sisters had never existed. They hadn't. Not in the way that Katie Linton existed. Not since that long-ago day when they sat on the drying Buffalo grass behind the oak tree, just out of sight of that nervous schoolteacher, had Willie been able to forget Katie Linton for a single day.

Even now, stretched atop cords of tree roots, one leg gone dead and the other too cold to feel the breeze pushing an iridescent fog down the river, Willie remembered only Katie.

She became a town girl a couple of years after that teacher whacked her. Too fine for country living, her father had bought a dry goods store in Wolfe Flats, an up-and-coming town that straddled the railroad tracks and boasted five cotton gins.

At fourteen when he had grown taller than his pa, too big to lick, Willie rode his horse ten miles to town every Sunday morning just to sit on the back row of the Methodist church and watch Katie. She looked like one of those imported French dolls in her father's store window, all pink and white, flouncing down the aisle in silk too ruffled for Methodists.

Willie heard guarded talk about Katie as "uncontrolled." The obscenities that spewed past her rosy lips might have suggested Coprolalia, a tendency toward Tourette's. Except, they were perfectly timed for the maximum effect.

At Thanksgiving, when the new Methodist preacher's son came to visit from the school back East where he was making something of himself, he greased himself into the Linton's pew next to Katie as though proprietorship had arrived on the same train with him.

Willie watched Samuel Pennyworst inching his thick haunches closer to Katie, the fat lobes of his ears wobbling like a boar's testicles. Then one hand snaked past her swan-like throat to settle like the swollen neck of a cobra on her left shoulder. Samuel's fleshy lips moved toward the side of her face and whispered something.

"Keep your gob-smacking mouth away from my ear, you half-wit!" Even in fury, Katie Linton's voice sounded like a trumpet from heaven to Willie.

To her grim father who marched her down the aisle and past the back pew where Willie sat, flushed with delight, the morning's teaching from Proverbs seemed prophetic. "When the wicked perish, there is jubilation."

The female wraith twisting in her father's firm grip would spend the day locked in her room as Mr. Linton fashioned apologies for the preacher and his promising son.

To cover the commotion in the church, Agnes Moore arched her spidery fingers over the keyboard and pounded out: "A charge to keep have I, a God to glorify," as John Wesley had proclaimed. The faltering sounds of the congregation concluded: "A never-dying soul to save and fit it for the sky." Few of those singing believed that Katie's soul would ever be fit for heaven.

Willie shifted to ease the pressure of the roots on his back. Under the magical, luminous dawn, his feet, crammed sockless into boots that looked unfamiliar, angled like those of a discarded puppet. The muscles in his pale thighs, honed from years of busting broncs and squatting to build fences, arced below the short hospital gown like panicles of yucca.

He squinted down the riverbank toward the ruined shafts of Tucker's Ferry. Katie might be along any time now, just as she had so unexpectedly arrived at the River after her performance in church that long-ago November day.

Her pa's fantasy that Katie would remain locked in a room while that preacher's porky son ranged free lasted as long as the second call to come downstairs for Sunday dinner. Silence and an empty place where Katie should have been greeted the resentful Pennyworst guests.

Scrambling down the Wisteria vine outside her upper bed-room window and flinging herself bareback onto her roan gelding were not purposeful acts. Where she went and how she got there didn't matter.

Escape was her only goal.

Then, Katie remembered Willie on the back pew of church that morning—Willie whose face flushed with barely suppressed anger as her pa dragged her down the aisle. She had noticed him most Sundays as he crept in late and sneaked out early, avoiding any contact with Methodists. Willie knew the meaning of escape. That hint of complicity that flushed his sober face was directed at her. She dug her bare knees into the sides of her gelding and pointed his nose toward the Red River.

Willie's father thumped him on the back as he mechanically split kindling after returning from church that day, wondering about Katie Linton's pa and whether his fury would transform itself into the blows of a man like his own father.

His taciturn father had a scrappy notion of fair play—pushing his family toward the edge of starvation with his erratic farming habits, and then belting his children if they seemed displeased. After the departure of his sisters, the belt hung on his father's bedpost as a grim reminder that it held their share of lashings for Willie.

Without turning around to acknowledge his father's fist against his back, Willie lightened in spirit as he thought about the Anatobys as true parents. Sadie had brought him into this world. Lester was the father he never had. Neither the Anatobys nor Willie were the kind of people to talk about their feelings, yet the silence between them blossomed with devotion.

"That Linton gal's here." Willie turned toward his father, holding the axe aloft.

"She's run her horse into a lather. I don't want trouble with her pa. We're beholden for stores. Tell her she had better g-g-git." Lazlo stuttered his command.

The girl had issued her own blunt directive to "find Willie." She didn't seem the type to take orders.

Willie sprinted around the corner of the lean-to, axe still in hand, and there she was. Just like one of those incandescent girls in fairy tales, her hair gleaming as though touched by Midas. Her gelding trembled with fatigue, but she sat atop its sagging muscular back, her face bright with anticipation and said: "I thought I'd come visit the only person who wasn't happy to see me punished in front of everyone in town."

"Every Methodist in town," retorted Willie.

He remembered the peal of her laughter. Laughter ringing out during all those other visits. She never came inside the lean-to. He would have been ashamed to let her see the poverty that his father wore like a cloak of righteousness. The odor of turnips had been replaced by the stench of rancid pork and unwashed blankets.

Only the grave of Lazlo's wife held pride of place just below the giant hickory where a swing had once dangled, the only plaything he'd ever built for his children. He'd carved Anna's name and something in Polish on sandstone. Willie feared to ask what. The sandstone wouldn't last. Cows knocked it over every time they grazed nearby.

Willie's home was a woebegone place where no person or animal showed respect for the dead. He read somewhere that elephants hide the bones of their dead in a great gathering place that always remains secret.

The only gathering place he could think of that November day when Katie arrived was at the Anatobys, so he took Katie there when she got tired of walking along the River and searching for windfall pecans. It was a mistake.

She adored the Anatobys. On days too cold for rambling about the countryside or when she tired of waiting for Willie to finish his long days of work, she would go directly to their house. That's where she met Tansey Yellowbird, that nephew of Sadie's cousin.

Sadie disapproved of Tansey but had to offer hospitality. "Not really kin. His ma was a Blackfoot. She kept Tansey with her people somewhere in Idaho. He got in trouble up there. A lazy boy with big ideas is alays trouble."

The only "big ideas" that Tansey Yellowbird showed Willie were on a faded newspaper: "Bronc Busters Needed for Wild West Show."

Willie stretched his good leg and tried to settle into the warmth of the packed mulch as he thought of what he might have missed in this world: great desires and great disappointments—the stuff of good stories. He wondered if the littleness of his life made the blame of his sadness about Katie such a burden. Sometimes the memories of Katie hung about, the way that sapless redbud leaves cling to branches in the fall, dazzling the world with unexpected shafts of gold.

When Willie was younger and could not keep those memories at bay, he thought he loved Katie most for her guilelessness, her trusting and straightforward self. He believed that her flippancy was just posturing, a way to get under the hide of her puffed-up father—or that Blackfoot drifter Tansey who had disappeared by the time of the next snowfall, taking Katie with him.

Willie knew that Lester grieved quietly over his "primrose gal," as he called Katie and said the only harsh words to Sadie that Willie ever heard him utter. "You knowed he come from the thievin' side of yore family. You put on blinders when it come to family."

Katie's disbelieving father forced the sheriff to deputize half the able-bodied men in Wolfe County, but the only trace of his daughter was a set of deep ruts made by his own missing Model T as it carved a swath through his manicured yard.

That long-remembered ache of loss still pained Willie. For all her coziness, her flutterings—like an unnested bird not ready to choose—Katie became unreachable.

Willie's half-shod foot angled sideways like the stirrup on a saddle left in the rain. He thought of that long-ago day when that nitwit roustabout had left his beartrap bronc busting saddle uncovered in a downpour at the depot while he was loading the horses for the New York trip. His prized Frazier with its fifteen-inch back swell, its five-inch cantle, its solid nickel horn treated like a piece of junk. The thought of it still riled him. Spanish rigged with circle dees, the beartrap was a gift from Lester—actually two gifts. A bronc saddle and a reminder not to wait for Katie.

He had been only sixteen, but claimed to be eighteen so the Millers would take him on. With broncs exploding between his thighs, he could still remember the shouting of strangers as he hung on and on against the punishing muscles of a desperate horse. Had he been happy then? He thought not. Those horses' eyes rolled white with fear—the same fear he could see in Joe Miller's eyes as he tried to revitalize the 101 Ranch show after the British confiscated his stock and wagons on the last trip to Europe.

With over a hundred thousand acres, the Miller boys needed ranch hands—and hands that could double as performers if Joe Miller wanted to keep his Wild West Show on the road.

Crowds loved watching Bill Pickett clamping down on a steer's nose like a het up dog and wrestling it to the ground. Along with steer wrestling, people favored bronc busting over calf roping. The staged extravaganzas of the two Bills' shows now seemed as dated as the Custer wigs Claudius Buth kept in his trunk: one with springy yellow curls and one with a bright red swath down the middle.

Yet, in the pale dawn of this day, it was Claudius and his elfin granddaughter that kept coming to mind, troubling the chronology of what his memory was trying to order as Willie lay on his back amidst tree roots.

He didn't regret what he'd done, just wished he had done it sooner. But, he kept seeing the shape of Valentine Buscetta's mouth popping soundlessly as a landed catfish as he clutched at the slatted sides of the stock car on that moving train.

Willie smiled ruefully up through the leafless pecan trees. Maybe Valentine's gaping mouth had been flinging up silent pleas for forgiveness for his sins of bestiality and pedophilia as Willie's foot hastened him through the gaping door to Hell.

He remembered how Claudius, hunkered down behind the bale of hay with his sobbing granddaughter, had put on his actor's rueful face and bellowed so that anyone in the next car might hear: "Don't look Miranda. Mr. Buscetta accidentally lost his grip."

Tonight, the moon, drifting west, was so heavy that Willie thought it might drop into the river to join its craters and hills with those of Wolfe County. At this moment, the moon's rays illuminated the world with a kinder light than he could ever remember. Even the crows swooping down, blasting the silence with their raspy calls seemed to dip their wings toward him, acknowledging him.

"They murder sleep." Claudius Buth said that, repeating Shakespeare. Sleep doesn't matter now, thought Willie. All sense of time seemed to have disappeared with his stroke. Willie thought of time as fabric, sometimes dense and comforting as Sadie's homespun blankets, or silken and perfumed as Katie's church dresses, or spangled with tin stars like the cowboys in the Wild West grand stampede opening.

Willie pulled the cheap cotton hospital robe across his chest as he watched the wind ruffling the Red River, pushing up tight pleats in the silt, reminding him of the way Sadie labored over bib shirts for him and Lester. That's when he was most happy.

People don't recognize small moments of happiness when they settle around them, in just the same way that the thousands of tiny droplets in the morning fog were obscuring the bend in the river that Willie knew was certainly there.

He could only sort out happiness when he looked back and saw Sadie, her needle flashing like some live thing into the tucks and folds of fabric, listening to everything he said, erupting in giggles just when he hoped she would. Those were absolute moments of happiness when the expected came into being with no hard edges or disappointments.

GOOD MORNING, YOUNG LADY

Katie's "good gracious" as he moved off of her didn't measure up to her usual Sarah Bernhardt exclamations, but she wasn't unhappy when it happened that day in the woods. He couldn't be sure, but the place where he was lying now might have been the same place, just under this tree. He had been drowning in the depths of blue eyes and exploding somewhere in flesh too soft for remembering.

Her flushed face, her small hands clenched into fists, and her eyes trying to look fierce with blame might have been a prelude to remorse, but Katie couldn't constrain the flicker of a smile and the burst of laughter that followed. Pleasure had filled him to the brim.

Now, Willie felt a wave of adrenaline surge through him, fearful in its intensity, and thrust his head back against the unforgiving bark of the tree. At that moment, he knew that he was running out of time and was not done with living.

There was an ordering and weighing of thoughts that should have been measured out all those cold evenings when he sat in his cement-block shed on the Sheller ranch, burning old rubber tires to keep warm.

Willie didn't mind the sparseness of the room, the sagging couch, a dresser handed down through three generations of Shellers. If he resented anything, it had been the cold.

After their father died, the Sheller boys put central heat and air into that old Victorian he had once shared with the family. The opened shafts were like living things, arteries pulsing heat while he huddled in a shed with no insulation against the raw Oklahoma winter wind sweeping down from Kansas.

Like a mole clawing its way down past the freeze line for warmth, Willie had duct taped old magazines over his only window and tossed rubber tires on a multipurpose fireplace cook stove he'd designed from pieces of a cast iron stove.

Jasper and Harry—Horace Sheller's boys—brought to mind the noxious odor of burning tires, a smell like rotten eggs or farts. Graceless, lumbering boys. Making their five-dollar bets for hitting buzzards on the wing. Brutal with the stock. Careless with the land. Takers. Never enough white meat to go around. "Brown is sweeter, Willie. We left the back and a drumstick for you."

Yet, Willie had tried to be the father that their father could never manage to be—teaching, comforting, and ignoring their sleights when they were old enough to know better.

"I can't tolerate disrespect, Willie. Or liars. I managed to hatch two, and shiftless ones to boot. You been like a member of our family and never asked for what you deserve. When I get around to making out my will, I won't forget. I give you assurance that you'll always have a place here."

The minute Horace used the word "assurance," Willie had a sinking feeling. He remembered a hymn that troubled him as a teenage boy watching Katie Linton from the back of the Methodist Church: "Blessed Assurance, Jesus is mine; O what a foretaste of glory divine!"

It was that "foretaste" business. The suggestion of glory nestled just at the midpoint of the cervical curve along the nape of Katie's neck. The morning light filtering through the stained-glass window above the Linton pew fired Katie's hair into dazzling brightness. Watching the sun turning her yellow hair into particles of light, Willie was assured that the divine sat only three pews ahead of him, almost, but not quite, within reach, like a foretaste.

A stroke on the day of his sixtieth birthday wiped Horace Sheller's memory as clean as a whistle. When he died a year later, no will was found. Jasper and Harry squared off like brain-damaged boxers, their only buffer zone a mutually shared resentment of a hired hand who had probably been overpaid by their father and sat at their table as though he belonged to the family.

When Jasper married one of the Sibley girls from out in the West End, they took the downstairs; Harry commandeered the second floor and told Willie he could take over the shed by the barn. Willie could see him now, over compensating for his five and a half feet, like Napoleon with his hand inside his shirt where he might or might not have been passing on secret Masonic signs.

"Nice little cement block shed, Willie. Just been used for old plows and sech since we give up on brood sows. You can tie onto that outlet in the barn. They's a pot-belly stove somewhere in that mess. Throw anything you can't use down a sinkhole. You need to do for yourself. Your work ain't changed, but Jasper's new wife is particular."

That meant he had a roof of sorts over his head, eggs and milk when he did the milking and kept the hens up at night so the coyotes couldn't get them. Sometimes Jasper remembered to pay him part of his wages before the month had passed. Willie did odd jobs for neighbors for extra cash.

For the last few years, regular as a seven-day clock with two sets of cannonball-like weights, Willie had eased his re-heeled polished Justin Ropers into the stirrups and ridden alongside Highway 77 into Wolfe Flats for the seven o'clock Saturday night picture show. Nine times out of ten, it was a Western; the grainy celluloid comforted him with curls and loops squiggling across the screen as a reminder of unreality.

The possibility of reality was there in the way that Hopalong Cassidy sat so confident atop his horse. Yet, no self-respecting cowboy would wear spangles like Gene. Hollywood had trans-formed Italians into Indians and boys named Leonard into Roy.

The movies didn't help dispel the absence he had always felt, the vacancy, the darkness, and the void of what might have been.

Nothing could transform a life that started out bold and weathered down to a nub. Willie squinted into the rays of sunlight casting a silver sheen across the river and tried to remember what he should no longer forget.

The weathering down started after he left the 101 Ranch and got wind that Katie was back in Wolfe Flats, back at that house where her bigoted pa could remind her daily that a Blackfoot Indian had brought shame to his household and a tinker from Madill hadn't been worth a "tinker's dam."

But Katie was past repairing. Willie had tried twice. On the outskirts of Twin Falls in a shack down by the great chasm of the Snake River, three years after she left Wolfe Flats, he had found Katie Linton. Yellowbird she was then and as wounded in spirit as in body.

"We married the day we left Wolfe County in Daddy's car. Tansey had an eye on my daddy's bank account from the get-go. And another wife on the rez." The crusted blood on her split lip teased a wobbling incisor to distract him from the bruises that wrapped her thin neck as regular as the splotches on a copperhead.

When she had opened the door, she reached for the side of Willie's face with tentative fingers, as though searching for the boy who had been replaced by this grim-faced stranger. "Tansey won't take kindly to you interfering, Willie. He says he wouldn't mind putting a bullet through Daddy's head if he could be sure that I haven't been cut out of his will."

Eyes the color of drowning looked up at Willie. "Tansey's found me every time I've run. Says he comes from a long line of Blackfoot trackers." She held up her left hand. The three middle fingers curled inward like the claws of a small bird angling for a safe branch.

"One broken finger for every time I've run. Someone as culpable as me is not worth your bother, Willie."

It was righteous anger that swatted the life out of a Blackfoot who had shamed the Anatobys and tortured Katie. Willie knew that some people who try to live considerate lives—just as he always had—hide killers inside, waiting for something to goad them into showing their dark selves.

During his entire life, the assassin within him had only popped out twice; both times, Willie had welcomed him. Bringing him to mind, even now, he felt a kind of hesitant gratitude that something so menacing within him had exacted justice only twice.

When a gaudy, yellow, Thunderbird-embossed boot with a two-inch slanted heel kicked the door open with no consideration as to who might be standing behind it, Willie showed the same regard.

The hand-forged poker lanced a tidy fissure right alongside the line of his scalp where Tansey greased down his hair in that old style, a sense of his doom already in his eyes the minute he recognized Willie.

All these years later, cold now under this layer of thin cotton, Willie recollected the heat of his fury as he watched Katie cowing in a corner of that filthy room. The blood boiled right up into his eyeballs, thick, hot and venomous—and he recalled only the faintest sense of surprise that Tansey crumpled into such a small, unmoving mound.

The turbulent Snake River accepted those fancy boots and the body that came with them gracefully with the gentlest kind of splash.

Willie shifted his pale shanks against the tree roots, thinking that they now resembled the legs on a puppet, not the sinewy legs of the killer who came out of him to exact justice on Valentine Buscetta.

That night on the train Willie remembered that his eyeballs felt as cold as lumps of coal in a snowman's head. An icy calmness had come over him in that stock car where a tortured donkey, a wounded child, and a weeping grandfather formed a kind of Greek chorus of woe.

My Foot's in the Stirrup

When thirty horses, six mules, a dozen steers, and that mouth-flapping Italian's trick donkey were loaded into the Keystone cars, Willie chose the railroad car with eight stalls for the pick of the saddle horses, Buscetta's donkey and his bedroll.

The train had just pulled away from the depot in Ponca City when a small shadow moved from behind a stack of alfalfa bales where Willie had stashed his gear and slipped between the bars into the donkey's stall. At first Willie thought it was simply light flashing between the slats louvered for ventilation. It moved again. This time, it was carrying carrots.

"I have a little shadow that goes in and out with me." Willie's voice carried softly over the thump and grind of metal on metal.

"And what can be the use of him is more than I can see." The tinkle of the young girl's voice reminded Willie of that clear prairie geyser splashing so surprisingly out of gyp rock when he had gone across what was back then Indian Territory with Lester to buy horses from Kiowas.

He had seen this young girl with her grandfather, an old actor who had traveled Europe years ago with the two Bills' shows. Now, her grandfather put together costumes and did fake war paint for the 101 Wild West Show.

At the 101 Ranch, the old man kept to himself, but the little girl often perched atop the corral when Willie worked the broncs. He hadn't bothered to ask her name. That might encourage her. He needed to discourage her now.

"Won't your grandfather be worried about you? This space is just for the stock. I'm one of the assistant hostlers. I can ride here. Mr. Buscetta should have given you tickets for one of the cars up front."

"For fear of bespeaking badly of my employer who let Mr. Buscetta assign sleeping cars, I will just say that Miranda and I prefer the company of a donkey. And you, of course, Mr. Joy, if you'll allow it. Claudius Buth. That's B-U-T-H. No relation of the actor that felled Mr. Lincoln." A gaunt man with a sclerotic twist along his upper frame rose from behind the hay bales.

"Miranda and I had hoped to travel incognito with the horses. I've traveled incognito for most of my life if the truth be told. Which it can't be." The thin man with the sunken jaws of a cadaver well past a respectable burial date stuck out a limp hand and brushed past Willie to hang over the pen with the donkey.

"So this is the scabby little beast who's been getting my vegetables. Miranda says donkeys give off a comforting odor. She spent a lot of time with this donkey back at the ranch. Then, she stayed away from it. Something about Valentine Buscetta. Donkey tricks. She couldn't make sense of it." His voice trailed off, and he appeared to age perceptibly.

Willie could feel his eyes narrowing as he watched Claudius leaning over the stall. That little girl clinging to the donkey had a haunted look about her as she listened to her grandfather. Willie knew that look. He had learned it when he was two years old from his father's belt.

"Is there something I can do to help you, Mr. Buth?" Willie hoped for a moment this old man would take his granddaughter when they stopped for water up the line and go back to a passenger car.

He played cards occasionally with a few of the hands, but didn't socialize with the other staff, particularly not a man like Buscetta whose clandestine night visits to his donkey had not gone unnoticed. No one dared to venture a rumor about this squared-off, swarthy man with cantaloupe biceps who lifted a 400-pound donkey as part of his act.

"Matter of fact, you can, Mr. Joy." His voice boomed with the clarion call of restored hope. "It appears that my granddaughter has gotten herself crosswise in a certain fashion with Mr. Call-Me-Val Buscetta. He should have been called Caliban."

Willie's single raised eyebrow suggested a curiosity that he was reluctant to reveal. Buscetta's clown act with his trained donkey took second place to his expertise with gunpowder for the Indian War. No one fiddled with an expert in explosives, even one who might be fiddling with a donkey.

"Caliban?"

"The monster that Prospero nurtured when he was shipwrecked on that island. Tried to assault his daughter, Miranda. She was so full of hope. One of Shakespeare's most hopeful characters. You'll have to forgive an old hack, Mr. Joy. We tend to ramble." Mr. Buth sank down on a bale of alfalfa, propped his fist under his chin, and bent his head as though he might be waiting for a curtain to drop.

"We had a family of Mirandas. My wife. My daughter. Now, my granddaughter. Not much of a family except for the nomenclature of naming. The stage does not propagate family solidity. My wife left me for what she called stability with a Norwegian farmer down by Ponca City when our daughter was two years old. My child was eighteen when I saw her again and fairly well along with this one."

He pointed toward the child stroking the donkey's ears. "I was doing Lear down in Fort Worth. My daughter came by train to see me. She asked me to come see my grandchild, but I couldn't leave the troupe for fear that I'd be replaced."

Claudius Buth pulled out two slivers of straw and stuck them into his thick, silver hair. "I did four bit parts in *Hamlet*. Couldn't play that old fool Polonius for fear I'd weep at the wrong time— for a daughter I didn't visit until a tornado gave me all that was left of her—a five-year-old frightened child."

He glanced ruefully up at Willie. "She's now eleven, but looks younger. Played the screaming child in the Attack on a Burning Cabin. The Bills took us in. I did Custer in a blond wig. Not quite in a league with King Lear. But that was in another country and with another playwright."

The curtain-coming-down-forever expression intensified on his face. "You'll have to forgive an old man, Mr. Joy, for sharing his troubles. But, that child is frightened again. And I'm at my wit's end."

My Pony Won't Stand

Willie stretched his good leg over to readjust the numb one that felt like a log with a boot diverging off the end of it as though it might be taking a path in the wrong direction. If time could be measured in intensity, Claudius Buth's "wit's end" filled Willie's wits with the pleasure of Shakespeare from the depot in Guthrie to the train's final stop in New York. Miranda and Willie sat wide-eyed as Claudius felled the enemies of Hamlet and Prospero.

Now, as he watched the turbid river lashing the Texas shore, Willie noticed a faint line of pink just toward the east. Maybe the sun would warm him soon. This chill night had scrambled his memories, memories he needed to reckon with in the time left to him.

From the moment Willie saw Valentine Buscetta jam a hidden safety pin into the stifle of his dancing donkey so that it would spin and bellow with pain in front of the audience, he knew to avoid the man with the call-me-Val phony smile. No one would dare associate him with hearts and flowers.

Willie remembered how anger black as new tar had welled up into his head. Maybe the stallion in that nearby stall stomped Valentine into a bloody pulp of something less than human. Willie feared that it was Lazlo's son who might have slain a man with the jawbone of an ass, the small donkey that Miranda loved.

He had found the child bruised and weeping behind a bale of alfalfa, her frightened heart beating like a trapped bird. He saw something else lying alongside the fear in her eyes, something that welcomed menace in the way that a gothic novel marries innocence with culpability in its heroines.

Then the face of Miranda became that of Katie Yellowbird when that Blackfoot Tansey had finished with her or Willie had finished with the Blackfoot.

Willie squinted through drooping fronds of cedars into the edge of morning. Things were always clearer at dawn, easier to understand, kindled by the repetition of daybreak, the same way that Claudius Buth had made things clear by speaking twice with every character's voice before the train pulled into New York.

After the evening that Valentine disappeared from a moving train, and he watched Claudius trying not to notice that his granddaughter couldn't stop crying, Willie remembered the tone of vague brightness Claudius used when he spoke about Miranda. He projected his voice in the way a minor actor does when preparing the audience for a heroine's entrance, as though her grandfather was casting an aura of hope about her.

Claudius had spoken only once about what had happened or what might have happened that night. "Hubris, my boy, is much more dangerous than a violent act. Cocky people create havoc that never touches them. Killing to save the innocent is a different kind of killing. Shakespeare tells us that, and he makes it all right in the end by clearing bodies off the stage."

Even when deserved, murder aligns with dishonor for both the victim and the perpetrator. Shakespeare's characters make that clear. That fact troubled Willie, even with the bodies cleared away. His victims had been complicit in their murders: Tansey pushing the door open in the pathway of a poker; and, Valentine creeping around a bale of alfalfa to work his evil in on a young girl.

For many years, Willie had kept the characters in his head, working his way through *Hamlet*, wondering about ghosts of fathers with poison in their ears and a son who seemed too fond of his mother. Princely as he might be, Hamlet didn't bring comfort to anyone he loved.

In the end, Hamlet's friends and relatives were scattered all over the stage and Ophelia as lost to him as if a Blackfoot had sweet-talked her away. As for his own relatives, their leaving never troubled Willie more than it should have.

When he found his father stiffened against the lean-to, there was nothing much worth keeping in the shack, only his mother's painted box with photos of people he couldn't identify. She had left them behind; in bitterness, she had refused to name them to her children. Willie had the nose of one and the ears of another and could only witness in sepia tones his connection to another world.

Willie knew that it would have been better if his disappointed father had died with an ear leaking poison into the grass rather than drifting so slowly into those last years of senility, locked into mute disregard with a son who found visiting him to be a trial.

Flexing his good leg against the tree root for assurance that he could still feel its solid roughness, Willie considered how he himself had become a hard man on the outside, the kind that people skirt around, making pleasant sounds of dismissal as though his welcome wore out before he came in the door.

Those great black holes in his life spread like oil drips in his memory, as he tried to think of the rainbows that reflect in spilled oil.

He'd had fake wives but just for a night of pleasure or a home-cooked meal. Some of those women had tried to cling like cockle burs that catch in horses' tails. You crush them with gloves on. That's the only way to splinter the little hooks that won't let go.

Pushing himself into an upright position, Willie scrabbled in the leaf mulch, hoping to find a few windfall pecans. Hunger wasn't a need now. He just wanted a diversion so he could retreat from some memories.

If he had a world map, one of those old, pull-down maps from his grade school, he could try to remember where the Wild West Show had gone in Europe just before the war. Miranda and Claudius had stayed behind. Miranda couldn't stop crying—even though the reason for her tears was mashed flat as those little pins that children placed on train tracks to make tiny scissors.

They put on a regular circus with ill-tempered buffalo instead of elephants for those folks who spoke a strange kind of English. Then, a startling memory came to him. He had visited a ruined abbey in England. It spoke to the very heart of him. It had been a place where holy men went about the business of planting and harvesting and singing.

They didn't sing Methodist hymns but praises from the soles of their feet to the great arching stones above them. It was the roofless space of those giant, abandoned walls that he had loved.

Willie thought about all the piles of rusting junk on the farms and ranches he had worked on during his life. Poverty, or the fear of it, fed the human impulse to collect: coils of rusting barbed wire, cistern covers, anything made of metal that might fill a gap on a roof or knit a broken fence.

Those derelict piles depressed him. They closed in space. He dreamed of space, remembering those great expanses of grassland rimmed only by mesas with hidden paths to the other side. He could almost feel the sugar-foot trotting of Lester's mare like the rocking of a cradle that he should remember but couldn't.

Willie looked up at the pale lavender moon retreating from the night and considered the kind of afterlife that might await a dutiful man like himself who never complained or bothered people with his ailments.

He didn't intend to stay beyond his purpose and become one of those old men endlessly cataloging their diseases. He rarely thought of where he might go but envisioned heaven as a circumscribed place, hemmed in by cedar and pecan trees, and beyond it acres of flat prairies of native grasses that no plow had touched.

Like an ancient goddess of the hearth, Sadie would be there amidst tubs of boiling laundry, the air dense with lye soap, an odor dearer to him than incense. Lester would be sitting in his rocking chair watching a pot of beet greens simmering on a blackened stove.

And Katie. She would flounce away from him—her own prickly self not changed at all by eternity—then, she'd look off into the distance just so he could admire the perfection of her chin before she turned those depthless blue eyes toward him.

Willie could feel his heart giving out. It had begun beating at the end of the last century and had served him well. Only Katie had broken it. Three times: running off with Tansy Yellowbird; settling into dullness with a religious tinker; and, giving in to a terrible illness that drained Katie of herself.

Willie had borrowed a pickup from Joe Miller when he heard that Katie had the cancer and headed for that shabby little bungalow in Madill where rows of wilted plants drooped along the porch steps like harbingers of abandonment.

A melting reproduction of Katie from Madame Tussaud's wax museum pushed open the lop-sided screen door into the 110-degree July heat and grinned impishly up at Willie.

"You might have paid me a visit before the lymphoma did, Willie. I would have been more hospitable. This heat takes it out of me. I got a couple of fans stirring the air inside." She moved close to him as she held back the screen door; the rough patches on her cheeks stood out like garish blotches of rouge against her colorless skin.

Two brass-bladed fans stirred dust around the darkened room. Two claw-footed Morris chairs stood like sentinels at the end of the couch where Katie lowered herself, her face mask-like as she stretched her feet toward a fan.

Six months earlier, Howard Carter had opened a pharaoh's tomb to show the world that Egyptian gods had stood guard for centuries over that young king. Willie thought of the newspaper photograph, as he stood helpless in this tomb.

Only the carved wooden feet of lions on Morris chairs stood watch over a dying Katie in a house smelling of stale food and soiled laundry.

"Get up, Katie. I'm taking you to Oklahoma City. To a specialist who will know what to do for you." Willie knew that the optimism in his voice struck an unconvincing note in the breathlessly hot room.

"I've been, Willie. Done that. Seen as many specialists as Daddy wanted to afford. Surprising really that he spent so much money, considering that he gave up on me when I stole his precious Ford years ago. My husband gave up on me too. He's a Christian Science Reader. Thinks sin causes cancer. Worse than any Methodist." Katie's coarse burst of laughter struck Willie as a poor facsimile of the light-hearted giggling he remembered.

"I don't see nothin' to laugh about, Katie. We can find someone who can help you get well." Willie had continued to stand by the couch, fearful that if he moved closer, the doubtfulness that had settled in her eyes would spread over her body like a shroud.

She swung her feet to the floor. "You have a kind of perverse complacency, Willie. You have always seemed to be too easily satisfied. But I know that you are nettlesome just beneath the surface."

"I'm feeling like a cocklebur now, Katie, if it's any satisfaction to you. Tore up inside and out."

She reached for his hand and tucked it against a chest that seemed almost concave. "I never meant to hurt you, Willie. You were the best one. Cancer comes after the culpable. Just like the Tanseys of this world. You saved me once. You can't do it again. You can't even see this culprit. It doesn't wear outrageous boots." With just the hint of a smile, she dropped her eyes as though to hide from him the lack of promise in them.

Willie remembered the heart-stopping grief of that moment. Katie could always be relied upon to say the most unsuitable thing for the occasion. The yellow Thunderbirds on Tansey's boots had long-since been washed away in the Snake River. At that moment, Willie regretted that Tansey had died so quickly, with only a brief premonition of his death.

"Remember that old song I used to sing? About riding the prairie that we love best? That's how I want you to think about me. The way we used to be before the bad things came along. We'll be that way again somewhere."

Willie stood stock-still, afraid that he might speak unbidden words. Katie met bad things with a smile and had waltzed out of his life with them. Purposeful. First, a Blackfoot. Then, a Bible-thumping tinker. Now, her partner, this cancer that had claimed her for a last, lingering dance, was taking his pleasure from the inside out.

Willie felt overwhelmed by the injustice of cancer, the way it had sidled into her body like a blood-sucking leech. Seeing the hopelessness in her eyes like a vast, blue summer sky cleared of clouds, of anything, he watched her pain preceding her into the room as she smiled cautiously, so as not to offer him hope.

At that moment, Willie knew that the pain of what they call eternity had visited him, but he could not make too much of that knowledge without injury to Katie.

Driving the back roads to Ponca so that he could hear only the sound of gravel, not the thump of his own heart that should have stopped beating when he held a frail, listless copy of Katie against him for the last time, Willie looked into the dog days of summer.

Late goldenrod soared up from ditches alongside the road. A red-tailed hawk wafted on a hot wind against a sky so blue that it could not be defined as color.

Suddenly, Willie knew what Katie was looking for and couldn't find. It was rapture.

And, she was taking her search to a place where he couldn't find her.

Now, in this lonely place near the river, watching the late November sun inching its way through a thick stand of cedars, Willie thought about the small pleasures of his life. Sometimes, they filled him to the brim—like one of those swirling vats of cotton candy at the county fair. Too sweet, too sticky, and vastly satisfying.

I'm Off to Montan'

Early mornings like this one caused a body to mull over fine moments in this world. The blood-red sumac had turned a rich orange, like a fox's ruff. The moss tucked into the riverbank glowed emerald in the sun. Willie felt a wave of adrenaline surge through him, fearful in its intensity, insisting on life.

This longing for life put him in danger. Willie had learned long ago not to hanker after what would surely be denied. He might disappear now right into the roots of this old tree—like one of those carnival magicians who walk into a box and leave it empty to amaze an audience who knew all about hidden trap doors but long to be mystified by a vanishing act.

When he had returned from the last Wild West Show, he found the Anatoby house sodden with dust—as though Sadie and Lester had faded away and regrouped as wispy particles clinging to every surface.

He remembered Sadie talking about how she could still hear the howl of the red wolves that were no longer around. "The spirits never leave. Everything that dies comes back in one way or t'other," she'd insisted.

Katie had died this very month over fifty years ago. Slowly. Not like Katie at all. Cancer came calling like an unexpected visitor and had turned the fall of every year into a eulogy for her. The bursts of late sunflowers, the sky repeating the blue of her eyes. The loss of her tugged on him in a way that unmanned him. Made him feel like a child again, helpless to find a way out of loneliness.

It didn't start with the cancer. When Tansey Yellowbird took her away, the ache started, a nagging thing like a splinter under the skin so deep that a bacon fat wrap couldn't bring it up to be dislodged.

Katie wouldn't have been happy with the meager slice of life Willie could offer her. He knew that she was meant for grander things. Not Tansey Yellowbird who could break the spirit of a horse with one swipe of his spurs. Not that shiftless tinker who promised shelter and meant a cage. She was like Dickens's Oliver with his bowl of gruel saying, "I want more," knowing she would be punished for the asking.

Willie had grieved so much for Katie that his brain hurt. He could only remember small parts of her now. Her perfect clavicle. That dip in her throat that quivered like a small bird just before it darted away. The flirtatious smile that appeared when you least expected it. The rest of her, the whole of her had faded.

Pushing himself up so that his back was erect against the rough bark of the tree, he gasped at the jab stabbing his heart. No different than winter's meat. Hard and fast to end consciousness. The pain would be less than Tansey felt when Willie split his skull with that poker. Or Valentine Buscetta just before that half-light in his black eyes suggested that some dark thought was surfacing, something involving helpless animals or an innocent child.

No regrets for Tansy or Valentine. The breeze lifted, dropping crimson sumac leaves like splashes of blood all around him. The sense of waste hovering about his last few years had tainted his memories of better times. The breaking darkness dropped low like a vulture's wings, beating back the morning sun.

Willie thrust his left leg forward, angling his toe into his boot. Cowboys should die with their boots on, not slowly decay into a riverbank. He watched the glorious silver moon wobbling across the night sky like the lid of a trash can rolling against the curb of eternity.

Even as Katie was dying, her face, waxen and thin, she had held on to the edge of the earth with such ethereal beauty.

Pulling Ventnor's crutch under his arm, Willie forced the muscles of his thighs and calves to hoist him to his feet, to clench the sides of the heaving bronc for one more minute.

Miles of unplowed prairies were going on forever under a clear blue sky in the east. Somewhere Katie went on. She must have strolled out for a late afternoon walk and forgotten to come back. Forgotten the time. Forgotten that he would be waiting.

Any minute now, she'd burst through the Anatobys' door and remember and laugh like a hundred church bells, making everything in this world right again.

November 11, 1993, the *Wolfe Flats Messenger* consigned a single column to the news that "a body believed to be that of Willie Joy surfaced this week in a heavily wooded area near the old Tucker Ferry crossing. Asaline Pouts and Jimmy Winders came upon the bones. Wild animals had disturbed the body, but the boots on the skeleton have been identified as those of Mr. Joy."

The End

www.ingramcontent.com/pod-product-compliance
Lightning Source LLC
Chambersburg PA
CBHW031321170626
46807CB00002B/517